MW01154007

GUARD DOG

J O E   H A J D U K

ISBN: 1979013268
ISBN-13: 9781979013260
Library of Congress Control Number: 2017916543
CreateSpace Independent Publishing Platform
North Charleston, South Carolina

For all my family and friends who have
heard many of my stories,
Here is one that you have not heard.

CONTENTS

Chapter 1
GUARD DOG

Gus Shepard was a man of extraordinary talents and mediocre achievements. He was an average-looking guy, five feet eleven inches tall with a thin but muscular build. At thirty-two years old, he was an only child who had been born to older, very accomplished parents. His father was a Special Forces army ranger who had fought in the Korean War. His mother was a North Korean childhood genius who, at the age of ten, was smuggled to South Korea by his father and became one of their most respected scientists.

At thirty-two years old, Gus was doing OK. He had a bachelor's degree in Chemistry from a local university. He obviously had inherited his mother's brains, but instead of pushing himself, he preferred to use his intelligence to do as little as possible. College was very easy for him, and in his opinion, he was very smart because he was not stupid enough to spend any extra time studying. He had a decent job at a local biotechnology company. He owned his own home, had a classic car on payments, and had a good-looking girlfriend he was almost serious about.

It was a sunny Saturday afternoon, and Gus had plans to go to the flea market. His girlfriend was busy, and his limited number of friends had not called or texted, so he decided to go alone.

He parked his car and started walking the booths. He was not really looking for anything special, more or less just killing time. As he was walking, he came across an elderly Asian man with a dog. The man stared at him, and Gus got this overwhelming feeling that the man knew him.

Their eyes locked, and the man said, "Finally, you are here. I have been waiting for you."

Gus smiled and replied with a somewhat cocky tone, "Well, I am here. Do you have something special for me?"

"Yes," the man replied. In his broken English, he said, "I have for you a god dog."

"A god dog?" Gus replied with a slight laugh. "What is that?"

"A god is a dog that will protect you. A god is a dog that will protect you with its life. A god is a dog that has only one master, and that master is you!"

"Oh," Gus said. "You mean a guard dog."

The Asian man smiled and said, "Yes, a god dog. A god dog."

Looking at the dog, a very lean but muscular German shepherd-pit bull mix, Gus replied, "I am sorry to disappoint you, but I don't want a dog. I just don't have the room or time for one."

The Asian man stared at Gus with a very serious look. "The god dog was put on this earth for you. He has a destiny to fulfill, as do you. These things I know. We are all tied together in this life. My destiny has been to raise this special dog and bring him to you. Your destiny is unknown to you, but as it unfolds over time, you will understand your relationship with this special dog."

Gus snickered. "OK, Master Po. Nice try, but I think l will be moving on."

The dog immediately walked to his side and sat, almost at attention, with a military-type style. It kind of reminded him of his father.

The Asian man replied, "See, the dog knows. Why do you not know? Walk this dog for me to the end of the booths and back. If you do not like this dog, maybe you are not the one."

How hard could this be? Gus thought. The man handed him a leash, and Gus attached it. He walked the dog to the end of the booths. The dog stayed at his side as if it were part of him. Even the stride of the dog's walk appeared to match his own. He actually had a slight eerie feeling of confidence. As he reached the end of the booths, he decided he would circle back around the booths and come up from the other direction.

After completing his lap and arriving back where he had started, the old Asian man was gone! His spot was completely empty.

He must be lost. Gus retraced his steps several times, always ending up in the same place.

Oh, great, he thought to himself. *Now what am I going to do with this dog? If only I had been more assertive, I would not be in this mess. Guess I will just take him home. The flea market will happen again next week. I guess I am stuck with this dog for a week, but that shouldn't be too bad. I'm sure he will be here next week. He had a lot of stuff. I'm sure he's a regular. Besides, I didn't pay him anything, so I am sure he wants money or his dog back.*

Gus took the dog home. As it turned out, he was able to work from home that week, so taking care of the dog wasn't too much trouble. Just walk him and feed him. A large park was right down the street from Gus's house, so every night he started to walk him.

The dog was quite a sight to see. He had the long, lean body of a German shepherd and the large head, muscular physique, and short hair of a pit bull. With its long tail, the dog almost resembled a prehistoric animal. While Gus felt very comfortable with the dog, it had a very intimidating look to it. The black coloring around its face, similar to that of a German shepherd, combined with its pearl-black eyes, was very intimidating. From a distance, it gave an appearance that the dog was staring at you.

Gus watched the way the dog walked. With confidence. Not aggressive but not weak. As he passed other people, he noticed that the dog did not look at them but did not look away, either. It seemed as he passed them that he was in a calm state of heightened awareness. Aware of his surroundings, calm but ready to react if necessary.

Gus thought to himself, *I should be more like this dog. If only I had this kind of attitude. Too bad there's no way to transfer his personality to me.*

As he walked, pondering this thought, he noticed the dog was staring at him with its pearl-black eyes. It was almost like the dog was reading his mind. In a sign of acknowledgment, the dog blinked its eyes, then looked forward again. Gus had this overwhelming feeling that the dog understood him. It was like a soldier who had been given a command.

A week had gone by, and it was now flea-market Saturday. Gus liked the dog, but being the honest guy he was, he decided that he now should return it. If nothing else, he should at least give the guy some money. Deep inside, he knew he actually wanted to keep the dog, but he was a common-sense guy who analyzed everything and took very few risks. His conclusion was that this was a great dog…for someone else. It was too big, he had no time for it, and his home was too small.

As he got into his car, he had the strangest feeling that something was not right. With the dog in the back seat, Gus headed for the flea market. Every time he looked into his rearview mirror, he could see the dog. Its pearl-black eyes stared at him but in an unusual way. Not angry, not sad, but confident, almost as if it knew Gus was doing the right thing.

As Gus was driving down the freeway, an eighteen-wheel truck switched to his left lane and passed him. Within an instant, a car cut directly in front of the truck, causing the driver to lock up his brakes. Its brakes screeching and smoke rising, the truck veered to the right and began to jackknife!

Almost in slow motion, Gus saw the rear portion of the truck lift completely into the air, tumbling over the cab of the vehicle. The rear portion of the truck slammed to the ground, blocking two lanes of the freeway. With his hands tightly gripping the steering wheel and traveling at a high rate of speed, Gus was headed directly at the large obstacle in front of him. He knew he was in serious trouble.

At that instant, the dog gave an extremely loud, vicious bark. Immediately startled, Gus whipped the steering wheel to the right, slamming into a guardrail on the side of the road and then down an embankment. The grade was steep, and his classic 1965 Mustang went into a roll. It was all happening very fast, but to Gus it was in slow motion. As the car went into the first flip, Gus saw the dog jump over the front seat. He felt his head slam forward hard, but it was cushioned by the dog's body. He was thrown side to side, but each time he felt the dog's body in between him and his point of impact. At some point during the roll, Gus had instinctively put his hand out of the car window and grabbed the roof to support himself. As the car went into its final roll, Gus felt the dog's teeth grab his arm and pull it back into the car, saving it from certain amputation from the crushing weight of the vehicle. Then everything went black.

As he awoke and his vision became clear, Gus realized that he was in the hospital. Standing in front of him was his mother, a small, thin Korean woman, who at the age of seventy-two, was still attractive. Anyone looking at her might have thought that she was a female executive for a music company. She dressed young and cool. She did not look the ultra-intelligent semiretired scientist that she actually was.

Gus looked at his mother and said, "Mom, what happened?"

His mother replied, "You were in a terrible accident. You're lucky to be alive. The police showed me pictures of your car. It's totally destroyed. They even say that it's a miracle that you're alive."

Gus replied, "How is the dog?"

"What dog?" his mother replied.

"I picked up a dog at the flea market from an old Asian man. I was returning him. The dog cushioned me and is probably the reason that I'm still alive."

"There was nothing in the police report about a dog. Are you sure that it's not your imagination playing tricks on you?"

"No, Mom, it was real," Gus replied. "It was of the most fantastic dogs I had ever seen. It was strong, intelligent, and obedient." He was now sitting up, his eyes wide open with obvious excitement.

His mother stared at him and asked, "The Asian man who gave you this dog—did he tell you anything about it?"

"Not much," Gus replied. "He said it was a guard dog. Actually, he said it was a god dog." Then Gus laughed.

To his surprise, his mother was not smiling. Instead, she looked very serious. She left Gus's side and went over to close the door. She returned to his side, still looking very serious.

"What's wrong, Mom?" Gus asked.

She said, "Son, your true journey in life has just begun. I believe that you have been given the power of a god dog. Upon the death of this dog, it transferred its energy to you. Its energy has been transferred so that you will someday do something in this world that the spirits need done. They are the spirits of good and sometimes send help to those who are destined to perform some great task. I feel honored, my son, that they have chosen you. I know that this must sound very confusing to you. You look very tired. Rest, and I will explain more tomorrow when we take you home."

"Can't you tell me more now?" Gus asked.

"No," his mother replied. "Your father is flying back from Washington, DC, now. I would like him there when I tell you my story."

Gus laid his head back and closed his eyes. He needed to absorb what he had just been told. While listening to his mother talk, he fell asleep. The next day he awoke, was given a thorough checkup, and was released. His mother picked him up and drove him home. Gus was now at home, waiting for his father to arrive. His mother appeared calm but had a seriousness to her. She kept their conversation to small talk and was obviously avoiding the conversation that they had in the hospital.

There was a quick knock on the door, and then it opened. It was his father. At eighty-two years old, he was ten years older than Gus's mother. With a full head of short gray hair, his father was one of those men who looked important. A Special Forces army ranger, he was very disciplined in everything he did but was not hard-driving when it came to Gus or his mother. He was a great husband and a very understanding father. He never talked much about what he did as a consultant for the US government. All Gus knew was that he had a top-secret security clearance and that he flew to Washington, DC, several times per year. Sometimes his mother would go with him and assist him.

After all the initial hugs and kisses, his mother and father sat down on the sofa in front of Gus. His father started the conversation. "Your mother told me what happened. I've read all the police and fire department reports. You're very lucky to be alive."

"It was the dog, Dad," Gus said. "Mom said there was nothing about it in the reports. Did you find anything about it?" Gus knew that when his dad had said that he had read all the reports, it had been nothing less than a thorough investigation. It was how he did everything he considered important.

"No, son, I found nothing. But I did not expect to after talking to your mother. In fact, if what we believe is true, you will not find anybody who has seen this dog. It was only visible to you."

Gus looked puzzled, but he knew by his father's tone that he should keep quiet and listen.

"I have had a similar experience in my life, which your mother and I have never told you about. In fact, if you hadn't had such an experience, we would not be telling you this story. I will let your mother start, for she is also very much involved in this story."

His mother had been sitting patiently, but Gus knew she was anxious to talk. She leaned back in her chair and slowly started the conversation, choosing each word carefully, the way she always spoke to him when it was a matter of importance.

"My story begins long ago, when I was just a little girl living in Korea. When I was very young, I knew I was different than all the other kids. I was able to read and understand books by the age of three. When I started school at the age of five, my teachers were so amazed with my abilities that they moved me up two grades. I did not like being away from all my friends, and my new classmates were all so much older that I started making mistakes and failing on purpose to hide my intelligence. They eventually moved me back to the lower grade, and I was with all my friends again.

"I was happy doing as little as possible, as school was very easy for me. Much like your own attitude toward school, my son. My father—your grandfather—was very wise and recognized what I was doing. He obtained several scientific books from local universities and gave them to me to read. I read as many books as he would bring me.

"By the age of eight, I was writing my own scientific equations to find solutions to diseases. The Korean War between the North and the South had just started. My father had told me to keep my intelligence a secret and not to let anybody know what I had been doing. I was a young girl, and I did not understand the importance of this and shared this information with my best friends. In a war such as this one, people chose sides, and even neighbors turned on one another. My friends' parents chose the North, and my family chose the South. My friends had told their parents all about me—innocently, of course.

"It was rumored at that time the North had developed a deadly disease that they would spread throughout the South. They had the cure and would only give it to those in the North. They only had one small problem. I had developed the scientific equations for a cure. My father had known for some time that Northern authorities would soon find out about this. He knew he had to get me deeper into the South. If he did not, they would most surely come take me, and I would be killed.

"Unknown to me, my father had been planning my escape for years. My father was a master in *Hwa Rang Do*, a very ancient and mysterious Korean martial art. He had been teaching a young American soldier everything he knew. He had told me many times that this man was his most trusted and talented student. The man your grandfather was talking about was your father.

"I was ten years old when your grandfather woke me in the middle of the night. He had packed my bag and told me I must leave immediately. I would be leaving with his favorite student, this man he trusted, and I must do everything he said. My father and I both knew that it would be a difficult, if almost impossible journey to the South. Most who tried had not made it and had been killed. In addition, he told me that in order to protect the rest of the family, in the morning he would report to the Northern authorities that an American soldier had kidnapped me. Them knowing who I was and who had taken me would make my capture their highest priority.

"I told my father that I was very scared. To this day, I still remember his reply. 'Do not worry, my daughter,' he said. 'I have prayed, and the spirits have answered. The man I am sending with you will be given the power of a god dog.'"

Gus's mother then looked at his father, who began to speak.

"I know this all sounds crazy to you, and I would never have believed it myself unless I had experienced it. Your grandfather gave me a small dog to take with me on my journey. He told me it was a special dog sent from the good spirits to protect me. On my journey, he said there would be many people that he had requested to help me, but in this time of war, he did not know if they could all be trusted. The dog he gave me would growl whenever I came upon somebody that could not be trusted.

"The journey he had sent me on lasted five days and left me little time for rest. I was very fatigued due to lack of sleep. The dog somehow knew when it was safe for me to rest and when it was time for me to run.

"On the very last day of my journey, the North Koreans bombed the entire village where I had been staying in an attempt to stop me. The last thing I remember was an explosion and the dog jumping in front of my face, protecting me from a large piece of flying metal. I awoke in a South Korean hospital and was told that I had saved the little genius girl who had developed the cure for a disease that would save the South.

"I asked them about the dog who had accompanied me on my journey and saved my life. They did not know what I was talking about. Nobody had seen me with a dog. I contacted an old South Korean elder who told me that the dog did exist but only as a sprit inside of me.

"That experience changed me, and I found what this old man said to be true. Many of the traits, abilities, and instincts of a dog had become part of me. To this day, I still have retained these abilities. Over time, I have learned to understand them and control them. I only use them for good.

"For some unknown reason, you have also been given this gift. You must now take the time to understand your new abilities and learn to use them. This gift has been given to you for a reason. The good spirits have given you this power to assist you in some great task you must achieve in the battle of good versus evil."

Chapter 2
HOUSE AT MEEKU FILBEECH

It had been a week since Gus had spoken with his mother and father. He had been home resting after the accident. He was supposed to take it easy, and he was feeling sore, but he had an overwhelming feeling of uneasiness. All this crazy talk about the guard dog or god dog was confusing, but he knew something was different within himself. He felt a burning desire to move, to get going, so he decided to go to his garage and work out.

His home had a large two-car garage, and Gus had dedicated one side to his car and the other side to working out. The garage had weights for strength training and a large open area to practice the katas, or forms, taught to him by his father. The forms were a series of martial arts moves that his father had put together. His father had told him that the forms consisted of the most effective moves and techniques he had found in all his years of martial arts.

When Gus was very young, he remembered his father saying, "These forms must be practiced over and over to develop the mind. If they are practiced daily with focus, the techniques will flow as a second nature. You will not have to think about 'Here comes a strike, I must block.' Your arm will just respond. Just as when someone throws a ball to you, your arms automatically position themselves to catch."

Gus went to the garage and started his workout with some stretching and then decided that he would go through his forms, lift some weights, and finish with a cardio workout by doing arm and leg strikes on the heavy bag. He started going through his forms but felt an intense focus that he had never experienced before. As he performed blocking techniques, he could see strikes coming in as if an imaginary opponent were in the room. As he performed imaginary counterstrikes, he felt a rage tearing through his body as if he were an animal going in for a kill.

Next, he moved to lifting some weights. Everything seemed lighter. Whereas he normally just stuck to his regular routine, he found himself adding more weight and doing more reps. He gritted his teeth and let out a groan-type growl at the end of each set, pushing his body to achieve that one last lift. This all felt so good to him, nothing like he had ever experienced.

Gus then finished up with some heavy-bag work. This was something he always liked because he got to use many kicks that he had learned on his own or from teachers other than his father. It was kind of his thing. Many times, his father had accused him of showing off and told him that those techniques were too flashy, but he could see in his father's eyes that he admired his skill.

Gus started to slowly hit and kick the bag. Then he started speeding up, hitting harder, moving faster. Energy surged through his veins. Normally at this point, he would be tiring, looking up at the clock to make sure he was not quitting early. But now he did not want to stop. As he was finishing his workout, slamming fast, hard, head-level roundhouse kicks into the bag, he caught a glimpse of himself in the mirror. He saw the snarling face of a wild animal. He blinked his eyes and did a double take and realized that was him like he had never seen himself before. What he saw made him feel good.

It was the first day for Gus to go back to work. Normally, he moved slowly on a workday, with his mind always preoccupied by other things. Today, he felt charged, sharp, and alert. It was Monday, which he normally disliked. Every Monday started off with a meeting run by the manager of the department, Hans. He was a large man of German decent. He was rude, arrogant, and never let anyone, especially men, forget that he was a large man. Gus did not like or dislike him. For the most part, Hans left

Gus alone because he knew of Gus's technical importance to the company. The one thing Gus did despise was the way he treated other people.

The meeting started at 8:00 a.m. sharp. Forget the fact that the company had flexible working hours and several employees attending the meeting had long commutes through heavy and unpredictable traffic. Gus showed up on time and sat in his regular spot. The meeting started as usual with Hans looking around the table for a victim. It was kind of a ritual. Hans would always wait until everyone was seated, look around the room, and find someone to embarrass in front of the others. Today, he set his sights on Molly, a young and shy secretary who just happened to be eight months pregnant. Hans sat back in his chair, staring at her with his typical sinister grin.

"Good morning, Molly," he started out. "Is that a clown suit you're wearing today, or is that the only thing that fit? I guess you're eating for two…but I think you're eating toooo much." Then he laughed.

Molly's eyes started to tear up, but everyone knew she would not say anything.

Normally, Gus ignored Hans's comments, but today, they drove him crazy. He could actually feel the hair standing up on the back of his neck. Unable to control himself, Gus blurted out, "What's a clown suit, Hans? Something that your tailor designed just for you?"

Everyone laughed. Hans did not. He immediately turned to Gus, obviously angry but still trying to be funny, and said, "Well, good morning, Gus. Molly should learn to eat less, and you should learn that it's a dog-eat-dog world. The big dog eats the little dog, and you better figure out which one you are."

Gus put his hands toward his crotch, then raised them as if he were holding his penis in the air and replied, "It's a dog-eat-dog world? Maybe it's time you tried eatin' on this dog."

Everyone laughed again, this time louder, as they truly enjoyed not the joke but Hans's red face, as he couldn't hide his anger. Gus knew he was in trouble. But unlike other times in his life, he didn't feel scared or worried. Instead, he felt like he was preparing for battle. He knew where this was going. Hans wasn't going to take it lightly. He was going to do something to try and embarrass Gus. If that didn't work, being the large man that he was, he would try to intimidate him with some aggressive action. He never backed down.

The meeting was half-over, and this was where they always took a break. When they returned, only management and the key technical people would be present. Gus left to use the restroom. While there, he could feel his brain racing like a supercomputer, analyzing every possible situation and outcome of what was going to happen when he reentered the meeting. As he looked into the bathroom mirror, he saw the face of a snarling dog. He blinked his eyes, and it was him again. He smiled at himself.

As he walked back into the room, he could feel Hans staring at him. He felt calm but alert. He knew his calmness would just make Hans angrier. Instead of sitting in his usual chair, Gus sat on the other side of the room. He wasn't sure why because normally he was a creature of habit. He felt like he was being guided by some new, strange instinct.

Gus noticed that in his new position sitting at the table that the sun shined through the window across his back and directly into Hans's eyes. Also, now sitting across from him was Dave, the gadget geek. Dave prided himself in having or knowing about every electronic device on this earth. Gus wasn't sure why, but everything felt perfect.

Hans entered the meeting last, as usual. It was his arrogant way of showing he was the boss. You could cut the tension with a knife. Everyone seemed to know that Hans was going to attack. He had to. He wouldn't leave this meeting until he had embarrassed or intimidated Gus.

Hans wasted no time. He looked at Gus and said, "How do you think you're going to get away with this?"

Gus looked at Hans and said in a German accent, "Hail?"

Hans replied, "I said, 'How?'"

Once again, Gus replied in a German accent, "Hail?"

Gus could see the anger in his face as Hans finally got it. Gus was mocking him by referring to the World War II salute to Hitler.

Gus could feel his adrenaline flowing. His senses seemed heightened. His hearing was at a level like never before. Gus heard the faint noise of a finger touching a screen. He sensed that the noise had come from across the table. Out of the corner of his eye, he saw that Dave had his hand on his phone. He knew that Dave had just started recording the action. It would only be an audio recording, as he knew Dave would never have the guts to hold the phone up and film it.

Knowing this was all now being recorded, Gus blurted out before Hans could speak, "How do you think we can all sit back in meetings and watch you mock pregnant women? Tell us, Hans, how?" Gus then raised his arm as if he were a World War II German soldier saluting his leader and said, "Come on, Hans. Tell us hail, tell us hail."

Gus knew what was coming next. It was time for Hans to get physical. Like always, he was going to switch to one of his big-man intimidation techniques. He knew Hans would charge at him like a bear and stop but be close enough to hit him. He had done this before to others. It was his way of saying, "You better back down, or I'll hit you." Nobody had ever taken the challenge.

Just like clockwork, Hans made his move. He slammed his hand on the table, kicked his chair back, and came charging at Gus. Gus's mind was turning like a high-end hard drive. As Hans approached, Gus waited until the sun shining over his shoulder was directly in Hans's eyes. With precision timing, Gus slightly moved the chair in front of him so that it caught Hans's foot as he was charging at him. Hans tripped and threw his arms up, but to everyone one in the room, it looked as if Hans was diving at Gus.

As Hans fell, Gus perfectly positioned his chair so that Hans's head would be at his knee level. Hans fell, and as soon his arms hit Gus's legs, Gus, out of the sight of others, slammed his knee into Hans's nose. Before Hans could rise, Gus bent over and grabbed Hans's head and whispered something in his ear.

Hans yelled and jumped back, falling onto the ground. His broken nose was twisted to one side and bleeding profusely. He stumbled to his feet in a feeble attempt to attack Gus, but the others jumped in, holding him back. Somebody yelled, "This is over. Get him to a doctor...now!" Everybody left the room, including Gus. But before he did, he turned at Hans and smiled.

Hans and Gus were sent home for the day so that Human Resources could conduct a thorough review. The decision was made that they both be fired. Human resources sent the paperwork to Hank Stewart, the senior vice president and second in command. As soon as Hank got the paperwork, he called J.P. Thorn, the president of the company.

J.P. answered. "What's up, Hank?"

"We have a problem. I am sure you heard about what happened today between Hans and one of our young scientists."

"It's the talk of the town," replied J.P.

Hank continued, "In a situation like this, both guys should be fired. Whatever action we take will be very visible. I know that you feel Hans is needed and is part of our inner circle of management, but he is an ass. Everyone hates him. The guy is an accident waiting to happen. We need to get him out of the day to day operations of the company before he gets us in a lawsuit. We don't need that kind of publicity and should fire him immediately. We can keep him on as a secret consultant and use him until he finishes what we need him to do. But he will have to work off-site. And as far as the company is concerned, he is fired.

"The other guy, Gus Shepard, is another story. He is a smart and talented young man. They have started using him on Project X. The team leader for the project is demanding we keep him. I think we should comply with his demand."

"What can you tell me about this Gus guy?" J.P. asked. "I've seen him in the hallway but don't know much about him."

Hank replied, "Well, to tell you the truth, he's kind of lazy. But he's probably the laziest genius I know!"

Both men laughed.

"I get it, Hank: big ass must go; lazy ass must stay. Make it happen, and keep us out of trouble," J.P. replied.

"You got it, boss," Hank said, and they both laughed again.

Hank had Human Resources interview everyone who had been in the room. The responses they got were vague. At this point, all he had was that two guys had gotten into an argument that had turned into a fight. Hank needed more information to do what he wanted to do. He decided he would personally interview Dave. Dave was always careful to say the right thing to keep himself out of trouble just like the others, but he always had some extra data. Hank brought Dave into his office, and they both sat down.

Hank wasted no time and jumped right into the conversation. "So, Dave, what happened?"

Dave replied, "You must have read my response to Human Resources."

"Sure did. It looks just like everyone else's. I can't seem to get anybody to speak up and tell me what happened. I get the impression that everybody is really afraid of Hans. Dave, off the record, give me one word that describes how you think the others feel about Hans."

Dave paused, then replied, "Ruthless."

"Now, one word for how you think they all feel about Gus?" Hank asked.

Dave replied, "Well, after yesterday, hero."

"Well, help me here, Dave," Hank said. "Nobody seems to want to answer my questions."

"Maybe because you're not asking the right questions."

"OK, what's a right question?"

Dave's face broke into an ear-to-ear grin. "Has anyone recorded in any way the incidents that happened on that day?"

Both men laughed.

"OK, Dave, hand it over."

Both laughed again.

Dave pulled out his cell phone and put it on the table. "This is how it was sitting in the room that day. The camera is facing down, so all that I have is audio."

"Let's hear it."

Dave turned it on, and they both listened. When it was done, Hank looked at Dave and said, "Why did Gus say, 'How do you think we can all sit back in meetings and watch you mock pregnant women?'"

"Maybe because it was what Hans said to Molly earlier in the meeting."

"The question is, what did Hans say to Molly, and was it offensive, therefore discriminatory?"

"I believe you have just found the right questions to ask," Dave replied. They both smiled, but Hank in a more sinister way.

After several interviews with employees who were in the meeting, it was determined that Hans had made discriminatory remarks toward a pregnant woman and had instigated the confrontation with Gus before assaulting him. Hans was immediately fired. Gus was sent home to recuperate from his assault.

A couple of nights passed, and Gus was still at home. He had been given the rest of the week off and would return to work on the following Monday. It was about 10:00 p.m., and the phone rang. Gus picked it up.

"Hello, this this Gus?"

"This is Dave from work."

"What's up, Dave?"

"You know I was the one who recorded part of the meeting and gave it to Hank. I saved your ass. You owe me."

"Yes, I know, so why are you calling me?"

"Well, I saw you bend down and whisper something in Hans's ear about the same time his head hit your knee. I analyzed my recording and deleted all the background sounds and heard you say, 'House at Meeku Filbeech.' I checked every record in both Germany and the United States, and I cannot find any address or name like that. I cannot figure out what you said, but it made Hans yell before he fell backward. It's killing me. What did you say?"

"How's that make you feel?" Gus replied.

"It doesn't matter how it makes me feel," Dave said, slightly annoyed.

"You're a smart man, Dave. Just think real hard about how does that make you feel. Think about it."

"Is that all that you're going to tell me?" Dave asked.

"That's it for tonight," Gus replied.

They both said goodbye and hung up the phone. About an hour later, the phone rang again. Gus picked up the phone, and Dave said with a German accent, "How's that make you feel, bitch!"

Gus let out a big laugh, followed by Dave doing the same.

"That was great! You whispered in his ear, 'How's that make you feel, bitch?' with a German accent. Not 'House at Meeku Filbeech.' Right after his head hit your knee. No wonder he yelled so loud. You are the man!"

They both laughed again.

"See you on Monday," Dave said.

"See ya," said Gus.

It was Monday morning. Gus arose, got his coffee, did his morning workout, got dressed, and drove to work. This was his first day back after the whole thing with Hans. Today was the first Monday of the month of the first quarter. On this day, they always had their quarterly meeting. Gus wondered who was going to speak. Normally, it would be Hans, but it was obvious that was not going to happen.

Gus drove into the parking lot and anticipated his normal five-minute search for a parking spot. As he made his first round in the parking lot, he saw a space very close to the front door. It was open. It had no special markings. But why didn't the guy in the car in front of him take it? Interesting. He pulled in and headed for his office.

As he walked to his office, he noticed everyone was smiling. They seemed to be smiling at him. Gus got to his office, opened the door, and sat down. When he looked up, across the back of his wall was a big banner that read in bold, uppercase letters THE HOUSE. He then looked down at his desk and saw a button about the size of a quarter. The button was the wearable type with a pin on the back. Curving around the top of the button, it said MEEKU FILBEECH. It also had a distorted face of a man with his head back and mouth open, appearing to be screaming. He had a bloody nose, and he looked a lot like Hans.

Gus was amused by all this but did not think too much about it. Occasionally, people at work played small jokes on one another. He knew today was going to be kind of awkward, as he was sure everyone knew about Hans leaving and why.

A couple of hours passed, and it was time to go to the quarterly meeting. As Gus walked to the place where he normally sat, he noticed a couple of people wearing the MEEKU FILBEECH buttons. The more he looked, the more of them he saw. Some were outside people's shirts in plain sight. Others were worn more discreetly, partly under a sweater or jacket.

The speaker of the meeting was Susan Smith. An unexpected pleasure. One of the nicest people one could ever meet. She had been Hans's second in command. She had always taken his abuse but had never passed it on. Everyone loved her.

She got up on stage and introduced herself. She presented the quarterly numbers, which were very good. The mood was upbeat. She was very enthusiastic. At the end of her presentation, she announced that Hans was no longer with the company and that for the foreseeable future, she would be assuming all of his responsibilities.

She thanked everyone for an incredible quarter. Her parting line was, "All this makes me feel really good." Then she yelled with a big smile on her face, "The question is, *How's that make you feel...bitch!*" The crowd broke into major applause. It sounded like the Academy Awards.

The meeting was over, and Gus got up and headed back to his office. As he walked back, everybody who passed him said something to him. People who knew him simply said "thanks" or "cool." Several whom he did not know but had seen around practically squealed *"Meeeeek"* or *"Meeeeekuuuu"* as they passed.

When Gus was almost to his office, he ran into Hank, the Senior Vice President who was responsible for firing Hans and keeping him. He came up to Gus and looked him in the eye. Then he said, "Too difficult to have been preplanned. Too perfect not to have been. You're a very interesting person, Gus Shepard. Very smooth."

Almost expressionless, Hank turned and started to walk away. He then looked back over his shoulder and, with a sinister grin, said to Gus, "Thanks."

Chapter 3
UNBELIEVABLY FAST

It had been a week since the quarterly meeting. Things had calmed down, and life was, for the most part, back to normal. It was Saturday, and Gus had decided to run down to the Mexican area of town and pick up a burrito. He had not had a burrito from his favorite little Mexican restaurant in several weeks and had woken up craving one. He understood this feeling, but something felt different. He wasn't sure why. His senses felt heightened. It was an edgy sensation. He was not sure what he was feeling but decided that he just needed some food in him. It was only 10:30 a.m., and he had no particularly important place to be that day, but Gus found himself hurrying. It was like he had to be someplace on time. He got into his car and started driving.

About a block from the restaurant, Gus saw a street vendor selling fruit. The fruit there was always fresh. Gus parked his car and walked to the fruit stand. Everything looked good, but the watermelon looked really good. He picked one, paid, and started back to his car.

All of a sudden, Gus felt the hair standing up on the back of his neck. His mind was racing. He sensed danger. His attention was immediately drawn to the street intersection. A middle-aged Mexican woman was waiting to cross the street. She had a baby in a stroller, a girl about six years old standing next to her, and she was holding the hand of a boy about four years old. She was obviously struggling, as any mother would be while trying to manage all three kids at the same time. Down the street, Gus saw an older-model Camaro approaching at a high rate of speed. The light was about to change, and Gus could tell the car was accelerating in an attempt to make it through the traffic light.

Then it happened. The four-year-old broke loose from his mother's hand and went running across the street, directly in the path of the speeding car. The woman was helpless. With a baby in a stroller and a six-year-old at her side, she could not chase the small boy. Gus could see the horror on her face.

Gus bolted across the intersection with blinding speed. He reached the boy an instant before the car was about to hit him. He had reacted so quickly that he was still holding the watermelon. With the watermelon under one arm and the boy safely cradled under the other, Gus jumped and hit the windshield of the car. The watermelon burst as it hit the windshield. It sprayed red upon impact. From where the helpless woman was standing, it looked as if the boy had just been splattered into a bloody mess. She screamed. Gus and the boy rolled off to one side of the car, unharmed, out of the woman's sight. The car slammed on its brakes and stopped.

The woman was screaming, "God help me! God help me!"

Gus stood up and let go of the boy, who went running back to the woman. She screamed again in disbelief. With tears in her eyes, she looked toward the sky and yelled, "Thank you, God! Thank you, God!" She then looked at Gus and said, "Thank you, God, for sending me this miracle man!"

Gus drove home feeling pretty good about himself. He had never saved a life before. The woman had begged him to allow her to do something for him, but Gus had refused. He could tell she was sincere and looked harmless, but he was hesitant because he did not want to get involved with some unknown Mexican woman off the street with three kids. She insisted that he at least allow her to make him a batch of homemade tamales. She told him that she would drop them off at his house; he did not even have to be home. How could he resist? Gus loved Mexican food, especially tamales. He gave her his address and headed home.

A couple of days passed, and Gus had just gotten home from work. The message light has flashing on his landline phone recorder, so he pushed the button to review his messages. There was only one, which said, "This is James P. Caldwell with Intellectual Design Systems. Could you please call me?" Then he left his number.

Gus assumed it was a job recruiter…aka…headhunter, because he got these calls often. He was happy with his job and did not plan on leaving and almost erased the phone number. But for some strange reason, he stopped. The guy did not sound like a typical salesman-type headhunter. To his own surprise, Gus found himself dialing the number.

The phone rang a couple of times, and then someone answered, "This is Caldwell."

"This is Gus Shepard. You called me," Gus replied.

"Oh, Mr. Shepard, thank you for calling back." The tone had switched from somewhat cold to enthusiastic. "Let me introduce myself. My name is James Caldwell. I am the most senior technical person and owner and founder of Intellectual Design Systems, or IDS for short. My company designs cameras and recorders for traffic-light monitoring. I've just been served with a subpoena to appear in court for a red-light-runner nearly hitting a small boy. I believe you are the man who saved the little boy?"

"Yes, your assumption is correct, Mr. Caldwell. What can I do for you?" Gus replied.

"Just call me James. I would like to ask a favor of you. I am being called to court as an expert witness on the video recording of the traffic violation. I have reviewed the video very thoroughly, and I have some unanswered questions. I was hoping I could get together with you and review the video so you could give me your perspective of the incident. As payment, I'll give you a copy of the video. After all, how often does someone get a video of themselves saving the life of a small child?" James replied with some enthusiasm.

"I'm not sure I want to get involved," Gus said with some hesitation.

"Whether you like it or not, you are involved because you're the man in the video. If I have some unanswered questions and the court decides they need them answered, then most likely you'll be called to testify."

"If I give you my input, I might be called to testify to clarify what I told you."

"Good point," said James, obviously trying very hard to be convincing but polite. "Once-in-a-lifetime chance to get a free video starring Gus Shepard; what do you say?"

"You are quite convincing, Mr. Caldwell—I mean, James. Yes, I'll meet you. Where would you like meet?" Gus asked.

"I would like you to come down to my company. If you have a cell phone, I'll just text you the address. I was thinking of tomorrow around this time. End of the day always works best for me. It's pretty crazy here for me during the workday."

"OK, sounds like a plan." Gus gave him his cell phone number, said goodbye, and hung up the phone.

The next day, after getting home from work, Gus drove to see James. It wasn't too far away, about twenty minutes from his house. Intellectual Design Systems was in a small building in a high-technology business-park part of town. Gus parked his car and proceeded to the building lobby.

As he walked toward the lobby, he knew he was being watched. He could sense it. On any other day, this might be a casual walk to one's destination. Today, he found himself scanning the building, recording every detail. He was able to see farther and with a greater level of clarity than ever before. In the two minutes that it took to get to the lobby, Gus counted six cameras. Even though they were covered in hard black plastic, he could see that four of the six cameras were panning and tilting to follow him. He could see the camera lenses adjusting inward and outward to improve their focus. Gus then knew that these four cameras were being manually operated and that someone must be watching him on a computer monitor.

Gus could also see someone watching him through the blinds on the windows. They were trying very hard not to be seen. Even though they only moved the blind a tenth of an inch, Gus could see it. He knew it was the same person moving from window to window; he could tell by judging the height, angle, and distance of the opening of the blind.

Gus entered the lobby and saw the letters IDS in a very large, red, circular format on the wall. Intellectual Design Systems was below that in smaller black letters. The lobby looked very professional. Gus introduced himself to the receptionist and told her that he was there to see James Caldwell. She called for Caldwell, and a few minutes later, the door opened, and an older man, about sixty years of age with slightly long gray hair, appeared. He was of average height and had a nonathletic build. He had a college professor look to him.

With a smile on his face, he said, "Hi, I'm James Caldwell. You must be Gus. I wasn't sure when you were going to arrive. I was downstairs in the lab working on a new design. I hope I didn't keep you waiting long."

Gus found his reply interesting. He knew James had not been down in the lab. By looking at James's height, arm length, and distance from his eyes to the ground, Gus knew this was the person who had been watching him through the window blinds. He was probably also the one who had been watching him through the cameras. Probably an unimportant fact. Gus just smiled and said, "Send it to the boys in the lab," like you might hear someone say in a detective movie. They both laughed.

Gus and James headed down the hallway to a room labeled Main Conference Room. They both sat down at a large conference room table. There was an extremely large ninety-inch TV screen on the wall at the opposite end of the table. James looked at Gus with a slightly serious look and said, "I would like to show you the recording taken by my traffic intersection cameras on the day of the incident."

"Do you have surround sound?" Gus asked with a smile.

James said nothing and started the recording on the ninety-inch screen. It was in slow motion. It went frame by frame, slightly pausing in between each of them. James began to narrate with the first frame.

"Here, you see the car entering the intersection as the light is changing. This is what triggers the camera to begin. On the other side of the street, you can see the boy entering the crosswalk. As we process each frame, you can see the boy get farther into the street and the car get closer.

"Now, watch this next frame very closely. This blurry object in front of the car is you. The next frame, the boy is gone. The next several frames are the car slamming on its breaks and sliding through the intersection."

James turned the TV to pause. He looked at Gus very seriously and said, "Do you realize what I have just shown you? You ran from the sidewalk, grabbed the boy, and were out of sight of the camera in just one frame! In human terms, that is physically impossible."

Gus looked calmly at James and said, "There must have been a camera malfunction."

"Exactly my first thought," James replied. "But I went through every slide. Everything correlates. The speed of the car, the rate of change of the traffic signal, the movement of the boy through the crosswalk. Even the speed of an airplane in the sky and the tire marks of the skidding car all match. The only thing that does not match is the rate of speed at which you moved to save the boy.

"Mister Shepard, I believe this may be one of the first recordings ever of superhuman abilities that sometimes come out during the fear and panic in a situation like this. I would like to take this movie public. I would agree to give you all monies gained from this as long as you give me the acknowledgment as being the person who was responsible for recording this."

He stared right at Gus, his eyes wide open, not blinking. Gus looked right back at him and calmly said, "No, thank you, Mister Caldwell. Not interested."

"Thank you," James replied.

"Thank you?" Gus said, somewhat puzzled at James's response.

"You just answered one of my questions about you. You are basically an honest man. You did not even consider the financial gain. That is hard to come by these days. I never really had any plans to take this public. I interviewed the Mexican lady who was walking with the boy whose life you saved. She thinks you were sent by God. She said she saw the boy get hit by the car and then explode in a bloody mess. I did not have the heart to tell her it was a watermelon. She said she closed her eyes and prayed, and when she opened them, the boy was running to her, and you were standing there. She thinks you are an angel.

"Mister Shepard, I do not believe in God, but I do believe in good and evil. I believe we as humans have a duty to recognize good when we see it. Once we recognize it, we must then support it. Gus, there is something very special about you. The speed at which you saved that boy is unexplainable. I will not let this be shown in court. I will just say the results were inconclusive."

Gus replied, "Do I still get a copy?"

Now James smiled and said, "Yes, one for me and one for you and none for anybody else." Looking serious again, he said, "Your actions have answered another question for me about you. This whole time, you never acted surprised over anything I showed you. You never denied that what I showed you was true. You are something special, and I think you know it. I truly believe you are good. I want you to know that I feel I have truly found good on a large scale. As a true believer in good and evil, I believe it is my duty as a good human being to support you. Whatever you need from me, anytime, anyplace, anywhere, I will make whatever capabilities I have available to you. I really mean it."

Gus looked him straight in the eye and said, "I know you do."

Gus walked to the front lobby, escorted by James. As Gus was leaving, he turned to James and said, "Forgetting something?"

James looked at Gus as if they were now good friends and said, "Of course not." He shuffled through an old leather bag he was carrying, reading the names on several CDs. "Here it is." He handed Gus a CD that was labeled UNBELIEVEABLY FAST.

Chapter 4
A WALK IN THE PARK

Gus had the day off. He had nothing in particular planned. As he religiously did four days a week, Gus decided it was a good day to do his morning workout. Unlike many children who start martial arts training as early as four years old, Gus was not allowed to study martial arts until he was fourteen years old. This was because Gus's father taught the type of martial arts used for war. It was only taught to highly trained soldiers. Its only purpose beyond self-defense was to injure, paralyze, or kill.

Gus was now training hard, like a soldier preparing for war. His speed and power had been increasing weekly. He had become lightning fast. Gus found the power of his strikes to be incredible even to him.

Hand strikes put indentions in the bag four inches deep. His foot strikes rocked the bag so hard, he knew that the bag would soon rip from the chains holding it to the ceiling.

After his workout, Gus went about his day taking care of those miscellaneous chores in life. He got some clothes washed, did some light grocery shopping, and kind of straightened up around the house. Normally, after a workout day, he would be tired and wanting to relax. It was the end of the day, and he still felt full of energy. He was starting to realize that he was not the man he used to be. He felt like he was a whole new man living in the shell of the human being he once was. One part of him knew he had changed. Another part of him knew that a lot of the things he was doing now he had always been capable of doing. He had just never had the motivation to do it.

Gus knew it was getting a little late, but there was still an hour or so of daylight left. He decided that he would go for a quick run through the park where he used to walk his dog. The mystical guard dog that had changed his life.

After putting on his sweat clothes and stretching, Gus headed for the park. He took the scenic route, and after about a mile reached a point where he was approaching the restrooms. As he approached, he saw two Mexican men with a large, muscular pit bull on a leash. They were drinking and laughing.

Gus slowed his run to a jog to give himself time to observe the situation, since they had not seen him yet. The man with the dog on the leash was of average height and husky, with a barrel body. His shaved head sat upon a neckless torso. He had a short beard shaved into a goatee, and looked kind of crazy. The other guy had a large athletic build, a larger nose, high cheekbones, and looked like a painting of an Aztec warrior that one might see in a Mexican restaurant.

Gus slowed his jog to a near walk. He could see that these guys had been drinking. Each had a glass quart bottle of some kind of cheap, high-alcohol beer in his hand. They were both laughing and yelling. It was hard for Gus to understand what they were saying because they kept switching between English and Spanish.

All of a sudden, the barrel-bodied guy yelled a command, and the pit bull jumped up over five feet in the air and clamped its jaw on an overhanging tree limb. And it just hung there! The Aztec-looking guy put down his beer and started punching the dog as if he were punching a bag in a gym. He was hitting the dog hard. Then he backed off and grabbed his knuckles, which were bleeding from hitting the dog. The barrel-bodied guy yelled another command, and the dog dropped from the tree. They both started laughing loudly and chanting, "Rocky, Rocky, Rocky," obviously referring to the old Sylvester Stallone boxing movies.

Gus had planned to keep on going, as this was none of his business and they seemed to be ignoring his presence. But something just was not right. He could sense the aggressiveness of the pit bull, but he could also sense the emotions of another animal in danger. As he was passing, he saw a small Chihuahua with a pink collar cowering by a retaining wall in front of the men. This dog did not belong here. The small dog was too scared to run. Gus decided to stop and watch.

The bigger guy who had been punching the dog was letting the pit bull lick his knuckles, and yelling, "Blood, blood!" Then the barrel-bodied guy started yelling, "Kill, kill!"

The pit bull was going wild. The barrel-bodied guy could hardly hold him. Gus realized the guy was about to let the pit bull rip the small Chihuahua to pieces. The small dog let out a loud yelp.

Gus could feel his adrenaline pumping. Then, from deep within his body, he let out an extremely loud, bloodthirsty, growling yell. It sounded like a prehistoric animal!

The pit bull stopped in its tracks. It turned and made eye contact with Gus. The dog then laid down and did not move.

The barrel-bodied guy holding the dog looked at Gus and then down at the pit bull. He angrily started yelling at the dog, "Kill, kill!" but the pit bull still would not move. He started kicking it in the head with all his force. He kicked it four or five times before Gus ran up and told him to stop.

The guy looked at Gus and said nothing. As Gus bent over to look at the dog, he heard the barrel-bodied guy say, "Maybe instead of the dog, I should kick you!"

Just as Gus looked up, the guy kicked him in the face. He instinctively turned his head, but the kick still brushed the side of Gus's face. He tasted blood in his mouth and felt an incredible rage flowing through his body. He flashed back to his father hitting him in the mouth during a martial arts training session and telling him, "Never take your eyes off your opponent if he's within striking distance."

Gus instinctively rolled with the kick and landed on his feet in a crouching position. Almost immediately, the next kick was delivered. Gus diverted the kick from the guy's right leg with a left-hand bent-wrist block and hooked his hand on the inside of the guy's ankle. He immediately grabbed the guy's other ankle with his right hand, then bolted to a standing position, raising his hands above his head and taking the guy's feet with him. He did this with such speed that he lifted the guy's feet above his head, spinning his body with a Ferris Wheel type motion. The guy's arms went out as he lost his balance. The back of his head, neck, and upper body slammed to the asphalt with a thud. He hit so hard that it knocked the wind out of him. Almost unconscious, he rolled to his side, gasping for air.

Out of the corner of his eye, Gus looked back and saw the Aztec-looking guy charging at him like a mad bull. Both his arms were stretched out, and he was going for Gus's head. Gus stepped toward him, pivoted, and delivered a solid back kick, the heel of his foot slamming directly into the guy's groin.

The force of the guy moving forward combined with the force of Gus stepping into him was like two cars in a head-on collision. The guy was hit so hard that his legs were lifted off the ground. He fell to the ground and curled up into a fetal position, his hands grasping his groin. Curled up like a baby on the ground, he loudly yelled, *"Fuuuuuck!"* Then he let out a smaller grunt. He had been kicked so hard that he pissed his pants.

Gus looked down at the pit bull that was still lying on the ground, and they locked eyes. The dog was an alpha male. He had to defend his master. The dog's honor was at stake. Gus knew and understood this. He snarled, then looked straight into the dog's eyes. In a communication unknown to man, he told the dog, "You must attack. Do it now."

The pit bull charged, its lean, muscular body coming at Gus like a bullet. Knowing what the dog had to do, Gus had positioned himself next to the bathroom. At the instant the dog leaped and became airborne, he stepped to the side, grabbed the dog's neck, and slammed its head into the bathroom wall. The dog fell to the ground with a loud bang. It had hit the wall so hard it had left a large dent in the side of the steel-walled bathroom. The dog's head was of solid bone and as hard as a rock, but it was now too stunned to react.

Gus then pushed open the bathroom door and went inside. He took off his sweatshirt and hung it over the bathroom stall door. He went into a stall, flushed the toilet, and quietly ran back to the main bathroom door. He quickly pulled the door open and stood behind it. Just as he had planned, the pit bull came charging in and ran straight for the bathroom stall. Gus slipped out through the door and closed the door behind him. The pit bull charged for the closed door, hitting hard with all its weight. Gus knew the door opened inward, and was aware of the character of this type of dog. He knew that its extreme anger would inhibit it from thinking clearly, and was sure it would take some time for the dog to get out. In fact, most likely the dog would not get out until one of the guys opened the door for it.

He looked at the small dog and, without saying a word, told it to leave. The small dog looked at him for just a second, then ran its fastest. It knew exactly what he was telling it to do. With the pit bull barking wildly from behind the bathroom door and the two guys rolling and moaning on the ground, he decided now was a good time to leave.

Gus ran home, looking back often to make sure he wasn't being followed. He got home, showered, and changed clothes. It was interesting to him how he felt. He felt good. Saving the life of the small dog had a special feeling. He had saved the life of a small boy, which was fantastic. This had made him a hero in many people's eyes. But saving the life of a worthless street dog had a special feeling. Nobody cared about that dog and probably never would. Possibly risking his life for something so insignificant would have seemed foolish to most people. But it was the right thing to do. Now that made him feel like a real hero.

All the excitement had made him hungry. Gus decided to go for a ride and get some food. For some reason, he thought to look out his window before he left. To his surprise, with his super-enhanced vision, he saw the two Mexican guys parked down the street from his house in a brand-new Ford Mustang GT. He recognized the bald head and goatee of the driver. It was the barrel-bodied Mexican guy. The bigger, Aztec-looking guy was on the passenger side.

Gus couldn't figure out how they had found him. Maybe it was just a coincidence. They were several blocks away and looking down the street, away from his house. For a second, he considered calling the police, but the crazy feeling he had wasn't fright. It was excitement.

Since Gus had lost his car in the accident, he had upgraded to a very fast Porsche 911 Turbo. He quietly opened his garage door and slowly backed out, constantly watching to make sure that they hadn't seen him. He slowly pulled up to them and, with his best Mexican accent, said, "*¿Como esta?*"

The big guy in the passenger side looked over, and his eyes bulged. Without saying a word, he slapped his partner on the shoulder, and he also looked over. Then Gus slammed the gas pedal to the floor. The twin turbos kicked in, and the 911 screamed as it took off.

He looked back and saw the smoking tires of the Mustang as it began the chase. Gus raced to an industrial area where there were no people. It was 8:00 p.m. and quiet since everybody had gone home. Now, it was fun time!

As Gus reached the industrial area, he slowed down just enough for them to catch up. Then he raced away just to see how long it took them to catch up. His adrenaline was pumping, his heart racing. He had no idea why he was doing this. He seemed to crave excitement and danger. As far as acceleration and cornering went, Gus knew he had a better vehicle. But these guys were good. It took him over five minutes to gain a substantial lead every time he let them catch up.

After several games of cat and mouse, Gus started to tire and decided it was time to leave. He didn't want them to follow him home and was pretty sure that they didn't know where he lived, so he came up with a plan.

Gus pulled out of the industrial area onto a main street. This time, he waited to make sure that they could see him and let them get really close. As they approached, Gus could hear the big Aztec guy yelling, "You're going to die, bitch!"

They were on a long, straight road. Gus had turned it into a drag race. It was American muscle versus German technology. Without having the advantage of being able to lose them on the turns, they were staying very close behind. Both cars screamed down the road. As they approached the next intersection, Gus slammed on his breaks and slid into a hard left turn, knowing that they couldn't make it. Just as he calculated, they raced through the intersection. The intersection where a cop always sat about that time. Gus saw the red lights and heard the siren. In his rearview mirror, he saw them pull over with the cop right behind them. Gus had a smile on his face. Now that was fun! He decided to take the long way home. Those guys were going to be tied up for a while.

Taking his time, Gus drove back home. As he was pulling up to his house, he realized a black Cadillac Escalade ESV Platinum with tinted windows was parked in his driveway. The occupant was not visible to the human eye. Using his superior vision, Gus was able to see that there was only one person in the vehicle on the driver's side. He could not see what he looked like. Parking in front of the house, Gus got out of the car and slowly started walking toward the Escalade.

All of a sudden, the two Mexican guys in the Mustang came racing down the street and came to a screeching stop, blocking his Porsche. How could they have known where he lived? When he had pulled out of his house, he had watched their eyes. They had never looked back or looked in their rearview mirrors. How had they gotten there so quickly? The traffic cop should have detained them for at least ten minutes, and he had gotten home in five. And who was this guy in the driveway? It didn't look good. Gus could have run, but some inner instinct told him not to panic.

The two guys got out of the car. They walked up to the driveway and stopped. They looked angry and tough. Gus turned and looked at them. They weren't within striking distance and had no visible weapons. He then turned to the Escalade. The driver's side door opened. Out stepped a short Mexican man with many tattoos. Gus saw something shiny on his seat. Possibly the shiny chrome of a gun.

Gus moved in closer to his opponent. He knew it was too late to run, and if this guy had a gun, he would be better off being close so he could attack before he fired. Out of the corner of his eye, he saw the other two guys moving in on him. Just when Gus thought it was going to get ugly, the guy who had gotten out of the Escalade put up his hand and sternly said, "No!"

The two guys behind Gus froze. This guy was obviously in charge. He looked at Gus and said, "Hey, man, do you live here?"

"Yes," Gus said.

"Amazing," the guy said. He quickly added, "My friends are angry and think they want a rematch. But now they can't have one. Let me introduce myself. Most people call me Mono, and I have something special for you."

He reached into his vehicle and grabbed the shiny metal object off the seat. Gus prepared for attack. As he turned toward Gus, he held a silver pan covered with aluminum foil.

Gus, quite surprised, looked at him and asked, "What is it?"

Mono replied, "Tamales! You saved a little boy's life. That woman who promised you tamales was my sister. That little boy was my son. I wanted to personally deliver these tamales and meet you. I want you to know, man, that I owe you big time. Whatever you might need from me that I can provide, you got it. I got your back." He then smiled at Gus with a used car salesman-type grin, exposing his front teeth, one of which was made of gold.

Gus could tell he was sincere, and felt a little more at ease. He smiled in return and replied, "I'm very happy that things turned out the way they did. I think maybe it was fate."

Mono then got a more serious look on his face and said, "I know what you mean, man. Fate, destiny—it was supposed to be. There's some reason our paths have crossed. My sister thinks you were sent by God. She's a very religious woman. She said she saw my son die. She said she saw the car hit him and blood flying everywhere. She closed her eyes and screamed to God, and when she opened them, you were standing there with not even a scratch, and my son was running back to her.

"You know, my sister has a gift. She sees things in her dreams. She says you're something special. That God has sent you and that I must help you. Sometimes I think she's crazy, but many times, what she sees in her dreams come true. I look at you, man, and I can tell, there's something different about you. Strange coincidence that you're the same guy who beat up my guys in the park. And after that, they're meeting me to deliver tamales to you. Then you beat them up behind the wheel of a car. Man, you outdrove Poco, my best driver, and he's really good. You know, if I wasn't bringing you these tamales, I'm sure we would have met one way or another. And when we did, it would've been very bad and painful for you."

Gus heard the two guys behind him laugh. He looked at Mono and said, "I'm happy that I saved your son's life, but I ask for nothing in return. I'm not sure I need anything that you provide. What are you, anyway—a gang leader?"

Mono quickly replied, "No, man, I'm a facilitator. You got gangs, cops, rich people, poor people, and politicians. I facilitate their needs. I bring people together and mix and match their needs. I help them all." He smiled his salesman grin, his gold tooth shining, and said, "Hey man, I fly just below the radar but high enough to stay out of jail. I'm very well connected and very helpful to many people in many ways. Just like the cop who pulled over my boys. I help him, he helps me. How do think my boys got here so fast?"

"That one did have me confused," Gus replied.

"Take this phone number. It's my private cell phone number. Call or text me anytime, day or night. I got your back, man."

Gus took the number and smiled as they both shook hands. They left, and Gus went back into his house.

Chapter 5
GRIN AND BEAR IT

Gus had been doing well at work. His pay had gone up significantly, and he had just received a bonus. He now worked in a secure part of the company reserved for only their top scientists. The company he worked for had a strong belief that employees should take quality time off. So when they offered Gus a paid vacation in the mountains for a week, how could he turn it down? He had always loved the woods, nature, and hiking.

Gus packed up and prepared to go. It was Sunday night, and he was leaving the next morning. As he was getting ready for bed, the phone rang.

"Hello, Gus! It's Dad."

"Daaaaaaad!" Gus yelled as he always did, followed by an immediate "What's up?" in a slight gangster tone.

His father laughed and said, "Gus, I have something important to talk to you about. The government, which includes myself, watches a lot of people who watch a lot of things. Your name has popped up on a list some people call an SIP list: Significantly Important People."

"Is this good or bad?" Gus asked.

"Don't know. It could be as simple as someone wants information on you because they're interested in hiring you. It could be as complicated as someone might want to kill you because your beliefs are different than theirs. Or sometimes you're just a pawn in somebody's twisted game of chess. They need to manipulate you to influence their game. This list you're on is put together by a group of people that pride themselves on their ability to gather information on everybody and everything. While they are legal, they're definitely not ethical. The same goes for the people who buy the list and other information from them."

"Should I be concerned?"

"Just stay alert. Keep your eyes and ears open. Your situation has changed. I sense that your journey is about to begin. I understand that you're going on a vacation tomorrow?"

"How did you know that? I hadn't told you yet."

"It's my job to know these things, and for some reason, I might be paying special attention to your situation. Let me think, what could that reason be? Oh yeah, you're my son."

They both laughed. Then his father said, "When you get up there, I'll have you meet a friend of mine. He's a short, fat, Eskimo man. If you get into any trouble, he can help you out. Oh, by the way—if you're in a bind and he asks you do things that seem awkward, just trust him."

"How will I find him?"

"Don't worry, he'll find you."

They talked for a while, then said good night and hung up the phone.

Gus flew out early Monday morning and arrived that evening. He checked into a local hotel. The town was small: two hotels, a market, a gas station, a bar, and a church.

While Gus was wandering around town, he noticed a cute little twentysomething-year-old girl. She had long black hair and was of American Indian or Eskimo decent. She worked in the market. The first time Gus walked in, their eyes locked. Gus had gone back to the store several times after that, but she would not look at him.

Gus wasn't very aggressive when it came to women. In his mind, he decided this was just another one of his make-believe romances. He would probably go home when his vacation was over without her name or phone number. Gus decided to stick to his plan. He loved hiking and nature. There were many good hiking trails, so he spent the next couple of days hiking and enjoying nature.

It was now the end of the day, and Gus only had a couple of days left. He had already eaten dinner, so he decided to go to the market and pick up a couple of microbrewed beers and then go back to his room and rest.

Gus went back to the market, and the cute little Indian girl was working. No one else was in the store, so she could not ignore him. She was nice and business like, but this time it was different. As he talked to her, he could feel his animal instincts kicking in. He could feel the heat. All his senses seem heightened. With his superior sense of smell, he could detect a slight scent pulsing from his body. A scent that was beyond what a human could smell. He also noticed a slight scent pulsing from her body. The smell from his body seemed to pulse and then fade. Each time his scent pulsed and faded, so did hers. As his scent pulses got heavier, her body responded the same way. The minutes he spent buying those beers seemed like hours. Gus left feeling something he had never felt before: He felt like a frustrated but determined animal.

Gus went back to his room. He had already eaten and had two big, tasty beers to drink. Normally, this would have made him happy. But this time, he found himself pacing the room. As he was looking out of his front window, he saw the little Indian girl again. She was going into the bar across the street.

Normally Gus wasn't a guy who drank in a bar. Sometimes after work, he might have had a couple of beers with some coworkers, but for the most part, he'd always felt uncomfortable with the bar scene. He had never liked drinking with people he did not know. Also, he was wondering, *Why's a nice girl like that going into a bar?*

None of this seemed to matter now. He was being driven by animal instincts. He was being driven by desire. Gus wanted to see this girl. Typically, he would spend some time cleaning up and shaving, and looking at himself in the mirror before going out, especially if he might see a woman he was attracted to. This time, he didn't care. He grabbed his jacket, and as he was leaving, he looked into the mirror. He snarled like a dog and smiled at the same time. A look he had seen before. A look he liked.

Gus crossed the street and walked into the bar. He was surprised at how many people were there and how lively it was. He thought to himself, *This is a weekday. Don't these people work?*

Gus scanned the room looking for the little Indian girl, still wondering what she was doing here. The bar was mostly filled with grubby mountain type looking men and a few rough looking women. They all looked like regulars. Then he saw her. She had on a short, tight, deer skin dress and high heels. She had looked good in the market, but now she looked extremely hot. She was carrying a tray full of drinks. She was a waitress! Obviously, this was a second job for her.

Gus sat down at a small table by himself. He knew she would have to serve him. He watched her move around the room. She was all smiles and talkative. She had not seen him yet. Then she did. She approached his table and stared directly into his eyes. Her eyes glared with the look of desire. Normally, Gus would look away, but this time his head wouldn't turn.

She came up to Gus and said, "Would you like a drink?"

Gus replied, "I'd like to know your name and a beer, in that order."

She smiled and said, "My name is Naomi."

"Thank you," said Gus then quickly replied, "I'll take an Amber on draft."

"Coming right up," she said.

Gus stared as she turned and walked away, her tight dress clinging to her toned and shapely body. Even though his brain was dizzy with desire, he found himself analyzing what she was wearing. Everything she wore now was different than what she had worn in the market except for her necklace. The necklace did not look like jewelry. It looked handmade and had a spiritual appearance to it.

She returned with the beer in a tall, frosty mug. Eagar to strike up a conversation, Gus asked, "I noticed that you changed your clothes from what you were wearing in the market. And I must say, you look stunning. But you're still wearing the necklace you had on in the market. Is it special?"

Her expression turned from smiling and flirty to somewhat serious. She said, "This necklace was given to me by my grandfather. He was an Indian Chief. He was the descendent of many great Indian Chiefs. I have worn it since I was a child. This necklace is sacred and blessed. He told me that whenever I am wearing this necklace, the spirits will watch over me."

Gus listened intently, then asked with a smile, "Do you take it off when you shower?"

She smiled and replied, "Stick around, and maybe you'll find out." She turned and quickly walked back toward the bar.

Gus could feel his pulse racing. He was intoxicated, and it wasn't from the beer. Gus watched her move around the bar. He downed a beer, then another one, and then another after that. Not to get drunk, but just to have the pleasure of having her serve him.

As Gus sat at his table, two men walked in through the front door. They had on thick coats that looked like something an Eskimo might wear. They checked both their rifles in at the door, as there were many hunters in the area and no guns were allowed inside the building. They looked like they were trying hard to appear like locals, but Gus could tell that they were not. Their hair was cut short, and they had a military look to them.

They both sat at the bar. Gus watched Naomi serve them. Her demeanor had changed. She seemed to be smiling, but to Gus, it looked kind of fake. He noticed that while she was talking to them, one guy looked directly at Gus, then quickly looked away. Gus pretended not to notice.

After about an hour, the bar got very busy. It was packed with locals, mostly men. Up until now, Gus had been getting good service from Naomi. He knew she was busy, but she seemed to be ignoring him. Finally, she came up to him and said, "Hey babe, I'm getting kind of busy. Why don't you come over to the bar? I can give you better service over there." She seemed a little bit less friendly, but Gus just thought to himself, *She's busy and concentrating on her work.*

Gus got up and walked across the room to the bar. He sat next to the military looking guys who were dressed like locals. Gus was starting to get drunk. Normally, by now he would start drinking water to sober up a little, but he was feeling good. So when one of the men sitting next to him said, "Would you like to join us in a shot of high quality tequila? We're buying," Gus said, "Sure, bring it on!"

They introduced themselves as Ike and Mike. Gus didn't pay much attention to which one was Ike or Mike. They had a similar military look to them, and he was more interested in Naomi. They did a toast and downed their shots. Gus tried to ignore them, but they kept trying to talk to him. Every time one of them tried to talk to him, the other one tried to hit on Naomi. It was starting to anger Gus.

Then one of them said, "Hey, you good at darts?"

Gus said, "No, not really. I haven't played much, but I believe that I can still kick your ass." Actually, he had played a lot as a kid, and sitting at the bar not being able to talk to Naomi was killing him. He had to change the situation.

One of them stood up and said, "Well then, I challenge you to a game."

The other one said, "Go easy on him, Ike." He smiled at his friend, which made Gus think, *This guy must be good.* In his mind Gus said to himself, *Ike is the dart guy, the other guy is Mike.*

They moved over to the dartboard. Some locals were playing, so when they finished, they moved to the side and decided to stay and watch Gus and Ike play. They played the first game. It was very close, but Gus won. He found that he was much better than he used to be as a kid. His precision, muscle control, and aim were greatly improved. He was able to land every dart exactly where he wanted to. The guys watching cheered. Ike acted irritated, but Gus could tell that he was much better than he was playing. He was holding back for some reason. Like he was some kind of hustler.

Ike immediately challenged Gus to another game. This time, Ike threw much better. The game was very close, but once again, Gus won. By now, six to eight guys were watching the game. They cheered loudly. Gus was drunk and was doing a victory dance. Ike seemed to be irritated by all the attention Gus was getting but kept his emotions contained.

Gus finished his dance and started to walk to the bar when Ike yelled, "One more game!"

Gus replied, "No thanks, I'm done."

"A hundred dollars says I can kick your ass."

"No thanks."

Ike quickly shot back, "Wimp!"

Gus realized that nearly the whole bar was looking at him, including Naomi. He then yelled, "Let's get it on!"

The whole bar was now focused on the game. Gus knew Naomi was watching, and he was feeling a little cocky. They started playing. Every dart Ike threw, Gus matched, except for one throw. Ike had a small lead. Then Ike threw his last dart and landed a bull's-eye. He got very excited and yelled, "Game over! Cough up the hunsky!"

Gus replied with a baby-faced look, "But I'm not done yet."

Ike said, "Just throw the dart...wimp!"

Gus then asked loudly, "Are we playing by standard house rules? Who knows the rules?"

Most people looked over at an old white guy sitting on a wooden stool, quietly watching the game. Gus walked over to him and whispered in his ear. The guy whispered back to Gus, then smiled and said, "Good luck."

Gus walked over to his throwing position, looked at Ike, and said, "Let's make it two hundred...wimp!"

Ike looked at him and said, "I'm not sure if you're just drunk or stupid or both. Sure thing, buddy, I'll take your money if you want."

Gus could hear people in the bar laughing at him. He raised his hand to throw, and the bar got quiet. Gus threw his last dart and hit the bull's-eye, and at the same time knocked one of Ike's bull's-eyes off the board.

The crowd was silent. They all looked over at the old man sitting on the stool. He smiled and said, "I'll be damned. The fallen dart counts as a zero." He pointed to Gus and said, "This young man is the winner!"

Gus started jumping around and dancing. As Ike began walking back to the bar, he blurted out, "Hunskies?"

Ike looked very irritated and said, "You'll get it." Then he mumbled, "One way or another." Gus, with his superior hearing, heard every word Ike said.

Ike went over to Mike, who was still sitting at the bar, and borrowed another hundred. Instead of handing it to Gus, Ike put the money on the bar in front of the stool where Gus had been sitting. Obviously, if Gus wanted his money, he had to go back and sit next to them. Both guys seemed a little tenser. It was clear that they did not like to lose. Mike was now sitting close to Gus, with Ike sitting on the other side of Mike.

Mike looked at Gus and said, "Are you a gambling man?"

"I don't gamble, but I've been known to take calculated risks." Then Gus laughed.

"Do you play poker?"

"A little."

"Ya, you play darts a little, too. How about a game: you, me, and Ike? Give us a chance to get our money back."

"Always willing to give a man a second chance," Gus said. "Let's do it."

They all got up and went to a small table in the corner of the bar. Gus was drunk but alert. He was starting to feel a little uncomfortable around these guys.

Mike got a deck of cards from the bartender and said, "I'll deal. Do you want to check the cards?"

"No, I trust the bartender," Gus replied. Mike just smiled like he knew something that Gus didn't.

The game started out normally, with Gus winning some, then losing some. Then Gus started winning. Mike was staying cool, and Ike was making a lot of noise. Ike was acting like he was getting mad, but Gus could tell he was faking. Gus could see that Mike and Ike were working as a team. They were trying to manipulate him. Gus decided to play his own game, and started acting drunker than he was. He followed their pattern. When they wanted him to bid high, they gave him good cards. When they wanted him to bid low, they gave him bad cards. Little did they know that Gus was counting cards. He had been taught this long ago, but it had always seemed difficult. Now he knew exactly what he was doing, and it took very little effort.

Ike then made his best effort to distract Gus, but out of the corner of his eye, Gus saw Mike slip a card into the deck. Gus said nothing. He knew he was being set up. Gus got dealt a low hand, a pair of tens, and knew that they expected him to bid low. But he also knew that his low hand beat theirs. So he yawned and said, "Aw, what the hell. I'm tired but feel lucky." He then pushed half of his money to the center of the table.

Mike looked confused. Mike knew if he backed out now, Gus might just stop playing. He looked at Ike, nodded his head, and then Ike said, "I fold. I'm out."

Mike was thinking, "If this guy will bet this much on two pair, I'll give him a really good hand next round and take all his money." So then Mike said, "I'll see your bet and call." Mike knew he was going to lose. He did not care. He would get Gus the next round.

Mike lost and gave Gus a substantial amount of money. Gus then yawned and said, "I think I'm done."

Mike quickly replied, "Come on—one more hand. One more and we're done."

Gus replied, "OK. One more hand, and that's it."

Mike smiled and dealt the cards. When the dealing was done, Gus looked at his cards. His hand was very good, but he knew Mike had a better hand and that Ike's cards were worthless. Gus could see the excitement in Mike's eyes. Gus sat up in his chair, pretending to show excitement over his good set of cards.

Mike said, "Your bet."

Gus then looked straight into Mike's eyes. He took all of his money and started to slide it to the center of the table as if he were going to bet it all. Then he slid the money back and said, "I fold. I'm out." He smiled with an ear-to-ear grin.

Ike immediately said, "You can't do that." He looked at Mike and said, "He can't do that, can he?"

Mike looked at Ike and said, "Shut up, you idiot." Then Mike looked at Gus with anger in his eyes and said, "Fuck you. You hustled us."

Gus said, "What are you talking about? It's not like I slipped an extra card into the deck or anything like that."

Mike then knew he had better be quiet. He still had to get the extra card out of the deck that he had slipped in earlier in the game. People would shoot you in a place like this for cheating at cards.

Ike stood up very quickly, knocking his chair over as if preparing for a fight. Mike just smiled and said, "I guess you won fair and square. Game over. I'd buy you a drink, but you took most of our money. Sure would be nice if you bought us a drink."

Gus replied, "As a small token of my appreciation, I'll gladly buy you gentlemen a drink."

They all got up and walked back to the bar. This time, Mike sat on Gus's left, and Ike sat on his right, putting him in between them.

Mike then said, "Let's play a drinking game. Just you and me. I pick a drink for you, and you pick a drink for me. We each tell the bartender and surprise each other. But we must promise to drink the drink that the other one has picked for us."

Gus knew Mike was up to something, and started calculating the possibilities. Gus said, "I'll try anything once and some stuff twice. Sounds good to me." He then looked at the bartender and said, "I'll take one of those small cigars and a lighter."

The bartender brought them to Gus. He grabbed the lighter, lit it a couple of times, and adjusted the flame up high, preparing to light his cigar. Then Gus leaned over to the bartender and quietly said, "Could you please get a twenty-two-ounce beer for the man sitting next to me?"

Then Mike called the bartender over and whispered to him. The bartender looked horrified. He looked at Mike and said, "Are you sure?"

"Yes, I'm very sure," he said.

The bartender came back and put the large beer in front of Mike. In front of Gus, he put what looked like a large glass of water. Gus looked at the bartender and asked, "What's this?"

With a sour expression, the bartender said, "It's rum. One hundred and fifty-one proof."

Gus looked at Mike and said, "You're kidding. I can't drink that."

Mike quickly pulled out a large hunting knife and put it up to Gus's neck. His eyes were bulging. Mike screamed, "Drink, you fuckin' asshole. Drink it, or I'll cut your fuckin' throat!"

Ike jumped away from the bar as if preparing for a fight. The bar was silent, and everyone was staring. Gus calmly replied, "OK, but I'll have to drink it in gulps. One mouthful at a time."

"Drink it!" Mike yelled.

Gus picked up the glass and filled his mouth. He turned and looked at Mike. Then, with one quick motion, he grabbed Mike's knife hand and spit the ultra-high-proof alcohol into his face. With the lighter in his other hand, he lit Mike's face on fire!

Mike screamed loudly but only for a second. Gus immediately kicked the bar stool out from underneath him and at the same time slammed Mike's head into the bar. He fell to the floor, nearly unconscious, with his face on fire.

Gus grabbed Mike's drink from the bar and said, "You forgot your beer." Then Gus threw the beer in Mike's face, putting out the fire, revealing Mike's burned eyebrows and eyelashes, and his bright red face.

Gus quickly turned, as Ike was behind him. He was about ten feet away on the dance floor. He was standing in a fighting position with his right leg forward and slightly crouched. In his right hand he had a large hunting knife. Gus slowly stepped into the middle of the room, keeping his distance. He knew that even an untrained man with a knife was dangerous, and Ike obviously had some training, making him very dangerous.

Gus unbuckled his thick leather belt, pulled it off, and wrapped it twice around his hand. With the metal buckle hanging at the end of about two and a half feet of leather, Gus had a weapon of his own. Ike lunged forward with the knife in his right hand attempting to stab him. Gus jumped back and, with a swift, tightly controlled swing of the belt, hit Ike in his right eye.

The buckle hit Ike hard. Ike stumbled backward and looked surprised, blood dripping down the side of his face. He lunged at Gus two more times attempting to stab him. Gus returned two more stinging blows. Again, the buckle end of the belt struck the area around Ike's right eye. Gus could see that Ike's right eye was swollen and nearly closed. He decided that now was a good time to end this. Gus charged in with a burst of rapid, close-quarter swings, of the belt hitting Ike in the face several times, while never taking his eyes off the knife. Before Ike could recover, Gus hit Ike's right arm, which was holding the knife, at the wrist with the belt. The belt wrapped tightly around Ike's wrist. Gus then yanked Ike's arm down, keeping the knife away from himself. With Ike off balance and the weapon temporarily under control, Gus landed a full-power left hook perfectly to the tip of Ike's jaw. Ike dropped to the floor like a rag doll. He was out.....cold.

Gus looked around. Mike was starting to get up, but he was moving very slowly. Ike was unconscious, lying on the floor. Gus kicked the knife away from Ike. Everyone in the bar stared. Nobody said anything. Then a skinny guy with a red flannel hunting shirt yelled with a smile, "You're one tough son of a bitch!"

Then somebody else yelled, "Yeeeeee haaaaaa!"

After that, everybody started talking and laughing almost like nothing had happened. Gus grabbed his jacket and headed toward the door. He stopped there, turned, and put his hand above his head in a wave goodbye. Everybody clapped, waved, and whistled as he turned and walked out.

Gus knew that this trouble was going to follow him. He headed straight to his room and started packing. Just as he was nearly ready to leave, he heard a faint knock at the door. Gus quietly walked over to the door and looked through the viewing hole. It was Naomi.

He opened the door, and in front of him stood pure beauty. They both stared at each other for less than a second. For Gus, it felt like an eternity.

She spoke first. "Can I come in? I must talk to you."

Gus let her in and shut the door.

"You must leave. Those men are looking for you. They mean you harm. The last bus for the airport leaves in twenty minutes. I will show you the way."

Gus caught himself being overwhelmed with her beauty, but then his protective instincts kicked in. He looked her straight in the eyes and said, "How do you know what these men are going to do? Do you know them?"

Naomi looked straight back into Gus's eyes and replied, "I do not know those men. They are not from around here. They paid me fifty dollars to get you to come sit at the bar. They said that they just wanted to talk to you. I did not ask why. When they were leaving, I heard them say that they were going to hurt you. They have guns."

Gus replied, "How do I know I can trust you?"

"Trust comes from one's heart. It cannot be determined by spoken words. Trust is a feeling that one must know. I could tell you to trust me, but my words would be meaningless."

Gus felt trust. He quickly said, "I trust you. Let's go."

He grabbed his things, and Naomi led the way down a narrow hall toward the back door. She opened the door and stood holding it, looking radiant. As Gus approached her, he noticed a door to the right of where Naomi was standing. Being careful, he grabbed the door handle and quickly pulled the door open. It was only the laundry room. It was empty.

All of a sudden, Gus felt the overwhelming need for a woman. Not just any woman. The beautiful woman in front of him. His animal instincts took over. He grabbed Naomi by the arm and pulled her into the room.

She said sternly, "What are you doing? You have no time. You must leave now!"

Gus firmly replied, "I leave when I want to leave, and I don't want to leave. I am not leaving now. Do you want to leave?"

Her eyes teared up, and without saying a word, she turned and shut the laundry room door behind her and locked it with both of them inside.

They fell into each other's arms. Gus felt passion like he had never felt before. He lifted her short skirt and found that she was not wearing any underwear. He picked her up and put her on the laundry table. She wrapped her bare, smooth legs around him. As he stood in front of her, they fell into a passionate kiss. She unbuckled and dropped his pants, then slid her arms up underneath his shirt, softly caressing his back.

As they became consumed into each other's passion, reality faded away, and they slipped into a world where only love and fantasy existed. Gus felt the power of a thousand horses racing through his body. His sexual strength was beyond even his own comprehension. Naomi held on to her man with her only intention to absorb his sexual aggressiveness. As they reached the plateau of desire, their minds screamed, and they held each other tight.

As their encounter subsided, they slowly came back to reality. Naomi softly said to Gus, "You have missed the last bus. What will you do?"

Gus looked at her, smiled, and said, "I will survive."

Naomi then unhooked the necklace she was wearing and hooked it around Gus's neck. "Wear this necklace and the gods will protect you."

Gus accepted the gift as they fell into one last passionate kiss. Reality set in, and he knew it was time to go. His instincts told him that those men would soon figure out where he was staying.

Just as he and Naomi exited through the back door, standing before them was a short, fat, Eskimo man. "A longer time than most," he said, looking at Naomi. Then he turned to Gus and said, "Mr. Shepard, I've been waiting for you. I'm a friend of your father's."

Naomi looked at the Eskimo man, and Gus could immediately tell they knew each other. She then turned to Gus and said, "I must go now." She briskly walked away before he could question her actions.

Quickly the man said, "I see you have met Naomi."

Gus replied, "She is the most beautiful woman I have ever met. I think I love her."

The man laughed and said, "Many men have loved her. They even love her after she rips out their hearts and shoves it in their faces before they die. She takes who she wants, when she wants, and then leaves. You must put her out of your mind for now, or you may never get the chance to return."

Gus knew he was correct and that it was time to focus. "What's your name?" he asked.

"I have many names, and I have no name. My name is what your brain sees when you remember me."

"Right now, I see a short, fat, Eskimo man."

"Then you know my name," the man said with a chuckle. "We must hurry. Those men from the bar are very angry and are looking for you. They have guns. Take this coat and put it on. Go down to the end of the main street. When you reach the end, look toward your right. You will see a hiking trail. Go to the trail, and run as fast as you can to where it ends. It's about four miles. Do not stop. Even if you hear noises in the bushes along the way, do not stop. When you reach the end, you will see a rock formation with a very large tree at the top. Take off the coat and drop it at the bottom of the rock formation. Then climb up the tree about twenty feet from the ground."

"How long do I stay in the tree?"

"When all the noise stops, wait for about thirty minutes. After that, get down and run back here as fast as you can. I will be waiting for you. And this is very important: Do not take the coat. Leave it there."

"What noises? What will they sound like?"

"You will know them when you hear them," the man replied.

"This sounds crazy. How do you even know those men will follow me?" Gus asked, slightly irritated.

"I know they will follow you because I will rent them ATVs and tell them where you went."

Gus remembered that his father had mentioned that this man had unusual methods and to trust him. "Leave now. You need a head start," the Eskimo man said, looking more serious.

"OK, I'll do it. But what kind of coat is this? It kind of stinks," asked Gus.

"It is a bear coat."

"What is that smell?"

"Bear piss. It is male bear piss," the man said with a big smile on his face.

Gus put the coat on and started running.

The Eskimo man did as he said. He met the two men from the bar. He gave them each a smelly bear coat and told them not to take the coats off because they would protect them from bears. Even their rented ATVs smelled like the coats. He pointed them toward the trail that Gus was running down. They fired up the ATVs and began the chase.

Gus did as the man had told him and ran down the trail. He could hear the ATVs in the distance. Gus started running faster. The faster he ran, the farther away the ATVs sounded. For this to be possible, Gus realized that he had to be running at least thirty miles per hour faster than the ATVs.

Gus reached the rock formation, took off the bear coat, dropped it on the ground, and climbed the tree. After about twenty minutes, he could hear the ATVs getting closer. Then the ATVs stopped. Gus could tell that they were less than a half mile away. With his superior hearing, he could tell that they were on foot and walking up the path. He wondered, *Why am I staying in this tree? I should be running*. But his instinct told him to stay.

Then Gus heard a crackling sound close by in the woods. The sound was moving toward him. Out of the brush appeared the biggest grizzly bear he had ever seen. The bear slowly walked over to the coat that Gus had left at the bottom of the rock formation. It sniffed the coat; then it stood upright on its hind legs. It looked enormous! The bear pulled back its head and let out a very angry, loud roar. So loud it echoed through the woods. The bear dropped to all fours and thoroughly sniffed the air. It then headed down the path in a slow gallop.

Several minutes later, a gunshot rang out. A high-powered hunting rifle, by the sound of it. Then Gus heard men yelling and the bear growling. It sounded like a battle of man versus beast. Gus could tell the bear was winning. The commotion went on for about ten minutes, with more bear sounds and less man sounds every minute. It was quiet for about another ten minutes except for the bear making a strange grunting noise. Finally, all the noise stopped.

After several minutes, Gus heard a noise coming up the trail. As the noise got closer, he looked down and saw the bear dragging one of the men in a bear coat. It was Ike. Gus listened very carefully. He heard the bear drag Ike farther down the trail. The bear covered him with leaves and left him. Gus sniffed the air and listened. He could tell Ike was alive and not dying. After about twenty minutes, everything got very quiet. By Gus's approximation, the bear was nearly a mile away and was not moving. Just as the Eskimo man had told him, he waited thirty minutes, got down from the tree, and ran very quickly back to where he had met him.

"I am happy to see you," said the Eskimo man, then he laughed a jolly laugh.

"The feeling is mutual," Gus said, smiling.

The man then pulled out a cell phone, pushed a button, and said, "The eagle has safely landed," in a strong, military tone. Then he smiled and said, "Or should I say bear?" as he put the cell on speakerphone.

"Gus, It's Dad. Are you OK?"

"All in one piece," Gus replied.

"I've heard you had a quiet and restful vacation."

They both laughed. "Did my friend take care of you?" his father asked.

"He supplied everything I needed. Even an old, smelly bear coat."

"Did you pull the old bear-piss trick, my Eskimo friend?" Gus's father asked the man.

"Awwww…yes, I did," the man said. He and Gus's father laughed very loudly.

"What did you put on my son's bear coat?" asked his father.

"Male bear piss. That made the old grizzly very angry. Another male in his territory."

"Did you mix or match on the other guys' coats?"

"I mixed," the man said. They both laughed loudly again. When the laughing was over, the man said, "Those men both got young, virgin bear piss on their coats. It made that old grizzly very horny. I told them not to take off the bear coats. It would protect them from bears."

In a joking tone, Gus's father replied, "Ya, it'll protect them. Like one big, furry body condom. At least the bear won't kill them until he's done with them. Which will probably be sometime tomorrow."

"Don't worry, sir, I already sent out a rescue team to check on them and the bear. We will have them in the hospital soon. And I made sure that they had a rape crisis counselor on duty!" the man said. They both laughed loudly again.

This made Gus a little angry. "Is this the best protection you could give me?" he asked. "I could have died out there. This seems like some kind of big joke."

His father replied, "Don't worry, son. I had my own little animal-type aircraft waiting. An A10 Warthog. Airborne and in hot standby, machine gun ready."

"You must be joking," Gus replied.

Only the Eskimo man laughed this time.

Gus looked at him and said, "Do you think that's funny?"

He looked Gus straight in the eye and said, "What's funny is that you think your father is joking. He never jokes about a thing like that!"

Gus and his father said their goodbyes and hung up the phone. It was now just him and the Eskimo man. The man said, "You do not need to worry about those men. Go back to your room and rest. I will have someone give you a ride to the airport in the morning."

Gus softly said, "I would like to see Naomi before I go." He knew the man would know how to reach her.

With a stern look on his face, the man said, "Forget her. She is very beautiful and uses her beauty to satisfy her own desires. She is not capable of true long-term love. You will never forget her, but you will never have her. A joy and a curse all in one. The best thing for you to do is to put her out of your mind."

Gus opened his shirt and exposed the necklace she had given him. He said, "I at least wanted to thank her for the necklace that she gave me."

The man's eyes bulged. He immediately blurted out, "How did you get it? Did she drop it? Did it fall off her neck? Did she lose it, and you want to return it to her?"

Gus shyly said, "No, she took it off and put it around my neck. She said it would protect me."

54

The man's expression changed. He looked humbled. He then said, "Your father told me you were special. Your father is the most intelligent and capable man I know. But I thought maybe he was just being a proud father. I have observed your actions, many of which were amazing. But there is now something I must tell you that you may not believe or understand.

"Naomi is the goddess of love. She was put here in a human form for a purpose. When she put that necklace around your neck, she gave you the power of love and seduction. What she is able to do with men, you will be able to do with women. She has been searching the earth an unknown number of years, her beauty never changing, looking for the right man. You, Gus Shepard, are that man.

"Understand the intense desire you felt with her and the terrible pain you feel now that she is gone. You can have as many women as you desire. But in the process, you may destroy the hearts of the many women you touch. Used wisely, it can help you along your journey. You must learn how to control your new gift. You will feel your body making the connection. Yours talking to hers. Hers talking to yours. If you know harm may come out of it, stop the connection.

"Your intense desire for Naomi will never die. It will stay with you as long as you live. If you are about to take a woman, think about your intense desire for Naomi, and if you are leaving the woman you are about to take with an intense desire for you."

Gus asked, "Will I ever see her again?" His eyes tearing up.

"No. She is gone forever. Understand that the pain serves a purpose. It is to help you control the power of your new-found gift."

"Yes, I understand," said Gus.

The next day, Gus got up early before his morning ride back to the airport. He searched the town for Naomi, hoping that the Eskimo man was wrong. He went to the market and the bar. He even found out where she lived. She had quit both her jobs and left town. She had left no mailing address or way to reach her.

Gus felt devastated. His only comfort came from an old woman who had been her landlord. She was very old and feeble, but her eyes sparkled with life, very similar to Naomi's. When Gus asked her where Naomi had gone, she put both her hands around his. She had a warm and tender touch. She told Gus that Naomi had gone back to the village where she had grown up, back to her people. She did not know where that was. She told Gus that Naomi had said that she had finally found what she had been looking for and that she had reached the end of a long journey. She also said that Naomi was happy and that she had found her inner peace.

Chapter 6
THE GADGET GEEK

Gus got home and unpacked his things. Not quite what he had expected for a week in the woods. His on-again, off-again girlfriend, Karen, was coming over. She was very beautiful on the outside, but the inside was not so good. She had broken up with him but had been coming around a lot lately. She had said they were a couple again, but even before his trip, Gus had not been sure of this. She had told him several times that she was too beautiful for him and that he was just lucky to have her. She really seemed to be waiting for the BBD—bigger, better deal—and Gus was just a holdover guy until she found what she really wanted. Most of this did not matter now because Gus had experienced true love with Naomi. Even though Naomi was gone, he knew he didn't love Karen. He also knew that she definitely didn't love him.

Karen showed up, and Gus let her in. Gus immediately knew something was different. He had unintentionally memorized Karen's smell. She smelled different. Gus's sense of smell was now a thousand times more sensitive than that of an average human. They hugged and kissed and talked, but Gus's mind wasn't there. He was busy analyzing that smell. He kept his emotions hidden, but he couldn't understand why this smell was making him angry. His mind kept wandering back to the bear sniffing the coat, then standing up and roaring. Then it hit him. It was the smell of another man. Karen must be seeing someone else.

His first male animal reaction was anger. Gus understood this feeling but decided not to get angry. He had watched the bear get angry over territory and go charging down the path. It was lucky it hadn't gotten shot and killed. Gus had animal instincts combined with human intelligence. Now that he had the knowledge that she was seeing someone else, he should just confront her and get it over with. It would be the best for the both of them.

Gus and Karen were in the kitchen. He casually looked at her and asked, "Hey, babe, are we exclusive?"

"Sure thing. You know I love you," Karen replied.

"Are you sure we're exclusive? You know we don't have to be."

Karen said with a very beautiful smile, "I'm all yours, and you're all mine."

Gus was going to push it, for he knew she was lying. Instead, he decided to just keep quiet. He kind of enjoyed knowing what he knew. He watched her trying to hide it, but after several hours of talking, he could tell that she was going to break.

It was almost time for her to leave. Gus noticed that she was getting fidgety. Then all of a sudden, Karen stood up. Her face turned red. She looked at Gus and said, "You're a loser. I gave you a chance. I gave you time to improve yourself. I told you what you had to do to keep me. I've wasted a lot of time on you. If I were seeing someone else, it would be your fault. If you really wanted me, you should've worked a lot harder. But I guess you can't help it because you're a loser. My mother was right about you."

Gus smiled and said, "I guess we aren't talking about love, are we now, baby?"

She seemed angry that Gus wasn't angry. She looked at him and said, "You're disgusting, get it? Dis...Gus...ting." Then she laughed at her own joke. "I'm leaving!" Karen blurted out.

Gus just looked at her and said, "Cool."

Karen grabbed her jacket and purse and headed for the door. When she got there, she stopped, turned, and said in a sweet, ladylike tone, "Oh, by the way, I used my access to your bank account to withdraw money while you were away. Thirty-five thousand dollars, to be exact. I'd planned on paying you back. I have changed my mind! Just consider that the cost of the time you've spent with the most beautiful woman you will ever have."

Gus just looked at Karen and said, "Not cool."

She slammed the door and walked out.

Gus knew that there was a good chance that he would not get the money back. Karen was the kind of person who would keep it. She knew Gus wouldn't get physical with her or call the police. He was too nice of a guy to do that. He might sue her, but that was a long shot.

At this point, Gus didn't care about the money. It actually made him kind of happy. As a kid, he had always been kind of devious. Now he had a reason to be devious. He thought to himself, *Dogs get mad. People get even.* Knowing that the money was most likely gone, Gus's mind began to race. They could have just kissed and said goodbye, but instead, she basically had told him that he was a piece of shit, and had stolen his money. Payback was definitely in order. It had to be special. Gus didn't have anything in mind, but he remembered what his father used to tell him: "Before you implement a plan, make sure you do your research and have good intelligence." The first thing on Gus's mind was, "Who is she seeing?"

Gus decided he needed some help. He had become friendly with Dave, the gadget geek from work. Ever since the House at Meeku Filbeech thing, he and Dave had talked daily. Dave had joined Gus and a couple of guys after work for beer. Dave was kind of a strange guy. He had curly hair and glasses. At work, he was tense and serious. But get him to a bar and get a couple of drinks into him, and he became loud and funny. Almost a Jekyll-and-Hyde-type personality. Gus gave Dave a call and invited him to his house.

Dave showed up the next day. Gus invited him in, got him a beer, and started with some typical how's-it-going-type small talk. They sat down in the living room. Then Gus turned to Dave and said, "Remember after that House at Meeku Filbeech thing, you said if I ever needed your help to just ask?"

"Sure, what's up?" asked Dave.

"I know that you know a lot about electronics and computers," said Gus.

"They don't call me the gadget king for nothing," Dave replied.

Gadget Geek, Gus thought to himself. Then he said, "What I may ask of you is probably not legal or even ethical."

Dave smiled his crazy beer smile and asked, "Is it fun?"

"I'm not sure of my exact plan yet, but if it all goes well, yes, it'll be fun."

"As fun as House at Meeku Filbeech?"

"Maybe even more fun."

Dave said, "I'm in."

With a big smile on his face, Gus explained, "My girlfriend—actually, ex-girlfriend—has been cheating on me. That doesn't bother me, as our relationship has been rocky for some time. You would have thought that we could have just broken it off and said, you know, the typical girl's line, 'Let's just be friends,' and said goodbye. But that's not what happened."

He told Dave what had happened the night before. Then he said, "The first thing I need to find out is who this other guy is."

Dave's expression changed to his work-face personality. He looked at Gus and started firing off questions. "Does she have a cell phone, and does she text?"

"Yes."

"Is it a smartphone with GPS capability?"

"Yes."

"Does she drive a car with a navigation system in it?"

"Yes."

"Does she have Bluetooth in her car, and is it linked to her cell phone?"

"Yes."

"Great," Dave said. "I can easily hack her cell phone since it's tied into the Internet. All I need is her phone number. If I do that, I can see all her texts and phone numbers. I can match the phone numbers and texts she sends to the ones she receives. I can also track her location everywhere she goes as long as she has her cell phone with her or driving in her car.

"Once I find the texts or cell phone numbers that I believe to be our guy, I'll hack his phone. Assuming he has a smartphone, I can track his location. Then I simply match his location to her location. And last, but not least, I'll make sure that my theoretical data matches my lab data. I will spy on them. What I'm about to do is highly illegal. I hope you can keep us out of trouble."

Gus replied, "*No problemo…*I think." He could see the excitement in Dave's eyes. He did not seem scared. Gus was sure that Dave had done this before. Gus knew Dave would probably cover his tracks no matter what he did.

Dave smiled and in a German accent said, "I just want to know one thing: How's that make you feel bitch?"

They toasted their beers, took a big drink, and laughed a devious laugh.

A day later, Gus, feeling a little guilty, decided to give Karen a call. The breakup was final, but the thirty-five-thousand-dollar separation fee was a little stiff. Maybe she had calmed down. They could laugh about it, agree to stay friends, and she could return the money. After all, she did always brag about the fairly large chunk of money she had inherited from her late grandmother. She didn't need the money. Then Gus could forget about the payback scheme he was planning. He had not set it into motion and could just stop before it was too late. So Gus gave Karen a call. She picked up the phone. "Hello Karen, this is Gus."

Karen asked, "What do you want?"

"Well, I just wanted to talk about the other night. I wanted to apologize for anything I said or did and don't want to end it like this."

Karen sternly said, "Apology accepted." Then she continued. "But that doesn't mean that you're getting your money back. We were together as a couple, and you willingly gave me access to your bank account. You didn't tell me that there was a limit on how much I could spend. So I spent as much as I wanted to. You have no legal right to force me to return that money."

"No legal right? I gave you access to that account just in case of an emergency. You know I didn't intend for you to take all that money. I trusted you!"

Karen quickly replied, "Well, Gus, I guess you lose. Losers lose. Maybe you'll be smart and treat this as a learning lesson. Why don't you use this experience as something to motivate you to become a winner? Just like in the movies, the winner gets the pretty girl and the money. The loser doesn't get shit!" Then she hung up the phone.

Gus found this quite amusing. His guilt was gone. *Thank you, Karen*, he thought to himself. Yes, this will be fun.

Within a couple of days, Gus got a call from Dave. He wanted to meet somewhere. Obviously, Dave did not want to talk to Gus at his place. Just like Gus had suspected, Dave was covering his tracks. *This is good*, he thought. *He's smart and careful.* They decided to meet at the pub where they had gone several times before.

Upon seeing each other, they said hello, then sat down at a tall table and ordered beer. Dave started the conversation with, "I have some good data. I did what I said. I found our guy. I did some research into who he is and what he's all about."

Gus said, "I'm all ears."

"Well, he's six feet two inches tall. He weighs about two hundred and twenty pounds and is a competition bodybuilder. He's thirty-two years old, never married, and has no kids…oh, ya, almost forgot: he graduated from a big-name college on the East Coast with a degree in law. He's a successful attorney with a well-known law firm. I hate to tell you this, Gus, but compared to him, you're just a loser."

"Just a loser and a boozer," Gus said as he held up his frosty mug of beer. They toasted and laughed.

Dave continued, "But wait, there's more. He owns a nice new car and a big house in a country club environment. All on payments. He's almost one hundred percent mortgaged. He owes big student loans. This guy has a lot of debt. He's on steroids and competes in bodybuilding tournaments. This guy spends a lot of time in front of mirrors. If you looked up 'sleazebag' on the Internet, I'm sure he would be the first thing that pops up."

"Well, it explains a couple of things. I know where Karen got her legal advice about the money from. Also, it might explain why she wants it.

They both are big spenders. Both of them want to appear to be rich. It's part of the image each is trying to portray to the other. She needs it to impress him. He needs it because he's cash poor. She's temporarily supporting their lifestyle with my money."

Dave jokingly asked, "Well, what's the plan, Stan?"

"The plan is to teach each of them a lesson and save them from themselves. Both of them are phony people and are always looking for the BBD: bigger, better, deal. Neither of them has considered love in their equation. They'll never be happy. I'll help them see themselves for what they are. As the Dalai Lama once said, 'I will help them find true happiness in life.'" Then Gus bowed his head, hands clasped together.

"Did the Dalai Lama really say that?"

With a laugh, Gus said, "I don't know, but it sounds like something he would say." He continued. "I'd like to present each of them with a new BBD. Of course, a fake BBD that we have made up. We need to create fake his and-hers BBDs and start communicating with them. Can you create fake people and hack into their Facebook accounts?"

"Creating fake BBDs is no problem. But I wouldn't recommend Facebook. Too much of Facebook's information is shared with other people. I suggest we hack into their personal e-mail accounts."

"Sounds good. I'll also need to know someplace where they meet and are seen by other people."

Dave quickly replied, "They meet a lot downtown."

"By all the high-rise buildings?"

"Yes."

"Perfect!" Gus said.

Dave looked a little confused. Gus explained, "I want you to get in touch with both of them. Start out with 'I work in one of the high-rise buildings downtown. I've seen you in the street from my office with my telescope. I can't get you out of my mind.' Then tell them how fantastic they look. Lay it on thick. Throw out lots of ego-building compliments. Then tell them that the person who's contacting them is very rich, important, and attractive but doesn't want to give them their identity until they know a little more about each other. Get them interested and get a conversation going.

"After they're both hooked on their new bigger...better...deal, we go to Plan B. Tell each of them that you've seen them with someone else. To him, you describe Karen. To her, you describe her new boyfriend. Tell them that if they're serious with someone else that the BBD doesn't want to get involved. I'm sure that they'll say they aren't serious because neither of them will want to lose their new BBD. Then start complimenting them and telling them why the person the BBD has seen them with doesn't seem good enough for them. Get them to open up. For instance, you might tell him that the woman the BBD sees him with is very beautiful but looks angry and uneducated. Or a stupid bitch. However you want to word it."

They both laughed, and Gus continued. "Get the conversation going and get him to start talking shit about Karen. Next, do the same to her. Maybe tell her that the guy that her BBD has seen her with is in very good shape but looks like an arrogant ass. I'm sure Karen will open up. She loves to complain and ridicule people."

Dave smiled a devious smile, then said, "I get where you're going with this. Get each of them to knock the other one down when confronted with a better prospect or bigger...better...deal. Let me guess: after we get all this information together, you get the pleasure of presenting the information to them. You get to see the look on their faces when they realize that their new BBDs are fake and are manufactured by you. This does sound like fun. But he's a big guy. I hope if he gets angry that you can take him. Even worse, he's a big attorney, and what we're doing is highly illegal. Do you have a good Plan C?"

"Not exactly. But I don't plan on getting beat up or either of us going to jail, or even court, for that matter. I have a possible Plan C, but it depends upon the results of Plan B. Are you still in?"

"Can't wait to start."

A week went by. Gus and Dave played it very cool at work. They barely talked to each other except for an occasional "How's it going?" from Gus. Dave would always reply, "It's going good." They didn't even communicate after work. Then, one day at work, Dave said, "Hey, we should get together for a beer sometime."

Gus knew by the look on his face that Dave had good data to share. He responded with, "How about tonight? Brew pub down the street?"

"Sure thing. See you around six."

They met at the bar, ordered their beers, and began to talk. Dave started out with, "They both went for it...hook, line, and sinker. It's working just as you expected. Much quicker than I expected. It's barely been a week, and they're already taking trash about each other. I got some really good stuff. He's called her stupid, a whore, and not the kind of woman a man wants to have kids with. He even said that fucking her was a valuable waste of his sperm. But the comment I liked the most was that he said he would consider her dumber than a stump, but that would be an insult to the stump, because stumps aren't that dumb!"

They both laughed, and Dave continued. "She was just as bad. She said he has a weird smell to his body that makes her want to vomit and that his breasts were bigger than hers. That he should join 4H and enter himself into the dairy cow competition. She also said that the only reason she would ever marry him was that she could divorce him in five years and make some money. Better than going to college. But the one of hers that I liked the best was that she said he's a natural-born asshole. He doesn't wake up in the morning, look in the mirror, and say, 'I'm going to be an asshole today. He doesn't have to. He already is one. He was born that way!'"

They both laughed loudly. Gus said, "She's good at tearing people down."

Dave leaned forward and said, "OK, I'll put this all together into two nicely presentable printed packages. One for him and one for her. But before I do that, I bet you can guess what I'm waiting to hear about."

Gus leaned back, smiled, and said, "Plan C."

Dave said with a Spanish accent, "*Si, si, señor.*"

Gus took a big gulp of his beer and said, "Time to initiate Plan C. The icing on the cake. I've found a real BBD for each of them. For her, a wealthy real estate investor. For him, a successful marketing executive working for a large corporation. Both work downtown in high-rise office buildings. I'll give you their names and addresses.

"I want you to tell Karen and her new guy that their BBDs are ready to reveal their identities. But considering that they've revealed so much personal information about themselves, they'll want something personal in return as an act of good faith before they're ready to meet in person. His BBD wants a picture of his cock. Tell him that she doesn't want an e-mail. Take a picture, and print it on a large sheet of photo paper. Put it in a plain paper envelope with her name and address on it, and personally drop it off in the mailbox at the building where she works. And tell him not to put his name on it. Just sign his initials. Do the same for Karen using her new BBD. Tell her that he really likes her ass. He's an ass guy. He wants her to sit on a copy machine and take a bare-ass picture. I know that she always wanted to do that. Have her send it in the same way: delivered, not e-mailed, with only her initials on it."

Dave looked at Gus, a little concerned, and said, "I'll do it, but I'm not sure I follow where you're going with this one. Just tell me we're covered."

"No risk, no reward…yes, we're covered."

They finished their beers and left.

Two days passed, and then Dave called Gus. It was a Friday night. He wanted to get together. They decided to meet at a restaurant in a quiet part of town.

As they sat down, Dave said, "Done deal. They were very enthusiastic once they learned the identities of their new BBDs. They both have personally delivered the envelopes to the offices of their new BBDs."

"Great! Do you have my his-and-hers e-mail correspondence packages ready? I'd like to pay them a visit for lunch tomorrow. I know where they meet."

"The packages are ready. Do you care if I show up and watch? Kind of like a fly on the wall."

"Sure, why not? You've earned the right."

The next day, Gus went to where Karen and her new guy were having lunch. Gus walked up to them and said, "Fancy meeting you here."

Karen replied, "Hello, Gus. What are you doing here? Get a second job as a waiter?"

The guy puffed out his chest and said, "Is this the loser? He looks a little thin. Maybe we should buy him a lunch."

With a smirk on his face, Gus said, "I'm not really hungry. I just stopped by to drop off some packages for you." He handed them each a large envelope.

Karen asked, "What's this?"

Starting to smile, Gus said, "Oh, just something I thought you both might like to read. It's what you both really think about each other."

Karen, starting to get angry, said, "What the hell are you talking about?"

Gus replied, "Both of your new high-rise office-building friends. You both know what I'm talking about. Your new e-mail friends. The real estate developer. The marketing executive. They're both me. And you've both told me so much. I loved how you both complimented each other. I loved it so much that I put together a package of each other's e-mail correspondences so that you could both sit together all cozy-like and compare notes."

Karen turned red, and her new guy looked very pale. All of a sudden, he jumped up and said, "Do you know who you're fucking with? You will fry! Your ass is going down for this!"

Gus looked at Karen, smiled, and said, "Hopefully, my ass isn't going down on a copy machine."

The guy then yelled, "Do you know who I am? I will guarantee that you're going to do some jail time."

With a laugh, Gus said, "I know who you are...you're a dick! And I know someone else that knows that you're a dick, because you sent her a picture. Same for you, Karen. I know who you are. You're an ass! And I know someone else who would probably agree with me, because you sent him a picture. Luckily, you both only put your initials on your envelopes and not your full names. They don't know your true identities. I could change that. Would you like to take me to court? It'll all come out."

They both looked stunned. They were speechless. Then Gus looked at Karen and said, "I may be a loser, but you're an ass, and he's a dick! See you later."

Gus walked away, thinking, *That felt good. Real good.* As he walked out, he winked at Dave, who was sitting by himself at a nearby table. Dave slyly gave him a thumbs-up.

Several weeks went by, and Gus had not heard anything back from Karen or her new boyfriend. It looked like it was game over. Gus and Dave had now become good friends. They had completed Gus's devious plot, and everything had worked out well. They were like two little kids who had gotten away with something. It had bonded them together.

Gus was getting tired of sitting home alone and decided to go get a couple of drinks and see if he could find a woman. He invited Dave, and they hit the bars. Gus was interested to see if the Eskimo man from his mountain vacation was right or just plain crazy. Did he truly have the power of seduction? Could he get any woman he wanted?

Gus and Dave got to the first bar. The night was early. Many people were stopping in for an after-work drink. They sat down at a small table and ordered beer. Gus looked around the bar and said, "I want her!" as a good-looking group of women walked in.

Dave looked at Gus and said, "Good luck. She's really hot and with a group of friends. First of all, you'll have a hard time getting her away from her girl pack. Even if you did, it's early in the evening, and she's not even drunk yet. It's like big-game hunting. You have to plan it out and slowly hunt down your animal. It only enhances the thrill of the kill."

Gus leaned his head to one side, slightly closed one eye, and said, "You sound like you got some moves."

Dave leaned back in his chair and said, "I've been around, dude. Some guys are the limp shrimps. Others claim to be the stout trout. Well, I'm known as the slammin' salmon!" They both laughed loudly.

"What do you recommend?"

Dave quickly replied, "Here's what you do. It's just three easy steps. First, you make eye contact. Second, you get her far enough away from her friends so that you can talk to her. Then third, you talk her into fucking you as soon as possible!"

They laughed again.

"OK, Einstein, sounds like a good plan. I think I'll try it," Gus said jokingly.

They had a couple more beers, then Gus said, "OK, boss. I'm going to try your big game-hunting approach."

He started making eye contact with the woman he had seen come in earlier. She got up to use the restroom, and Gus followed her. He returned from the restroom smiling.

Dave asked, "Did you talk to her?"

"Yes. I told her that I couldn't take my eyes off her and that I wanted to have sex with her as soon as possible."

Dave looked surprised and asked, "What did she say?"

Gus leaned into him and said, "She told me to meet her at her car in five minutes."

Dave said, "Yeah, sure. You're lucky she didn't slap you."

Gus immediately said, "There she goes. I'll be back." He got up and followed her outside.

Gus came back looking like a man who had obviously just had sex. His hair was a little messy, his top shirt buttons were unbuttoned, and he had an ear-to-ear grin. Dave looked a little stunned.

The woman and her friends asked Gus and Dave to join them. They partied the night away. The woman that took Gus to her car and had sex with him never left his side. He now knew that he easily had the power to get women. But he could also see that this woman was falling in love with him. Gus talked Dave into sneaking out of the bar when the girls weren't looking. He didn't exchange phone numbers, so the girl he had met had no way to reach him. Dave acted like he didn't want to go, but Gus knew he was actually doing him a favor. It was highly unlikely that any of these girls were going to go home with him.

As the weeks went by, Gus and Dave hit the bars. It was like the movie *Groundhog Day*. The story kept repeating. It was like shooting fish in a barrel. Every time they went out, Gus would end up having sex with some beautiful woman. Then he and Dave would sneak out without leaving any contact information.

Each time, it appeared Dave came up empty-handed. Then one night, Dave said to Gus, "You probably think that I don't enjoy this, but I do— the drinking, the laughter, and the people. And some day, I might just meet the right girl. I may not be as good-looking as you, but I also have sex with a beautiful woman before I go home. I stop off and visit a hooker. I know some really gorgeous ones. In reality, our situations aren't very different: drinking, socializing, having sex with a beautiful woman, and then leaving without taking or giving any contact information. It's great sex, but it's not sex with love."

Gus went home and couldn't quit thinking about what Dave had said. He knew Dave was right. All the sex Gus had experienced in the last couple of weeks was great, but it paled in comparison to what it had been like with Naomi. There was an empty feeling in his stomach. He longed for the way it had been with her.

It was Friday again, and Gus decided to go out alone this time. Going out with Dave was fun, but tonight, he wanted something more than sex. Tonight, he would not use his power of seduction. He wanted to find a woman who would like him for who he was. He would be happy just to find one that he could communicate with. Something mentally deeper than his most recent female encounters.

Gus got dressed up and headed for the bars. Tonight he decided to go to a tamer part of town. He didn't want to run into any of the women who he had previously had sex with. He found a wine bar where the music was a little quieter, which would make it easier to talk. The bar had more women than men. Gus went inside and sat down. He talked with a couple of women, but it was nothing special.

Then he saw a woman walk in by herself. She had long red hair and a slender build. He couldn't take his eyes off her. She looked wholesome but sensual. When she walked into the bar, it was like all the other women disappeared. There was just her.

Gus really wanted to meet her, but nothing was working. Every time he looked at her, she looked away. She seemed to be happy sitting by herself, listening to the music. The night was starting to get late, and Gus was afraid she might leave. He couldn't let that happen. He decided to use his power of seduction.

Gus made eye contact and turned on the charm. He walked across the room and introduced himself. Soon they were talking and laughing. It all seemed so natural. Just like they were old friends. Gus decided he would have sex with her just like all the others. But this time would be different. He would make sure that they traded phone numbers so that they could contact each other after tonight.

Gus turned on his power of seduction. He could feel the passion. Gus could sense she wanted him as badly as he wanted her. Just when he was about to ask her to have sex with him, she seductively stretched out her arm and put her finger on his lips. He knew that this meant she wanted him to listen and not talk. She stared into his eyes with her soft blue eyes and spoke.

"I haven't been totally truthful with you. I told you my name is Carla. It's really Lisa. Also, I said that I hadn't ever seen you before tonight. That's not true. I saw you several months ago in the park walking your dog. A very magnificent animal. A lot like you."

Gus listened, but all that was on his mind was sex. He asked her to have sex, using every ounce of his persuasiveness. She agreed and told him to meet her in front of the bar. She needed to use the bathroom and would be there in five minutes. Gus went outside and waited. Five minutes went by. Then ten minutes passed. Gus went back into the bar. She was gone!

He thought to himself, *How could this be?* He had used his power of seduction. He knew she wanted him as badly as he wanted her. He could feel it. This was the first woman who had been able to reject his advances. And to rub salt in the wound, she'd left without getting or giving a phone number! Gus left the bar confused. How could this have happened? Maybe he was being paid back for all the girls he had left without trading phone numbers. What this was, some kind of poetic justice?

Feeling frustrated and a little angry, Gus headed back to his car. He had parked his Porsche 911 Turbo at the very back of the parking lot to avoid scratches. As he approached his car, he saw a guy wearing a hoodie spray-painting his car window.

Gus quietly snuck up on the vandal and noticed that he had spray-painted the word *Loser* on the driver's side window. He quickly grabbed the guy's arm and twisted it into an arm lock, forcing him to drop the spray-paint can. He lifted him up, spun him around, and slammed a knee strike into his groin.

The guy crouched over in pain and fell to the ground. While he was moaning, he said, "You're fucked now."

The guy was not very big and looked helpless lying there on the ground. This left Gus a little confused. He pulled out his cell phone to call the police. Just as he started to punch in his unlock code, he saw a big guy get out of a car and slam his door. The guy was about six feet tall and about five feet wide. He was walking fast and staring straight at Gus. All of a sudden, he yelled, "Time for a little ground and pound, you skinny piece of shit!"

Gus put away his phone. He had already been frustrated by a woman and had his car vandalized. He felt like hitting something, and now seemed like a good time to do it. The large man came running at Gus and swung one of his massive arms, attempting to hit him in the face. He sidestepped the guy, blocked his strike, and directed the force of his attack into his car window. The window shattered, and the guy yelled. Blood dripped down his arm from the cuts in his knuckles.

Gus moved out into an open area of the parking lot. He did not think it was wise to fight this big guy close in. The guy charged at Gus. He swung a couple of times, missed, and then attempted a takedown. Gus easily moved out of his way, avoiding the attacks. Then Gus smiled a sinister grin and said, "Did you mention 'ground and pound?' Well, you have to get to the ground before you can pound. Would you like me to help you to get there?"

The guy said, "Come on, you loser sissy. Fight back."

Gus thought to himself, "Loser, that sounds familiar." While they both kept moving around in their dance of battle, Gus said, "Do you like bull fighting? Don't you just love how the matador frustrates the bull and injures it before he puts it down? I'll tell what. Let's play bullfight. I'll be the matador, and you can be the bull."

"Fuck you," the guy said, immediately charging at Gus as if attempting a takedown. Then threw a sneaky haymaker punch. He was going for the knockout. Leaning back and avoiding the strike, Gus shuffled and slammed a roundhouse kick into his left thigh.

The guy smiled and said, "Is that all you got?"

The big man attempted several more swings and missed. Each time, Gus slammed roundhouse kicks into his thighs. The guy was moving much slower now. Gus knew his tree trunk-size legs must be hurting. The guy moved into a left-leg-forward stance and was crouching, looking like a wrestler going for a takedown. Gus slammed a roundhouse kick, hard, into his left thigh. Gus could see him wince in pain. The guy couldn't block or avoid Gus; he was too fast. The big man stood helplessly as he slammed another and then another. Then a flurry of full-power roundhouse kicks to the same leg. The guy's leg collapsed from underneath him, and he fell to the ground on one knee.

Gus then yelled, "*Olé!*"; jumped in the air; and landed a flying roundhouse kick to the side of the guy's head. The big man crumpled to the ground, unconscious.

Gus looked at him, smiled, and said, "Did you say, 'Ground and pound?' I thought you said, 'Ground and downed.' Sorry for the misunderstanding...loser. Bullfight is over."

Gus decided not to call the police and just leave. But before he left, he went over to the guy who had been spray-painting his car. He had recovered but had not left yet. Obviously, he had expected a different outcome. He put out his arms and said, "Hey, man, I'm sorry."

Gus grabbed one of his arms, twisted it, and started bending back one of his fingers. The guy started crying and then yelled, "I *am* sorry, man! They paid me to do this. I needed the money."

Gus pulled his finger back even farther. The guy screamed in pain. Gus let up a little, then said, "Keep talking."

The guy whimpered, "Some bodybuilding lawyer dude wanted to get you angry, man. Fuck up your car. Maybe even rough you up a little. He wants you to come after him. It is a setup, man. I was supposed to put a tracking device on your car. He would know when you're coming for him. He and some other guys would be waiting for you to kick your ass. On top of that, he would have witnesses that would say you attacked him first; then he would press charges against you for assault."

Gus let go of his finger but kept his arm in a twisted position. Speaking slowly, he said, "OK, here's what you're going to do now. Put the tracking device on my car. Tell your buddy over there that you heard me say, 'I know who did this: Karen's new boyfriend. I'm going to find him and kick his ass.' And if you tell anybody about our little conversation, I'll track you down and cripple you. Do you understand?"

"Yes."

Gus twisted his arm back even farther, and the guy screamed, "Yes!"

Gus now knew for sure where this was coming from. It was from Karen's new boyfriend. He had known Karen was mean, but this was beyond her. It obviously was not game over.

Chapter 7
MONO LISA

Gus went home that night with his mind racing. He needed a plan. He didn't really want to beat this guy up. He wanted to beat him at his own game. This guy was smart and was willing to break the rules. It would be tricky.

Gus decided he needed some help. Someone with connections who might also be willing to break the rules. It was starting to get violent. Gus didn't think that Dave was the guy to call for help in this situation. He decided to call Mono. The guy who had delivered the tamales, the Mexican guy who was the father of the boy he had saved. Gus called him that night. It was late, but Mono picked up on the first ring.

Gus told him the story and his problem. Mono listened quietly, then said, "Let me think about it. I'll call you in the morning."

It was around 11:00 a.m. Saturday morning and Gus got a call. He picked up the phone. He knew it was Mono by his phone ID. *"Buenas días, amigo,"* Gus said.

"Good morning to you also, my friend," Mono said. "I have a plan for you. Later on today, your lawyer friend is going to the county fair. He's going there looking for you. He has very good information and knows you'll be there today. Someone who's monitoring the tracking device on your car will let him know that you've parked in Lot C at the very back of the parking lot at four o'clock. He will come looking for you, and you and my people will mysteriously end up meeting him and his people."

Gus listened intently, then asked, "What happens next? Do I get to kick his ass?"

"I know you can fight, my friend, but no, you just get to watch. Just sit back and enjoy the show. It should be very amusing."

"Are you sending over some tough guys?"

Mono laughed. "Trust me, amigo—it will be very amusing. Hey, I need you to get there about twenty minutes early. Stay in your car. A friend of mine will come meet you. His name's Tony."

Later that day, Gus drove to the county fair and parked in Lot C near the back. As he sat in his car, he saw a county fair golf cart coming toward him. A kid was driving, and an old man with a golfing hat was on the passenger side. He was a small but muscular black man with a shaved head and a big scar running down the side of his face.

The cart parked near his car, and the old guy got off. He slowly walked up to Gus and said, "I'm Tony, Mono's friend. You must be Gus."

Gus got out of the car and replied, "Yes, I am."

They shook hands. Gus was surprised how firm his handshake was. He asked, "So why has Mono asked you here today?"

Tony replied, "I'm going to kick someone's ass."

Gus looked at him, smiled, and said, "How does it work? You start the fight, and then the cavalry comes in to back you up?"

Tony jokingly punched Gus in the arm and said, "Don't need no stinking backup. There ain't nobody showing up besides me for the fighting part. I'm all you need."

Gus laughed, and then Tony laughed even louder after him. They made small talk for a while, and Gus noticed that it was already 3:50, and no one else had shown up. The action was supposed to start around four, and it was still just him and Tony. Gus was getting a little nervous. He decided to go back to his car and give Mono a call.

Mono picked up the phone. "Gus, my buddy, what's up?"

"Well, it's almost four o'clock, and I was just wondering, what's the plan, and what do you want me to do?"

"Everything is in place. I think you should just sit in your car and watch."

"Mono, the only person here is some old guy named Tony. He says he's doing all the fighting. Is he just messing with me?"

Mono chuckled and said, "Don't under estimate him. He's old-school tough. He's a boxing instructor who grew up on the mean streets of Harlem. The scar on his face is from a hatchet fight that he won. This guy was declared the toughest guy in New York State all four years he was there."

"New York State University?" Gus asked.

"No, man, New York state prison!" Then he laughed a crazy laugh before continuing. "The guy does four hundred push-ups per day. Sets of one hundred at a time. Bare knuckles on the concrete! He moves a little slow in the beginning, but once he gets going, look out. Hey, it's almost four. Your friends should be showing up soon. Sit back and enjoy the show."

Gus soon saw Karen's new guy walking toward his car. He looked large and muscular. Walking with him were two other large white guys. Both were very buffed bodybuilding types. Gus could feel the hair standing up on the back of his neck. His body was preparing for battle.

They were now about thirty feet from his car and glaring at him. Just as Gus was about ready to get out of his car, Tony came walking up and cut in front of them. Tony yelled, "Are you the one harassing my client? I'm going to file charges against you for assault! I demand to know your name."

"Harold," Karen's guy replied, but before he could say more, Tony yelled, "I thought it was Dick! I heard you're just a dick."

Harold's face turned red. The two guys with him started laughing. Then Harold loudly said, "You're going to file charges for assault? I don't even think you can spell the word. And if you're too stupid to spell it, how could you even know what it is?"

The second Harold finished his sentence, Tony slapped him in the face hard. Then Tony said, "I know what assault is. *That's* assault!"

Harold got very angry and shouted, "Listen, asshole, if you do that again, I'll forcibly put you under a citizen's arrest. I'll call the police and sit on you until they arrive."

Just as Harold finished what he was saying, Tony smiled, then slapped him two more times. He hit hard, and he was fast. Harold's friends started laughing again, and one said, "Is this why you brought us?"

The other said, "Does Harold need some help?"

Harold yelled, "OK, asshole, that's it!"

He charged at Tony, attempting to grab his arms. Tony shuffled back and forth and avoided Harold's attempts. With Harold chasing him, Tony moved the fight to an open section of the parking lot. Coincidently, two average looking Mexican men and a woman came out from between two cars. Looking like surprised spectators, one of the men and the woman pulled out cell phones and started filming. Then Tony started yelling, "Get away from me! Leave me alone! What's wrong with you? Are you crazy?" Tony carried on for about a minute, then yelled, "You're forcing me to defend myself. You may be bigger than me, but I'm going to give you everything I got. I'll teach you not to pick on old people!"

All of a sudden, Tony quit dancing around. He transformed into a fighter. He crouched down like a panther going in for the kill. Harold blindly came charging in, his arms outstretched and trying to grab Tony's arms. With lighting speed, Tony threw three fast punches, hitting Harold in the face. They were solid hits. Gus could hear the slapping sound even the in car. Harold snapped with anger. He bellowed a loud roar and charged at Tony swinging. Then Tony let loose and started swinging back. He threw a flurry of punches, three to four at a time, momentarily hesitated, and then repeated the attack. He did this three times. He was quick. Gus was impressed.

Tony faded back for a second as Harold slowed down, then stepped in and slammed a kick between Harold's legs. He continued swinging like a mad man and beat Harold down to the ground. Then he backed off about ten feet and just stood there. The fight was over.

Harold looked bloody and confused. As he tried to stand up, he started yelling, "I'm going to kick your ass!"

One of Harold's friends started helping him up, and Harold said, "Where is he? I'm going to kick his ass. What happened? Where'd he go?"

His friend started laughing and said, "I'll tell you what happened. You just got the shit kicked out of you by a little old man."

His other friend said, "Get up, you asshole. You're embarrassing me."

Within seconds, two county fair police cars showed up with their red lights flashing. As they got out of their cars, Tony started yelling, "Officers, this bully attacked me!"

Harold's friends quickly left. One cop went over to Harold, and the other went over to the Mexican people who had been watching. Gus could see the Mexican spectators showing the cop their phones. He was obviously looking at their cell phone videos. He was smiling. The two cops got together and talked for a couple of minutes. Then one of them went over to Harold, handcuffed his hands behind his back, and put him in the back seat of his car. He drove away with his lights flashing. The other cop stayed. He and Tony shook hands and then hugged. Tony and the cop walked over to the Mexicans. They all started watching the video and were laughing. Tony turned to Gus, smiled, and waved. Gus waved back and then drove away.

That night, Mono called Gus. The phone rang, and recognizing the number, Gus picked up the phone. Mono asked, "So how did you like the show?"

"Five stars," Gus said.

"I think your problems are over, my friend. Your buddy Harold is moving back to the East Coast as long as Tony will drop the assault charge against him. And you don't have to worry about him after he moves away. The phone video shows him angry, yelling, and chasing around an old man. Then it shows the old man beating the hell out of him. It's very funny. I'll get you a copy. We threatened to put it on the Internet and let it go viral. Maybe call it 'Don't Fuck with Grandpa.' Or 'Better Mind Your Elders.'" Then Mono laughed and said, "Hey, man, even all the cops are watching it. They love it. In addition, Harold feels very sorry for what happened, and out of an act of forgiveness, he's decided to pay you back the thirty-five thousand dollars that your ex-girlfriend borrowed from you and five thousand more in interest for a total of forty thousand dollars. One of my boys will drop off a cashier's check at your house."

Gus sincerely replied, "Thank you, Mono. I'm sorry that I doubted you. I'm truly very impressed. You are the man! What do I owe you? Split the money? Hell, take all the money. What you did was truly priceless."

Mono replied with the same level of sincerity, "You risked your life to save the life of my son. *That* was truly priceless. You are now my brother. You are family. Anytime, anywhere, if you need help, I will do my best to help you."

Gus could hear the truthfulness in his voice, and his inner instinct could feel his sincerity. He got a little choked up and simply ended the conversation by saying, "Thanks, Bro."

Several weeks had passed, and as far as Karen and Harold were concerned, it truly appeared that this time, it was game over. Gus had not had sex with any other women. He had gone out looking for Lisa several times, but she was nowhere to be found. There were many beautiful women out there, but Gus could not get her out of his mind. It was ironic to him that he could go out and get any woman he wanted, but he didn't. He wanted something he couldn't have. Maybe this was just human nature. It really made him think. Maybe his power of seduction was not a gift but a curse. Or maybe he was just learning some sort of cruel lesson. Possibly a lot of the women he had seduced had woken up the next morning missing him. Maybe they were hitting the bars looking for him, feeling the way he felt about Lisa. His power was a special gift, but was he really any better off than Dave? Why not just go out and have sex with beautiful women that you pay for? Sex with no emotional damage to anyone.

But what bothered him the most was how Lisa could have turned him down when none of the others could. How was she feeling now? Did she miss him like he missed her? His mind was going in circles with no answer. Gus decided to call the person he always called when it came to women and feelings: his mother.

It was a lazy afternoon, and Gus decided it was a good time to call his mother. He called, and she answered the phone, "Good morning to the world's greatest boy."

Gus replied, "The greatest in the world?"

"The greatest in the universe!" his mother said with a giggle. This was kind of a little ritual they went through every time Gus called.

He started the conversation with, "Mom, I'm confused about a woman."

His mother replied, "Women are confusing creatures."

"It's a long story. Where should I start?"

His mother calmly replied, "Let me pour myself a glass of tea, sit down, and get comfortable. Then you can start at the beginning."

Gus told her the whole story about Naomi and how he loved her and that she had given him the power of seduction. He told her about all the women he had seduced, leaving out the details he knew she would not want to hear. And then finally he told her about Lisa. She listened intently with very few questions as she always did. Then she asked, "This girl, Lisa—do you love her?"

Gus sighed, paused for a second, then said, "I don't know. Yes, I think so, but I just don't know. I saw her for such a short period of time. I don't even know what she thinks of me. All I know is that I can't quit thinking about her. I go to bed thinking about her, and I wake up thinking about her. Some days I even make up little stories in my mind where I'm talking to her. Some days I even get mad at her for not making any kind of effort to find me. It's like she's already in my life, but she's not even here."

His mother spoke softly and said, "Close your eyes, think about her, and tell me what you see."

Gus excitedly said, "She is very beautiful. She is very real. She wears makeup but not too much. Just enough to enhance her beauty. That's also how she dresses. Not overexposed and in your face, but just enough to make you want to see more. Her smile makes you smile. Her laugh is funny and makes you laugh. But she is also intelligent and can hold an interesting conversation. In many regards, she is the perfect woman."

Gus's mother then asked, "At this very moment, look at her in your mind and tell me what you see."

"I see her eyes. They seem to speak to me. They are soft and blue and calming and beautiful."

His mother chuckled as if she knew something Gus did not and said, "My son, the eyes are the window to the soul. From what you have told me, I believe you love her, and I feel that she loves you. I also truly believe that you acquired the power of love and seduction. The story that you told me about Naomi and the Eskimo man are paths down your journey. I know of the Eskimo man you speak about from your father. He is a gifted and wise man. I believe what he told you is true. This girl you speak of, Lisa, was able to resist your advances because of a strong belief or reason. Possibly she is married or maybe even a virgin. Whatever her reason, she stayed true to herself. It must have been very difficult for her to leave. She resisted the power of the gods and is a very special person."

Gus listened quietly, then asked, "I have one other question for you, Mom. Dad told me about his story and the dog he saw. And just like my story, nobody ever saw the dog except him. At least nobody remembers seeing it. I had never even thought to ask before. You were with Dad. Did you see the dog?"

He heard his mother sitting up in the chair when she said, "Why do you ask, my son?"

"Lisa said she saw me in the park walking my dog."

There was a long silence.

"Mom, are you there?" Gus asked.

"Yes, my son, I saw the dog. I was the only other person besides your grandfather and your father. If this girl Lisa has also seen the dog associated with your journey, she is an important part of your destiny."

Gus excitedly asked, "How will I ever find her?"

"She is a part of your destiny. You do not have to worry about finding your destiny. Your destiny will find you."

Like always, after talking with his mother, Gus felt better. They said their goodbyes and hung up.

After the conversation, Gus felt calm and relaxed. He trusted his mother's opinions about Lisa. He knew he would see her again. He had been punishing himself, trying every way he could think of to find Lisa. Not being able to come to any conclusion had been driving him crazy. It reminded him of something his father had once told him. Sometimes when solving a difficult problem, you must slow down and let your brain relax. Many of the world's most difficult problems and significant discoveries came from the relaxed brain. He liked to tell him about the famous scientist Sir Isaac Newton. Many of his greatest ideas came to him while relaxing under an apple tree on a leisurely afternoon. Knowing that he would see Lisa again made Gus feel relaxed. He felt like a weight had been lifted off him and that he was now thinking clearly again.

The weekend had passed, and it was Monday. Gus headed to work in a good mood. He felt positive about things. He got to work and went down to the scientists' lunchroom and put his lunch in the refrigerator. He was early, and nobody else was in the room. Like a dog sniffing the air on a beautiful spring afternoon, Gus put his head back and took a slow, deep breath through his nose. He let it out, slowly sampling all the interesting smells of his surroundings.

A particular smell snapped him out of his calmness. He sniffed the air again. His gift of smell and analytical brain kicked into overdrive. He asked himself, *What is that smell?* It was very faint, but he recognized it. He took one more very quick sniff and felt the hair standing up on his arms. He knew that smell. It was Lisa! The smell was very faint, but it was unmistakable.

Like a trained hound dog, Gus began tracking her scent.

He grabbed a notepad and a pen from his leather briefcase. He wanted to track Lisa's scent but did not want to attract attention. Gus thought to himself, *Since I'm a senior scientist, I'll act like one. I'll walk around the building like I'm in deep thought. This way I won't have to make eye contact or say hello to anybody. I can move slowly, giving me more time to track her scent. If anybody asks what I'm doing, I'll simply tell them that walking helps me think.*

Gus started walking down the hallway, sniffing the air. Her scent was faint but was getting slightly stronger. It led him down the hallway to a set of locked doors. Gus did not see this as a problem because he had moved up to a very high position as far as the company's confidential information was concerned. With that position, he had been issued an electronic card access key that should grant him entry to almost anywhere in the building. He went through the locked doors and kept moving down the hallway. Her scent was getting stronger.

Following her scent took Gus down two more hallways and through two more sets of locked doors. He had never been in this part of the building before. Gus noticed that there were several cameras in this part of the building. There were very few cameras in most other parts of the building. He wondered, *What makes this part of the building need so much surveillance?* As he walked, he observed each camera's field of view and memorized the data.

As Gus reached the end of the hallway, he approached two more doors that were different than the others. They were made of steel as opposed to wood and had no windows. Gus hesitated to use his key because he knew the security system most likely records all attempts to enter or exit these doors. He did not want it to appear that he was sneaking around. Gus evaluated his options. Off to the left of the doors he saw a unisex bathroom. *Perfect*, he thought to himself.

He went inside, flushed the toilet, washed his hands, and came back out. Now he had an alibi for being in this part of the building. He was just looking for a clean and quiet place to take a shit. He thought, *Hey, what can they say? Scientists are weird.* Then he went over to the doors and attempted to open them with his card key. They did not open, just as he suspected. In addition, a small red LED above the door was flashing.

Gus decided to leave. He headed back down the hallway. Before he reached the last set of locked doors he had come through, two security guards came in. They were much more military looking than all the other security guards Gus had seen in the company. They stopped, blocking the hallway. Gus walked up to them. One was older and balding, and looked very serious. The other was younger and appeared junior in rank.

The serious one spoke. "What's your name, and what are you doing in this section of the building?"

Gus replied, "I'm Gus Shepard, senior staff scientist. And what am I doing? Well I'm searching the building for a clean and quiet place to take a shit."

Then he looked over at the bathroom, smiled, and said, "Eureka! I've found it."

The serious guard looked puzzled. The younger guard smiled, then said, "Did you say your name was Gus Shepard?"

"Yes."

"The House at Meeku Filbeech guy?"

"Yes."

The younger guard looked at the serious guard and said, "This is Meeku. You know—the scientist dude." The younger guard was smiling.

The serious guard did not look amused. Then the younger one said, "This is the guy who broke Hans's nose!"

All of a sudden, the serious one broke into a big smile. He extended his arm and said, "I would be honored to shake the hand of the man that broke that bastard's nose. We all hated that arrogant prick."

All of a sudden the guards loosened up and became friendly. They talked about Hans and his broken nose. They described many of the details about what had happened after Hans and Gus had been split apart. There was much laughter.

Then the serious guard said, "I see that you attempted to open the door to Section B. Not many people have access to section B. It leads directly to Section A. There's some weird shit going on in Section A. Even my access stops at Section B."

The younger guard added, "Hans used to go to section A all the time. We used to have to deal with that asshole a couple times a week."

The serious guard said, "The only people that I'm aware of that have full-time access to Section A are the president, J.P. Thorn, and the senior vice president, Hank Stewart. Some people get temporary access to Section A. Sometimes escorted contractors are allowed in. Our boss, Ben, handles all that. In fact, they have some contractors coming in this week. I have no idea who they work for or what they're doing. It's all very hush-hush."

Gus asked, "Ben? Is that the big guy with the beard?"

The younger guard replied, "Yep, that's Ben. He's intense. Twenty-five years in the air force. He spent all his time in the black world doing some kind of ultra-secret communication stuff. The guy is very precise. He lives by a clock. Everything he does is based upon time. Even his lunch break. He goes to lunch at exactly twelve o'clock and returns at exactly one o'clock. Every day, always exactly on time."

While they were talking, Gus had been sniffing the air. The scent of Lisa had led him to Section B. And Section B only seemed to lead to Section A. Gus had to get into section A. He asked, "What kind of contractors are working in Section A?"

The serious guard replied, "I don't know. Appears to be some kind of building construction. All I know is that Ben gives them some kind of special access key. He uses that to monitor where they are in the building at all times." Gus decided to take this information and investigate. He talked with the guards for a while longer; then they went their separate ways. Gus knew Lisa's scent was leading him to section A. He needed to figure out how to get into section A.

That day, Gus went to the main employee cafeteria a little before noon. He was actually there to spy on Ben and to see how the contractors got access to Section A. Just as the security guards had told him, Ben ended his lunch break exactly at one o'clock. Gus followed Ben. He watched the contractors come in. Ben took them to a special room, where he punched in a special tone code to open the door. With his superior hearing, Gus could hear the tones that Ben used to unlock the door. All the contractors entered the room with Ben and exited wearing brightly colored orange coveralls, and had access keys hanging from chains around their necks.

Gus went back to his office. Using a mathematical analysis of the difference in tone frequencies, he was able to decipher the code Ben had used to unlock the door. Gus now had a plan.

Gus waited two days and spent his time watching the movements of Ben and the contractors. He had noticed that one of the contractors wore a hat. Gus went out and purchased a hat just like his. He was ready to put his plan into motion.

Gus waited until the next day and went to lunch a little after twelve o'clock. He made sure Ben was at lunch. He went to the locked room where the contractors' coveralls and access keys were kept. He punched in the code and entered the room. He grabbed a pair of the brightly colored contractor's coveralls and an access key. Gus put them into his leather briefcase and left the room. He headed down the hallway to the bathroom that was located right before the locked entrance to Section B. He knew that there were cameras on the way, but he was just the nerdy scientist going to take a private shit. Gus walked to the bathroom, went inside, and put on the brightly colored contractors' coveralls. After that, he put on the hat he had picked up to cover his face. He took the contractors' access key, which was on a chain, and placed it around his neck. Now ready to leave, he hid his briefcase behind the garbage can.

Gus knew that there were cameras in the hallways and a camera on the locked door to Section B. But he also had observed that there was no camera monitoring who went in and out of the bathroom. No one would know that he had entered the bathroom as Gus and had left looking like a contractor.

Keeping his head low and the hat over his face, he walked over to the doors to Section B. Using the contractor's access key, he opened the doors and entered. Section B was one long hallway that turned to the right. Once he went around the corner, he saw the doors to Section A.

Lisa's scent was now very strong.

Gus walked slowly and opened the doors to Section A. To his surprise, there was a house, a lawn, and flowers. But it was all artificial. It was a totally enclosed artificial environment!

Gus thought to himself, *What the hell is this?*

The smell of Lisa was incredibly strong. As Gus stood in the doorway staring, he saw Lisa come out of the house. But her hair wasn't red this time. It was brown. She walked on to the front porch looking calm and relaxed. Then she saw Gus. Their eyes locked upon each other. Nothing needed to be said. She knew it was him, and he knew it was her. He watched her pleasant demeanor change to fear.

Gus knew something was wrong. He could sense it. All of a sudden, Hank Stewart, the vice president and second in command of the company came out of the house. He was smiling and put his hand on Lisa's shoulder. Lisa stared directly at Gus. Her look told him to leave. Gus decided to go. Just as he was shutting the doors, he saw Hank catching a glimpse of him.

Gus quickly made his way back to the bathroom and changed out of his contractor's disguise. He quickly stuffed it back into his briefcase and left the bathroom as Gus. He went back to the locked room where the contractor's coveralls and access keys were kept and put them away. He did this all while Ben was at lunch. Gus had succeeded in getting in and out of Section A undetected. And he had seen Lisa. But now he was more confused than ever.

Gus went back to his office. As soon as he sat down, the phone rang. It was a number that he didn't recognize. He picked up the phone and said his usual, "This is Gus."

There was silence. Again, he said, "This is Gus."

Just as he was about to hang up, he heard, "Gus, this is Lisa. Please pretend that you don't know me. I will call you tomorrow. I'll leave a cell phone in your desk tonight and call you on it at lunchtime. I'll call at twelve o'clock tomorrow. Do you understand?"

Gus simply replied, "Yes." Then Lisa hung up.

Gus went home that night with his mind racing. He kept playing back in his mind what he had seen and, analyzing the situation. He finally just decided to let his mind rest. He was happy that he had found Lisa and that he would be talking to her tomorrow.

The next morning, Gus went to his desk and opened the middle drawer. There was a small, older-style cell phone. It was not a smartphone. *Interesting*, Gus thought to himself. *An older-style phone like this has no GPS tracking capability.*

He waited until lunchtime and took the phone out to his car. At noon, the phone rang. Gus answered but did not speak.

Lisa spoke first. "I' am sorry for leaving you in the bar."

Gus answered, "If you're sorry, it was probably something that you didn't want to do. So why did you do it?"

"I wasn't supposed to be there that night or any night. I'm not supposed to leave my isolation. I have a potentially fatal disease. My immune system is very weak, and being around the general public could kill me. The company you work for is trying hard to find a cure for it. They created a sterile environment for me to live in while they look for a cure. Hank Stewart is my father. My mother is dead."

Gus asked, "How long have you lived there?"

Lisa paused, then said, "My whole life. But in the last year, they've been making some progress. They told me that my immune system is not as weak as it used to be. I've been sneaking around the building at night. When I went to the bar that night, that was the first time I had ever been out of the building."

"That was the first time you had ever been out of the building in your whole life?" Gus asked.

"Yes."

"But why did you go there?"

"I went to that bar that night because I knew you would be there."

"How did you know that?"

Lisa laughed and said, "I know a lot about you, Gus Shepard. The day you started here, I heard about a bright young scientist who was a genius. They said this new scientist was making major breakthroughs on finding a cure for my disease. I found out this scientist was you. I've been watching you for a long time."

"But how did you know that I would be at the bar that night?"

"Gus, your cell phone is paid for by the company. I track you everywhere you go."

Slightly taken back, Gus asked, "Who else do you track?"

Lisa shyly replied, "I only track you. I don't know very much about the world outside of my isolation. Only what I've been able to read and study. And I've always been very happy and content living in my isolation. This company has done a lot for me, and I am very grateful. I've always done what I was told and have never done anything wrong. Then I saw you."

Gus, with his sharp analytical mind asked, "I thought you said you saw me in the park with my dog."

"Yes, that was the first time I saw you. I know where you live. There's a county park near your house. There's a camera in the park on the hiking trail near the bathroom. It's available to be monitored by the public. I saw you on the camera."

"How did you know I would be there?"

"I didn't. I was researching you. I guess you could say I was spying on you. But honestly, it's hard to explain. I just had a feeling that day to watch it. It was like it was destiny. That was the first time I saw you. You and your dog looked magnificent. Now I have feelings I don't understand. I'm consumed with wanting to know everything about you. I've tried to stop, but I can't. Then I followed you to the bar. I've felt guilty ever since. Now I'm causing trouble for you. You must leave me alone and forget we ever met."

Gus said, "I'm having trouble understanding a lot of the things that you've been telling me except that I understand your feelings. I can't forget the first time we met, and I don't ever want to leave you alone."

Lisa softly replied, "Keep this phone and take it with you. Don't call me. I'll call you again. But Gus, you must promise to keep this a secret, our secret."

"I promise," Gus said. He said goodbye and hung up the phone.

The next day, Gus was walking down the hallway toward his office, and he passed Hank Stewart. As he was passing, Hank stopped and said, "Shepard, heard you're doing a good job. Just signed off on a request to give you access to the executive bathrooms. No need to have our top guys searching the building for a comfortable place to take a shit." Then he smiled his sinister grin.

Gus just smiled back and said, "Things just come out better when you're comfortable."

Hank looked straight into Gus's eyes and said, "The executive bathrooms are very clean and comfortable. In fact, they get cleaned all the time. Some of the other bathrooms don't get cleaned that often. And sometimes people from outside the company use them like...contract construction workers. In fact, I've even heard that sometimes the construction workers don't pick up the toilet seat when they take a piss. You haven't noticed any piss on the toilet seats, have you?"

Gus gave him a confused look and said, "No, they all look clean to me."

Hank smiled his sinister grin again and said, "That's what I thought you would say, Shepard. It's probably just a bad rumor about those construction guys. I don't think they use the bathrooms at all. I think they piss outside in the bushes."

Gus smiled and said, "I think you might be right." Then he continued walking to his office.

Chapter 8

VEGAS

It was Saturday, and Gus was tired from the previous week's events. He had just gotten up, drank his one cup of coffee, and was getting ready to work out. The phone rang. It was his father. Gus picked up the phone and loudly said, "Daaaaad."

His father replied, "Good morning, my boy. How are you?"

"Good. What's up?"

"Just wanted to see if you wanted to go to lunch. Maybe around one?"

"Sure, got any place in mind?"

"How about that little French sandwich shop downtown?"

"Sounds good. See you at one." They said their goodbyes and hung up the phone.

Gus thought to himself, *Interesting that Dad wants to go to lunch. Typically, he would just stop in with some food. He usually prefers to sit around at my place, eat some good food, and drink a beer.*

Gus drove to the sandwich shop downtown. He walked in and saw his father sitting in the back. They smiled and waved at each other. Gus went over and sat down.

They talked for a couple of minutes. Then his father said, "Gus, I asked you here because I needed someplace private to talk to you."

Gus asked, "Why didn't you just come to my house?"

"Well, because I found out that you're being watched at a much higher level than I expected. Let me explain and you will understand. Remember when I told you about the SIP list, Significantly Important People?"

"Yes, I remember."

"For some reason, you've moved much higher up on that list. I'm not sure why, but I'm working on finding out. The main point is that you're now a high-dollar target for people who sell information. Any and all information on you is now valuable. Even the big guys like the Internet-based and social media companies will be watching you.

"There are certain things going on that you're most likely not aware of. I want to make you aware of these things so that you'll know how to react. First of all, you can't completely hide from the people seeking information. You just need to understand that they are watching so that you can manipulate and control the data they receive.

"Let's start with phones. Any conversation on any regular phone may be listened to or recorded. I'm going to give you a nontraceable contract phone. Call me on that phone only when it's important and confidential. For all regular calls, your normal phone can and should be used.

"You should be aware that social media and Internet-based companies will be watching you. There are certain social media companies that exist mainly to keep and share data on people. One of the biggest ones now has the world's largest database of people's photographs. I bet you can guess who I'm talking about. They've also developed face-recognition technology. What this means is that once they have a picture of a person, they can find them every place that their picture exists in their database. They can also trace everybody associated with that person who's in their database. Be careful when getting your picture taken by people who are always posting pictures on the Internet."

Gus frowned and said, "Dad, this sounds a little crazy."

"Gus, for some reason, you've risen very high on the Significantly Important People list. You're up there with the presidents of some countries. Any and all information on you is now valuable. Even small things that you may consider insignificant will be tracked and recorded. It will all be up for sale. I don't really know what's going on, but I would guess that it's all related to the journey that you're now on."

Gus replied, "I understand, Dad. Keep going."

"I'm going to tell you about ways in which you're being watched, recorded, and tracked. I'll also give you some tips on how to avoid, confuse, or manipulate the data the people watching you collect. If your cell phone is a smartphone, then it has GPS technology and is tracking you. If your car has a navigation system, it has GPS technology and is tracking you. Be careful of anything that has a camera lens on it. Just as with any electronic device, it may always be on. Just because you turned the device off and the screen goes black or the little red light goes out doesn't truly mean it's off. Did you just get a new smart TV?"

"Yes, about a month ago."

"Is it hooked up to the Internet?"

"No."

His father quickly said, "Keep it that way for now. Everything that's hooked up to the Internet can be manipulated. I'm familiar with your home alarm system, and I know it's not one that's connected to the Internet, so you don't have to worry about that."

Gus asked, "It is hooked up to a phone line, do I need to worry about that?"

"Well, it's a landline and goes to some alarm company. Those companies tend to be smaller and aren't usually involved in selling information. On the other hand, somebody can get data from your alarm system, such as when you're coming and going. They can get this by tracking when it's turned on and off. But getting access to that data would be risky and difficult to get. Plus, the data wouldn't be worth much and would be a bad return on their investment."

Gus, looking a little puzzled, asked, "Now that I'm aware of these things, what can I do about them?"

"Let's start with cameras. Many devices now have cameras. The easiest and most effective way to defeat a camera is to cover the lens or, in some way, block its field of view. Then you don't have to worry if the device is truly on or off. Now let's talk about cell phones. Not only does your phone have a camera, it also has the ability to listen and has GPS-tracking capability."

"Why don't I just get rid of my regular cell phone and only call using my contract phone?"

"The people who watch also watch for changes. They would notice that they don't have access to all the information they had when you had the regular cell phone. Not only would they try to find out why you aren't using your regular phone, they'll start looking for other ways to get the information. It's better not to attract attention and control the information they receive. For instance, you can manipulate your cell phone and car GPS tracking systems into thinking you are somewhere that you're actually not. Park your car and leave your cell phone in it. From there, walk, take a cab, or take public transportation."

"How about a ride-sharing service?"

"Only use that if you have no other options. I don't know if they're in the information-selling business, but I do know that they save the information. Any information that's saved is vulnerable. If you need to take your cell phone with you, there's a way to hide your location, at least until you make a call. This method also blocks the camera and significantly reduces the sound getting to the phone. Here is what you do. Go find a small metal box that your phone will fit into. It must have a metal lid, and all the sides of the lid must touch the sides of the box. A coffee tin or metal candy box will usually work. The box will block the camera's vision and reduce the sound to it. The metal will stop the phone transmission and reception."

"But how will I know if the box I choose works?"

"Put your phone in the box and secure the lid. Go to another phone and call your cell phone. If the box is working, it should prevent your phone from transmitting or receiving signals. It shouldn't ring. Take it out of the box and call it again. It should ring. You should keep in mind that this method works until you have to make a call. As soon as you do, your location can be tracked, your voice can be recorded, and your camera can take pictures."

"Speaking of cameras, there seems to be cameras everywhere. Is there any way to manipulate the data they collect? Many times, they're up too high, and their field of view can't be blocked."

"That's not exactly true. You block the field of view before it reaches your body or, most importantly, your face. It is called a disguise. They can be very elaborate or quite simple. Ask any criminal robbing a liquor store with cameras. A long-sleeve sweatshirt with a hoodie pulled tight and a dark pair of sunglasses seem to work fine!"

Gus and his father both laughed. Then his father continued. "It's interesting the way the world is changing. It used to be that data on people's names was easily available. Data on what that person looked like or their photo was not. Soon, data on everyone's photo will be easily available, and the hard part will be to match it to their real name. By real name, I mean the name that identifies who you really are.

"Once people realize that many organizations have photos of them, they'll start hiding their names or start using more than one. Hiding your name will become more important than hiding your face. It's actually already happening. With the satellite technology that exists today, they can take a photo of anybody, anywhere in the world, anytime they want. So they can get your photo, but then they'll want to know what your name is.

"As far as people hiding their names go, many people already create e-mail addresses or join websites such as dating sites and provide fake names. They may be willing to supply photos of themselves because they know that haven't used their real name. People who understand what's taking place in this world already hide their names. Remember the short, fat, Eskimo man you met on your vacation? He doesn't use his name. He's very hard to find. In fact, you don't find him—he finds you. If you're a stranger to him, all you can do is go to a place where you think he might be and ask around. He'll hear about it and make contact with you only if he wants to.

"Another thing I find interesting is that most people think that large Internet and social media companies make all their money from other companies that advertise on their sites. This is mostly true, but they also make a huge amount of money selling information on people. And information on people high on the SIP list pays the most. You wouldn't believe how valuable information on very important people is. Take the president of the United States, for example. Any little thing he does is important."

"But why?" Gus asked.

"Because if they understand his habits, his likes and dislikes, that'll help them understand and predict his decisions. The decisions he makes can be very important."

"People like me who watch what the people who collect and sell information are amazed by what's happening, and the general public doesn't even see it."

"Take the self-driving car for example—totally controlled by GPS technology. Why would any company want to invest in it? Where's their return on investment? It's the information that can be sold! Whoever has this information will know the locations of large groups of people all the time. What really amazes me is that the creators of the technology are already pushing for vehicles with no steering wheels so early in the creation of the system. You would think it would be safer to leave the steering wheel in case the system malfunctioned or failed. Why do they want to leave out the steering wheel? Because no steering wheel definitely means that you can't travel in your vehicle without them tracking you. This makes their data very valuable!

"Working for the government, I'm surprised how many companies don't want to unlock their phones or provide data when requested to do so by the government. They tell everybody it's private information and that we can't trust the government. Has anyone ever thought to ask, 'Why should we trust *them*?' Why are they collecting and saving the information? If they don't want to share the data, why don't they just quit collecting it? You can't be forced to share what you don't have!

"Another thing people don't think about is listening devices. I'm not talking about someone sneaking into your house and planting a listening device, aka...a bug. I am talking about anything that's voice activated or controlled. Take, for instance, things like your cable-provided voice-controlled remote for your television."

Gus replied "Ya, I just installed one. It's pretty cool. I just talk into my television remote."

"Exactly what I'm talking about. It has a microphone that has the ability to listen to you twenty-four seven. It communicates with your television, which is connected to a company-provided cable. That gives them a transmission line. They now have everything they need to perform audio surveillance on you. It's right in front of your face, and it's all legal. Sign up for any Internet, phone, or television service, and read the disclaimer on information and privacy. They're allowed to collect everything and do what they want with it. Your only choice is to not accept the service. It is take it or leave it!

"To sum it all up, Gus, like I said earlier, you can't hide from the people who collect information. But if you have a basic understanding of what they're doing, you can manipulate the data they receive. You can confuse them or manipulate them into believing about you what you want them too. That puts you in control of them instead of them in control of you."

Gus then said with a laugh, "Thanks, Dad. I feel like my eyes have been opened. I feel about as happy about this as I did when you told me that Santa Claus and the Easter Bunny did not exist!"

Then they both laughed loudly together. His father then said, "Gus, there's actually two reasons I needed to talk to you. The first was to make you aware of how closely you're being watched. But now that I have covered that, we also need to talk about those two guys you met on your trip to the mountains, Ike and Mike. They're low-end small-job mercenaries, but they're also involved in the information-selling business. When you moved up on the SIP list, a kind of information bounty was put out on you. It's kind of like a Wanted poster with a very large reward for information on Gus Shepard. Your meeting them wasn't accidental. They were there to collect information on you because it pays well. They were there to test your limits so that they would have good data for sale.

"I had suspected something. That's why I called my friend, the short, fat, Eskimo man. He came up with the bear thing all on his own. He did that because things like this that confuse the people who collect and sell information. A lot of those guys will now back off from collecting information on you. The word will get out, and the story won't make any sense. They won't know how to analyze the risk of collecting information on you. It'll become an unanswered question. A theoretical dog chasing its tail. They won't know what to think about it, so they will just think about something else. They will move on to collecting information on other people who are high on the SIP list.

"But Ike and Mike aren't going to back off. What happened in the bar didn't just confuse them—it pissed them off. You made them look like fools. They now need to redeem themselves. Those guys aren't high-end soldiers, but they *are* dangerous. They both have military training and have seen combat. They aren't as good as they think they are, which actually makes them more dangerous. They're more likely to do something stupid. Gus, these guys are pissed off, and they are out for revenge. I taught you many things about martial arts and hand-to-hand combat, so these guys are no match for you in a fight. The big problem is that these guys are going to come after you with guns. I need to prepare you for this. I need to teach you about guns."

"But Dad, you've always told me to never carry a gun unless I was prepared to kill somebody. Even in my martial arts training, you made it clear that many of the techniques I learned could kill. That a human life is the most valuable thing in the universe. That, as humans, we should try our hardest to avoid ending another human's life. If you're telling me I need to learn about guns, then you're telling me I need to prepare to start killing people. I don't know if I can do that. It goes against everything I know. Everything you've taught me!"

His father looked at him with a concerned, serious look and said, "I've always told you that the only time you take a human's life is in defense of your life or the life of someone with you; I have always told you that if you have the ability to leave or run, that you should do that if it means sparing another human's life. That hasn't changed. I also told you that the only other time that a man may be forced to take another human's life was in a time of war. Hopefully, the war is for a just cause, but many times, knowing that for sure is beyond the knowledge of the soldier. He unfortunately must kill or be killed.

"My son, I'm afraid that the journey you're on may be pulling you into a war. The war of good versus evil. Even I have sometimes questioned the things that I have become involved in. I would sometimes wonder who is right and who is wrong. I finally concluded that as my deciding criteria, I would ask myself, Is what I am about to do for good or evil?

I do believe in God, but I have a problem with many organized religions' perception of good and evil. Many religions use the worship of their God to do evil things. I used to be somewhat confused until I got involved in a major scientific study of God. We had many large supercomputers analyze everything that existed on all Gods and religions. The study came to two simple conclusions. If you believe in a God, you also believe in a Devil. And that if you add one letter to the word *God*, you get 'good.' If you subtract one letter from the word 'Devil,' you get 'evil.' The final conclusion was that the teachings about God and the Devil were actually the teachings of good versus evil. Understanding what's truly good or evil may not always be easy. That's why many religions teach about God and the Devil.

I've always asked myself when my actions could result in the death of another human if it's for good or for evil. Then I would let my conscience be my guide. My son, you may soon find yourself in a similar situation. Please remember what I've told you and let your conscience be your guide."

Gus hesitated, then said, "I understand what you're saying, but it'll take some time to sink in."

"Don't spend too much time trying to answer that question now. When the time comes, you may be forced to make a life-or-death decision. Only then will you be in a situation where you have to ask yourself what you should do. If you aren't in that kind of a situation, then there's no decision to make; therefore, no question to be answered."

"So I guess for now, I should just let it sink in and not think about it."

"You guessed right—for now, anyway.

Now that we have that out of the way, I need to know when you can take a couple of days off."

"It just so happens that my company shuts down for a week coincidently next week. But I bet you already knew that."

His father smiled and said, "Funny how information on somebody can be used to your advantage."

"So what did you have in mind?"

"How about three days in Vegas?"

"Sounds good, but why Vegas?"

"For two reasons. First of all, it's a good cover, so you won't draw attention to yourself. Second, that's where I've set up your weapons training. I have a friend that owns a one-hundred-acre ranch and has access to one of those gun places."

"You mean one of those places where you can rent any gun known to man and shoot them at an indoor range, even fully automatics? I must confess, I've always wanted to do that."

"You'll get to do that and much, much more."

Gus smiled and said, "What's the plan?"

"You'll leave Monday afternoon. When you get there, I want you to book a room, do some gambling, maybe even go see a show. Typical Vegas type stuff. To anybody watching, you have some time off and just flew to Vegas to have some fun. Make sure that your regular cell phone is with you and turned on. Your training will start Tuesday morning. A military-looking guy with a scar below his left eye will find you. Just go to the gambling area of the hotel around 7:00 a.m. He'll address you as Junior. He'll take you where you need to go. When you go with him, leave your cell phone in your room."

"Should I leave my cell phone on or off?"

"It doesn't matter. It's most likely now always on. But to make it look like you intentionally left it there, turn it off. Anyone watching will think you haven't gone far. Your absence won't arouse suspicion."

Gus and his father finished eating and left.

That Monday, Gus flew to Las Vegas. He did as his father said. He arrived around 6:00 p.m., checked into his room, went down to the casino, and did some gambling. He went to bed around 10:00 p.m. so that he would be rested and fresh for the next day. The next morning, Gus went back to the casino and started gambling. He left his cell phone in his room, just as his father had instructed him to do.

Just as his father had told him, a military-looking guy with a scar below his left eye approached him. He came up to Gus and said, "You look like your father. I can tell that you're his son. How about I just call you Junior?" They both smiled and shook hands.

Gus said, "So what should I call you?"

"Call me what you like. As your father most likely explained to you, many of us use no names. Only when it's necessary, and even then, we make one up. As you know, I have decided to call you Junior. What would you like to call me?"

Gus looked at him and said, "Let me think about it. How about Sarge, short for Sergeant?"

"Sounds good to me. Beats being called Scarface."

Gus jokingly said, "How about Scarface Sarge?"

"I think Sarge is good enough," the man replied with a smile.

Gus and Sarge left the casino and went to his car. They drove for about forty minutes to the outskirts of Las Vegas. They parked and got out of the car. Gus followed Sarge to an industrial building, which had been converted into an indoor shooting range.

Sarge said, "I get you for two full days. Today, we'll just work on guns. You'll get to shoot almost every gun in existence. You'll learn to load, unload, and shoot. I'll also show you how to quickly free up some automatics, which tend to jam."

Gus felt excited. He looked around the room at the largest selection of guns that he had ever seen in his life. Then they got started. Sarge had

Gus loading and shooting guns. He got to shoot many guns of all types: revolvers, semiautomatic pistols, shotguns, and high-powered bolt-action rifles. He then moved into more military-type weapons, such as the well-known AK-47 and its lighter American competitor, the AR-15. He was put through many drills. All were unique.

Then Sarge looked at Gus and said, "One last test. You've done very well so far. You catch on very quickly."

Sarge took thirty of the most popular guns. He put them in a big, messed-up pile on a table. Then he took loose ammunition and some loaded magazines matching all the guns and put them in a jumbled pile on a table next to the guns.

Sarge said, "You have sixty seconds to load and shoot as many guns as you can." He raised his hand into the air and said, "Are you ready?"

"I'm ready."

Sarge looked at a big clock in the room and waited until the second hand was at twelve o clock. Then he slammed his hand down on the table and said, "Go!"

Gus hesitated, staring at the guns and the pile of loose ammunition. He appeared to be frozen. But that wasn't the case. His mind was racing. His concentration was intense. Then he began rapidly loading and shooting weapons. It sounded like a war. He looked up at the clock and saw that thirty seconds had gone by. He realized that he wouldn't finish shooting all the guns in the time that was left. He felt his body kicking into hyperspeed. He started loading two guns as quickly as he had been loading one, then turning and shooting two guns at a time. In fifty-eight seconds, Gus finished shooting all the guns, turned to Sarge, and said, "Two seconds to spare. How's that?"

Sarge looked at Gus and said, "Damn. Your father told me you were exceptional, but what I've just seen is unreal. I've seen guys, very talented guys, spend months practicing and have not been able to shoot all the guns in sixty seconds. And on top of that, your accuracy was almost one hundred percent. The targets look like Swiss cheese! I can't wait to see what you do tomorrow at the ranch.

"OK, that was the last test for the day. You'll need some rest for to-morrow. But one question I always ask at the end of this session is, what gun did you like the best?"

Gus looked upward and said, "Let me see. The Uzi was cool. I like the way it rapidly fires. I think in close quarters, it would be very effective. It's a relatively small gun, considering the firepower it can deliver. But for some reason, I really liked the World War Two-era Thompson subma-chine gun. The military version of the Tommy gun. It was slower, but it felt powerful. I wouldn't think there would be many things that you could hide behind if someone were shooting at you with a Thompson."

"Good choice. Both have their own characteristics. The Uzi is eas-ily concealed. It holds a lot of shells, but they're of a smaller caliber. It's more suitable to a person who might not be a good shot due to its rapid firing capability. It's a very good close-quarters weapon. It is very well suited for urban warfare. If you want to shoot up the house, bring the Uzi. But if you prefer to shoot down the house, bring the Thompson. It's a .45-caliber beast. It will penetrate many walls in a typical house. Just point in the general direction of your opponent and destroy what's in front of you!

"I'm very impressed that you understand the personality of the weap-ons. They all have their strengths and weaknesses. Choosing the most appropriate weapon for the situation in many cases is the determining factor in a conflict. OK, let's wrap it up and get you back. I'll meet you at 5:00 a.m. tomorrow in the same area of the hotel. We'll have a busy day."

They drove back to the hotel, and Sarge dropped Gus off. Gus went back to the hotel and repeated some of the previous day's actions. He went out to dinner, did some gambling, had a beer at the bar, and went to bed early.

The next morning, he met Sarge, just as he had done the day before. Gus left with Sarge, and they drove for about an hour and a half into a mountain-terrain type of area to get to Sarge's one-hundred-acre ranch. They drove about four miles into the ranch down a dirt road until they arrived at a large metal building.

Sarge parked and said while getting out of the car, "This is where we'll start."

Gus got out of the car and they entered the metal building. Once inside, Gus found the building very well lighted with natural skylights and a large area covered with mats. There was also another section that had mats, a small bridge, padded logs, a fence, and a rope hanging from the ceiling. It was obviously some sort of obstacle course.

Sarge said, "Yesterday, you learned to load and shoot guns. Today, you'll learn to how to use a gun. I understand from your father that you're very proficient in martial arts."

"My father started teaching me when I was fourteen."

"How often do you practice your katas or forms?"

"I practice my forms in every workout I do, which is usually four to five times a week."

"Good. Then you understand that they combine eye, hand, and muscle coordination with mental concentration. Studies have shown that this type of continuous practice over time actually develops growth in parts of the brain that normal people don't have. It's this type of practice that lets your body react upon impulse. Your brain actually develops the ability to have your body react to a situation before it has had time to analyze it. The same way your brain and hands react when someone throws you a ball and you automatically catch it.

"The first part of today, I'll teach you a new form. It's known as the kata of the gun. It's performed with an unloaded weapon. First, I'll teach you each individual move. Then I'll combine them into a set of moves. Once you learn this kata, you must perform it at least once per day and more if you can."

Gus asked, "How long should I continue to practice this kata? A month, a year?"

Sarge got a serious look on his face and said, "If I were you, I'd practice it until I die."

By the look on Sarge's face, Gus could feel his seriousness. It inspired him to try to absorb as much as he could. He knew this was not a game.

Sarge started teaching Gus the individual moves. This was a handgun kata. It was based upon the fact that the handgun was most likely the first gun to be used when encountering a surprise attack. Sarge preferred to use a Beretta 9 millimeter. Each move he showed Gus was unique. Shooting straight in front, over the shoulder, and under the arm to the back. He also had Gus switching the gun between hands and repeating the moves. Then he went into body-movement shots. Forward flip and shoot. Backward flip and shoot. Spin and shoot and even rolling while shooting.

Sarge combined all the moves into a sequence of moves which became the basis of the complete kata. After Sarge ran through the kata twice in its entirety, he said to Gus, "Your turn. Do as much as you can remember."

Gus walked to the center of the room and started performing the kata of the gun. He was spinning, turning, and flipping while pretending to shoot. His focus of an imaginary opponent was intense. He performed it flawlessly.

Sarge looked at Gus when he was done and said, "After what I saw you do yesterday, I thought nothing you would do could amaze me. But you just performed the kata of the gun for the first time perfectly. I'm truly amazed again. Not only were all your moves fluid and correct, your focus was intense! The focus is the most important part. I could tell that you were imagining a true opponent. That's the part of the kata that develops the brain over time. You look as good as guys who have practiced this kata for years! Let's take a break and eat. The next part of your training will be physically demanding."

After the break, Sarge took Gus to the obstacle course. He had Gus jumping off a bridge and shooting, going up and down a rope while shooting, and even diving into water then coming up and shooting. Sarge emphasized the need to keep moving. He told Gus, "A moving target is much harder to hit than one that isn't moving. You must never forget that while you're shooting at someone else, they'll be shooting back at you."

The end of the day was nearing, and Sarge had Gus take another break. After the break, Sarge said, "This time, we're going to add some realism to your training. I'll give you a handgun that holds fifteen paint-filled rounds. In the other half of the building, I've constructed a small simulated city. In that city, there are fifteen people who also have weapons with paint-filled rounds. They'll try to shoot you. I've also included several people who don't have weapons and aren't there to shoot you. They're there to deceive and confuse you. Your goal is to shoot fifteen people who are trying to shoot you, using only the fifteen rounds you are given. You are to do this without being shot by them. In addition, you can't shoot any people who aren't carrying weapons. If you miss your target or get hit, keep on going. We will tally up your score when it is over. I want you to remember one very important thing: Do not trust anyone until I tell you that you're done. Do you understand?"

Gus smiled a kind of cocky smile and said, "I got it."

Sarge handed Gus a gun and took him over to the other half of the building. Gus walked in and shut the door behind him. It truly looked like he was in a city in a bad part of town. Gus saw what appeared to be a group of homeless men sitting by a burning garbage can. As he approached, the action started. Two were decoys, and one was an opponent. Lights started flashing, loud rock music began playing, and smoke started pouring out of the garbage can. All this was to add confusion. Then one of the men turned with a gun. Gus fired fast and hit him before he could shoot.

Each situation was different. An old lady and an old man each shooting weapons at the same time. A hot-looking woman jogging by to distract him with an ambush from behind. One by one, Gus eliminated his opponents without getting hit by them.

When it was nearly over, Gus counted thirteen simulated kills. All were direct hits. He knew he only had two rounds left. Then an artificial sun began to brightly shine. Out of the sun came a man and a woman pushing a stroller. They were heading for Gus. He started thinking, I *have two rounds left. Is it the man or the woman or both?*

As they got closer, Gus noticed that the man was pushing the stroller, not the woman. He could also see that the man's forearm muscles were tight. Gus could tell that they were tight because he was pushing something much heavier than a baby. They approached Gus and stopped. They were both smiling.

Gus immediately fired directly into the stroller!

A dwarf man with a gun pretended to fall out dead. The man and woman ran. Gus could tell that the man's forearm muscles were tight because he was pushing something much heavier than a baby. That, combined with instinct, told him to shoot.

Suddenly, all of the distracting noises and lights shut off, and the overhead stockroom-type lights turned on. Sarge came in carrying a clipboard and smiling. He yelled, "Good job. Let's add up your score and see how well you did."

As Sarge approached, Gus fired directly into his chest!

Sarge, looking a little stunned, said, "Why did you do that?"

"You said fifteen rounds and fifteen opponents. I had one round left and had no opponent except you. You also told me to not trust anyone until you told me we were done. You never said we were finished."

Sarge looked at Gus, kind of irritated, and said, "You son of a bitch. You just ruined my new shirt! But most of all, you bruised my ego. You're absolutely right. I was going to shoot you."

He turned over the clipboard and exposed a gun he was holding, which was taped to the bottom.

"Nobody has ever passed this part of the test except you. I didn't fool you. That means that you're better than me. Your training is over. I have nothing more to offer." He smiled a big grin and said, "Let's go get a beer, you son of a bitch."

They shook hands and left.

Chapter 9
HOOVER DAM

Gus went back to his room. It was about 8:00 p.m. He was tired from to-day's training session. Tomorrow was a day to himself before flying out that evening. Gus ordered food to his room, watched some TV, and then went to bed.

The next morning, he got up early, ate breakfast, and decided to go see Hoover Dam. This time, he would bring his regular cell phone with him. It would be turned on so that anybody who might be following him could track him. Anybody that was watching would most likely conclude that he had two days of drinking and gambling, and his last day was a slow day. He was just taking it easy, checking out the local sights before flying home that evening.

Gus drove to the dam, paid, and entered. It looked massive. There were very few people there that day because it was the off-season. Gus didn't like guided tours, so he decided to walk around by himself. He had an eerie feeling that something wasn't right. He decided to ignore the feel-ing. Gus thought to himself, *It must be the enormous size of this place that has me feeling a little nervous.*

Gus walked around, marveling at the tremendous amount of engi-neering and construction. He saw some pressure gauges, and crossed the room to check them out. Something only an engineer or scientist would do.

As he crossed the room, the lights went out, and the room went black. Then some sort of backup generator kicked in, dimly illuminating the room.

Gus saw an exit door light turn on, so he headed for it. He went through the door and entered the hallway. As the door shut behind him, he heard a familiar clicking sound. After his last two days of training, Gus knew exactly what that sound was. It was the sound of someone pulling back the hammer of a revolver.

"Freeze, motherfucker!" someone yelled from behind him.

Gus could feel two guns touching his head. He knew that were at least two assailants. Then one of the guys walked in front of him. In the light, Gus could see that it was Mike from his trip to the mountains.

"Remember me, asshole?" he said.

Cautiously, Gus replied, "How could I forget the same ugly red face I remember from the last time I saw you lying on the floor?"

Mike pushed the revolver in Gus's face and said, "You're a real smart ass, aren't you?"

Gus said with a slight smile, "Better to be a smart ass than a stupid ass."

Then Gus heard the guy behind him say, "Can't we just fuck him up a little before we kill him? No one will know."

Gus said, "Speaking of stupid asses, how you doing, Ike?"

Ike spun from behind Gus to in front of him. He kept his gun close to Gus's head. When Ike's face hit the light, Gus could see an ugly scar near the side of his right eye.

He looked at Ike, smiled, and said, "What happened to you? Someone belt you in the eye?"

Ike yelled, "Let me hit him at least once! No one will know. It'll just look like part of the accident."

Mike said, "I'd like to do that and a lot more, but we're professionals. The last time, we made mistakes. This time, no mistakes. A lot of people are watching this guy. They'll ask questions. And you know what'll happen if we get caught eliminating a person of significant importance. It must look like an accident, pure and simple. When it's all done, we can sit back, have a beer, and laugh like true professionals."

Ike smiled and said, "You're right, man. Cool. I'm the fire, and you're the ice. You're always thinking with a cool head. Let's do this right."

Keeping their guns aimed directly at Gus's head, Mike said, "OK, asshole, let's move."

They marched Gus through a small door and down a narrow hallway that led to a tunnel. Ike and Mike stopped and told Gus to walk to the end of the tunnel. Gus got to the end of the tunnel and looked down. It was easily a one-hundred-foot drop into a large cavern of swirling water. Obviously some sort of drainage system for the dam.

Mike yelled, "The power temporarily failed. The lights went out. In the darkness and confusion, you accidently went down this tunnel, slipped, and fell. Sounds good to me. What do you think about the plan, asshole?"

Gus yelled back, "Maybe you're just bluffing and won't really shoot me. Maybe if you shoot me, you'll get caught, and you don't want that. Maybe I'll just turn around and walk right out of here."

"Go ahead, asshole. You like games. You're a gambling man. You've been lucky before. Spend your nickel and take your chances!"

Gus's mind was spinning. He'd been acting kind of cocky, but he knew this was serious. He looked down over the side of the tunnel into the swirling water and mentally calculated his chances of survival. They were slim. Then he turned and faced Ike and Mike. They both had their guns trained on him. Gus could not only see the anger on their faces, he could feel their thirst for revenge.

Without saying a word, Gus did a backflip and dove off the edge of the tunnel down into the swirling water. He was hit with a force like he had never felt in his life. The first thought in his mind was, *I am going to die!*

Like an animal backed into a corner, Gus fought for his life. He knew he had survived the fall. He could feel his body being pulled rapidly in one direction by the force of the water. Gus wasn't sure why, but instinct told him to swim with the current but hard to his left. He soon hit a wall and grabbed a pipe. With all his might, he pulled himself up the pipe.

Unable to see Gus, Ike and Mike cheered. Mike said to Ike, "Follow me. I know a good place to watch him pop up out of the water. His body will be pinned against a drainage grate."

"What if he isn't dead yet?"

"Then we get to sit there and eat popcorn and watch him die. Any life that he has left in him will be no match for the force of the rushing water."

Ike smiled and said, "That's what I like about you, buddy. Always one step ahead of the game."

They both ran down to the place Mike suggested. There was no Gus. They waited about five minutes and still nothing. Then Ike looked off to the left of the drainage grate. There was a small maintenance area. He saw Gus climbing out of the water. Ike yelled, "Look, there he is!"

Mike whined, "Damn, this guy is lucky. OK, Ike, you get your wish. Let's go shoot him! We can't get a good shot from here. The only way out of here for him is up that ladder that's behind that large downward stream of water. Let's get about halfway up to another level to get a good shot at him." They took off running.

Gus climbed out of the water onto the maintenance area. There was no exit door, only a ladder upward. He knew the same thing that they did. His only way out was up the ladder, which had a very powerful stream of water rushing over it. Obviously, the ladder had been designed to be used when the water wasn't flowing over it. Gus anticipated that they would be shooting at him as he climbed up the ladder. He came up with a plan. He calculated that the force of the rushing water would deflect the bullets from hitting him. But every step he got closer to the top, the force of the downward stream would be stronger and would most likely tear him away from the ladder.

Gus's mind started spinning. He looked around the maintenance area. He found a large construction wheelbarrow type garbage dumpster. He found some tools and quickly removed the frame and wheel. Gus took an axe, punched two holes in the wheelbarrow, and ran a construction belt through it. He buckled the belt around his waist and pulled the hull of the wheelbarrow over his body like a turtle shell.

Gus moved into the water. The force of the water hit the curved surface of the wheelbarrow. It slammed the structure against the ladder with Gus underneath, protected like a turtle in its shell. The curved surface of the wheelbarrow deflected the force of the water allowing him to move upward. He began to climb. Just as Gus reached about halfway up the ladder, he heard a popping, swishing noise. First once, then twice, then several times. Just as Gus had calculated, they were shooting at him. The heavily flowing water was deflecting the shots.

Ike and Mike had strategically set themselves up directly across from where Gus was now. Ike yelled to Mike, "Is he dead?"

Mike yelled back, "No, I don't think so. We would have seen him fall. The stream of water is protecting him from the shots. It's like shooting into a pond but a thousand times harder to hit your target."

Ike asked, "Who *is* this guy?"

"I don't know, but I don't think he's just some very lucky, nerdy scientist. We need to step up our game, buddy. He's going to climb up the ladder to get to that small platform so that he can leave through that exit door. That's his only way out. Let's get to that door before him. When he gets out of the water, it'll be a turkey shoot. We'll unload on that motherfucker! Let the fire rain upon him."

Ike then yelled, "Yaaaaa, let's fuckin' rock 'n' roll!" They both took off running for the exit door.

Gus was tiring after climbing the ladder. He knew he was nearing the platform and that his only way out was through the exit door. He also knew that once he stepped out of the flow of the water, he would be unprotected from bullets and that Ike and Mike would be waiting for him. He was almost at the platform near the exit door. He could hear Ike and Mike yelling, screaming, and laughing.

Gus reached the platform but stayed behind the flowing water. Ike and Mike were eager for him to get out. Gus stayed behind the stream of water but continued to climb. He got about eight feet above the platform. He was in position. With every last bit of strength left in his body, Gus slammed his back against the inside of the large wheelbarrow. He pushed upward and to the left, directing the massive stream of water into Ike and Mike.

The water hit with such force that it knocked them to the platform floor. Mike was holding on to the railing, and Ike was clutching Mike's leg. Gus let out a massive roar as he pushed the wheelbarrow higher, slamming them with a more powerful stream.

Ike yelled to Mike, "Don't give up. Pull me up; we're a team!"

Mike looked down at Ike and shouted, "Yes, we are, but sorry, buddy, time to take one for the team." Then he kicked Ike in the face.

Ike let go of his leg and got blasted off the platform down into the swirling water below.

Gus's arms ached as he fell back into his turtle shell. Unable to move, he just clung onto the ladder. Peering through a small opening in the wheelbarrow, Gus saw Mike stumble up to the door, fall, and crawl out. He knew he was running away. He couldn't see Ike but knew he wasn't on the platform. That only left one other place: off the side and down into the water. Gus thought to himself, *I didn't want to kill you. I was only defending myself. I gave you the same chance to live that you gave me. Destiny will now determine your fate.*

Gus got to the platform and out of the water. He unbuckled the strap holding the structure to his body. Immediately he fell to the floor, exhausted from the energy he had just spent. He laid there for over thirty minutes before getting up and stumbling back to his car. Gus opened the car door and got in. He had left his phone inside. Just as he sat down, it rang. He didn't recognize the number but answered, "Hello, this is Gus."

To his surprise, the reply was, "Hello, Gus, this is Lisa. I called several times; finally you've picked up. I'm at the airport in Las Vegas. I'm here to see you. I'll explain more when we meet. I know you can't pick me up, so thank you for sending your friend. Hold on, Gus, he wants to talk to you."

Gus heard Lisa talking and handing the phone to someone. Then a voice came on to the line. "Hey, buddy, Gus, this is Mike. How you doing?" Then he laughed.

Gus yelled, "What the fuck?"

Mike then said, "I'm having some trouble hearing you. Let me take the phone over in this corner…there, now we have some privacy. Gus, my friend, I've been monitoring your phone. How do you think I found you, asshole? Lisa called and needed a ride to your hotel. And I sure am going to give her one. When I'm done with her, the biggest favor I could do for her is kill her. But I won't do that. When I'm finished with her, I'll deliver her to your room. The way I figure, even if your car was working—which it isn't—it would take you nearly an hour to get back to the hotel. And by the time you get there, I'll be done. I'll have her all prettied up and waiting for you in bed. This one's for Ike. An eye for an eye, motherfucker!" Then he hung up the phone.

Gus felt a pit in his stomach. For the first time in his life, he felt helpless and desperate. He thought to himself, *What am I going to do? I need to get to them before he hurts her.*

His eyes bulged, and his brain started spinning. Gus estimated that he had about twenty minutes to get to them before he hurt her. Mike wouldn't do it at the airport, so he would most likely take her to the hotel or somewhere close to it to do his dirty work. Gus must work fast.

He looked around the parking lot for the fastest car. Parked near a maintenance area was a 1970s-era Chevy Chevelle Super Sport. It was definitely modified for speed. He saw two guys in it smoking a joint and drinking a beer. They were obviously locals.

Gus ran over to the passenger side of the car. "How fast can you get me downtown?" he asked.

The guy on the passenger side smiled and said, "You got money?"

Gus said, "I'll pay you five thousand dollars."

The guy replied, "Woo, shit, you are in a hurry. We can get you there in twenty minutes, give or take five minutes."

Gus said, "I need to get there in fifteen minutes."

The passenger looked at the driver and said, "If we include Benny and break some rules, what do you think?"

The driver leaned over toward the passenger side of the car and said to Gus, "Make it ten thousand, and we'll get you there in fifteen minutes or your money back!"

Gus said, "Let's do it," and jumped into the back seat of the car.

The car ripped out of the parking lot. The driver looked kind of crazy as he yelled, "*Heeee haaaa!*"

Gus grabbed his phone and called the only man he thought might be able to find and track Mike and Lisa: he decided to call James Caldwell, the owner of the camera company that had filmed him saving the Mexican boy's life. Gus called Intellectual Design Systems and asked for him. He answered.

"Gus, my friend, what a pleasure. What can I do for you?"

"I need your help."

"You sound serious. Anything you need, I'm at your disposal."

"Someone very special to me has been kidnapped by a very evil person. He's going to hurt her badly unless I stop him. Do you have any access to cameras in Las Vegas?"

Caldwell changed the tone of his voice as if responding to an emergency. He said, "I don't have access to any cameras in Las Vegas. I have access to every camera in Las Vegas, including all satellite images, both commercial and military. Give me their descriptions and a starting point."

Gus provided the information.

In the amazingly short time of ninety seconds, Caldwell said, "I have them now. They're heading for the airport parking lot. I'll track them. Keep your phone on, and I'll also track you."

The Chevelle was flying. They were on a straight path doing a little over 160 miles per hour. They passed a police car that was parked on the side of the road. He turned on his lights and immediately began the chase. To his Gus's surprise, the driver slowed down to about 130 miles per hour. Gus looked at him and said, "What are you doing?"

The driver said, "Don't worry, pal. I don't want to lose him. He doesn't know it, but he's part of the plan." The driver looked at the passenger and said, "Call Benny and tell him to get ready. We're close."

Gus could see that they were just on the outskirts of downtown Las Vegas. All of a sudden, the driver yelled, "Hold on!" He flipped a switch on the console, and a nitrous oxide system kicked in. The car took off like a rocket, leaving the police car far behind.

Just as the nitrous system depleted its booster tank, they pulled up to the back of a small building. The driver yelled, "Get out!"

All of a sudden, an ambulance with lights flashing pulled up. "Get in the ambulance now!" he yelled.

They all jumped out and got into the back of the vehicle. The ambulance flew out of the parking lot. This was no ordinary ambulance. It was fast.

Within a minute of racing down the road, the police car that had been following them before pulled right up behind them. The driver of the ambulance hit a switch to talk to the cop. He yelled, "I have a Code Red. I repeat, Code Red. I need to get downtown now!"

The cop yelled back, "Is this real?"

"Big-time real!" the ambulance driver yelled.

"Let me get in front. I'll radio ahead. We'll have all green lights."

The driver hung up the phone. "Thanks, Benny," one of the guys said.

Gus loudly asked Benny, "What's a Code Red?"

"It means somebody big is down and needs help. It could be a senator, or a movie star, or even more importantly, a crime boss. It's our code for pull out all the stops. Break rules if you have to, especially if it's a crime boss!" Then he let out a loud laugh.

Gus could see that they were entering the main strip of Las Vegas. All the lights were green in their direction. Benny yelled to him, "We told you fifteen minutes, and we've only used up ten. Where exactly do you want to go?"

Gus yelled back, "Hold on Benny. Caldwell, where are they and where are we?"

Caldwell replied, "They just arrived at your hotel and entered a back entrance to the basement. You're one block away. Go one block and turn right, and you'll be entering your parking lot near the back entrance that they went in."

The guys in the car overheard what was going on. Benny yelled out, "I'll get you there in less than fifteen minutes, and as a bonus, I'll get you into any part of the hotel that you want. Put on one of those EMT ambulance jackets. I'll call it in." Gus heard Benny yelling into his phone, "Code Red! Code Red! We're coming in through the back door."

Gus yelled back, "Thanks, guys. Thanks, Benny. Caldwell, could you wire these guys fifteen thousand dollars? That's ten thousand for the ride and five for the bonus."

Caldwell replied, "It's as good as done! Gus, the male suspect, the girl, and a group of four additional men have all entered the back door of the hotel together. I'm following them using the hotel's surveillance system. I'll direct you when you get in."

The ambulance slid up to the back door in a screeching halt. The hotel staff had the back door open, leading to the basement. Gus jumped out looking like an EMT-Emergency Medical Technician and ran inside. He said to Caldwell, "I'm inside. Which way?"

Caldwell quickly said, "Make your first right and then your second left. That'll put you in a direct path heading right for them. They are entering a large room at the end of a hallway. Some of them are definitely armed and appear to be more military than civilian. You're only two hallways away from them."

Gus asked, "Can you kill the lights?"

"Yes, I can but only for a short period of time."

"I'm heading for them. I can hear them. Kill the lights when I get close to them. Just before they see me."

Just as Gus turned the corner, the lights went out. Like a dog, he had developed the ability to see in the dark. With lightning speed, he rushed the group in total darkness. In an instant, Gus shoved one into another, grabbed Lisa, and pushed her into a small room with the door locked from the inside. Then the lights turned on.

Gus turned toward his attackers, leaving Lisa in the locked room behind him. They were in an isolated part of the hotel basement. Mike's destination to do his dirty work. Standing in front of him were Mike and four other guys. They were unshaven military types. They looked like a mixture of a soldier and a convict.

Mike said with a laugh, "I don't know how you got here so fast, but you did. You must have come to watch. That's all I can figure. OK, guys, it's fun time. You get to beat the hell out of him, but you can't kill him. He is our significantly important person. But after you beat him to a living pulp, you get to have your way with her. And make sure he watches."

One of the guys yelled, "So what are our limits with her?"

Mike enthusiastically replied, "With her, you have no limits! In fact, I want it to hurt bad, real bad. And as an example of my excellent leadership, I'll let you guys have all the fun. I'll go upstairs and have a beer. I will return for the grand finale. I'll come back and put a bullet in her head while he watches." Mike looked at Gus and said, "I need to leave now, but I'll see you soon." He turned and walked out a door behind his group while yelling to his guys, "Call when you're done having fun."

The four guys started to circle Gus. He could feel the hair standing up on the back of his neck. He began to size up his opponents. Three of them had an evil twinkle in their eyes. They looked like hyenas preparing to pounce on their prey. One guy looked paranoid, almost scared. Gus saw an opportunity to mentally mess with their minds. He yelled out, "You follow this guy Mike? He's no leader. He killed Ike, and he'll kill you."

The scared guy loudly replied, "What the fuck are you talking about? How do you know Ike?"

Gus said, "I know who he is because I heard Ike yell for help before Mike kicked him in the face and let him die."

One of the evil guys said, "Why the fuck would he do that?"

Gus answered, "To save himself. He told Ike to take one for the team."

The paranoid one said, "That's one of Mike's lines. Mike said Ike will be back in an hour. It's over an hour. Ike's never late. He always texts when he's going to be late. We all would have gotten a copy!"

One of the other evil guys yelled out, "Don't let this guy fuck with us. We'll talk with Mike when we're done. Let's have our fun!"

The paranoid guy replied in a loud but controlled voice, "You guys know that I'm not into this kind of shit. I told you guys that back in Iraq, and I told all of you that when I signed up for this mission."

Then one of them blurted out, "We hear you loud and clear. So just like we told you back in Iraq, sit back, shut up, and watch the door."

The paranoid guy stood back as the three hyenas began to circle. Gus looked at them and said, "So you've done this before?"

One of the evil guys replied, "Whenever the opportunity had presented itself. The high was out of this world. The best part was always hearing her squeal in pain while he watched. It makes me hard just thinking about it."

Then one of the other evil guys looked at him and said, "I thought you told me that putting a bullet in her head with him watching was always the best part?"

The other guy replied back with a smile, "Hearing her screaming in pain with him watching was like fucking. Then finishing it off with a bullet to her head was like cumming. The best part is that there is no best part. It's all great!" Then he laughed loudly.

Gus looked at him, smiled, and said, "So I guess no matter how badly I hurt all of you, you probably deserve it."

The guy looked at Gus with an evil grin and replied. "I'm sure you guessed right. Take your best shot. Do what you can."

One of the other guys yelled, "Enough fucking around. Let's fuck this asshole up!"

Gus's eyes narrowed as he began to growl. He felt his mind slipping from the human world into the animal world. Normally a peaceful guy and a lover of life, Gus felt those thoughts slipping away. He knew this was a kill or be killed, or something even worse situation. The three guys circling him were evil scum of the earth. Gus knew in his heart that if he didn't stop these guys permanently, they would come back after him or someone he cared about.

For just an instant, Gus's mind slipped back into an earlier time in his life when his father was teaching him military-style hand-to-hand combat.

He remembered his father had shown him several attacks and told him, "Be very careful. These techniques were designed to kill."

Gus remembered asking, "How will I ever know if these attacks really work?"

His father had replied, "There's only one way to know. I hope that you will never be forced to find the answer."

At the time, Gus hadn't liked practicing those attacks. Now, he found himself wishing that he had practiced them more.

The paranoid looking guy had backed off and stood near the door Mike had exited. The three others had formed a half circle around Gus and were preparing to attack. Gus knew in an attack by three or more opponents to defend to the right or to the left. Never go for the middle, or you will be fighting all three at once.

The guy on the right had a small-bladed knife, which meant he wanted to cut, not necessarily kill. The guy in the center had a two-foot-long steel pipe, and the guy on the left had his fists up and was in a fighting stance. They started taunting Gus, teasing him, as one of them would attack first. He knew that he had to take the fight to them. Gus let the EMT jacket he was wearing drop to the floor, and kicked it behind him. He prepared for battle.

Suddenly, the guy on the right of Gus lunged at him with the knife in his right hand. That's when Gus made his move. He stepped back with his right foot, avoiding the thrust, and grabbed the guy's knife hand with his left hand. In one quick move, Gus lifted the attacker's hand above his head and whipped around in a full circle. Like a dancer being spun by their partner. As Gus completed the spin, he ripped the knife away from his opponent's hand and slammed the knife into the man's neck. The guy fell to the ground, gagging, blood squirting from his neck.

The other two guys stopped and stared at their partner on the ground. Then they looked at Gus. They were no longer smiling as before. Then the one with the pipe yelled out a battle cry and charged with rage in his eyes. With the pipe in his right hand, he swung it over his head and down on Gus with the intention of crushing anything in its path. Gus instinctively stepped forward and to the left, moving out of the direct force of the attack. He blocked his opponent's strike at his wrist with a right-arm open-handed block. Flowing with the force of the strike, Gus directed the swing and the pipe to come crashing down hard on his opponent's knee and lower leg. The guy leaned forward as the pipe slammed into his leg. With his left hand, Gus then delivered a full-power karate chop to the back of the guy's outstretched neck. The guy fell to the floor on his face and lay there lifeless. His neck was broken. Gus had delivered a fatal blow.

The only attacker left standing was the one with his fists up in a fighting stance. Gus immediately turned his focus to him. He realized that he was wearing a bulletproof vest and was reaching behind his back with his right hand. Just like Gus had learned in his Las Vegas weapons training, the body language meant gun. Being nearly ten feet away from his opponent, he knew he had to close the gap. Acting on instinct and his most recent training, Gus dove into a forward roll. Just as the attacker pulled the gun from behind his back and over his shoulder to fire at what should have been Gus's head, he came out of the roll. He was directly in front of him and underneath his opponent's gun-yielding hand. Gus grabbed the guy's gun with both his hands, securing the barrel. As Gus stood up, he snapped the guy's gun and wrist back, pointing the gun back into the guy's face. The movement was so fast that it forced the guy to pull the trigger on his own gun. It went off firing a single round, hitting the attacker directly in the middle of his forehead! Gus held the gun in his hands as the guy's grip let loose and he slowly fell to the ground.

Holding the gun, Gus quickly turned toward the paranoid guy who was standing near the door. He had his eyes closed and his head down. He was praying.

Gus asked, "What are you doing?"

The guy opened his eyes and said, "I'm waiting to die! I deserve to die! I've been involved in some evil shit, and now it's time to pay."

Gus stared at him for a moment and said nothing. He could feel his defensive animal instincts starting to calm. He knew this man was no threat to him. Gus then said, "Something tells me that you're not as evil as Mike and his friends."

The guy replied with a tremor in his voice, "We were all hardcore military. We all saw a lot of action. After working for Uncle Sam, we continued our military lives for private money. It all started out as same day, different boss. Then things changed. They started hurting people. They didn't have to. They only did it because they could. I didn't do what they did, but I didn't stop them, either. That makes me just as bad as them."

Gus replied, "Evil has a way of influencing people. Many evil people have convinced others to join them. Take Hitler, for example. A whole country followed him. I'm sure many who followed him where sorry for what they did after they understood the evil that they supported. I have only one question for you. If you were one of Hitler's followers and knew that you could stop all the evil by putting a bullet in his head, would you do it?"

The guy's eyes watered as he said, "Yes...fuck yes!"

"Mike is evil. I need your help to stop him. You could get killed. Would you be willing to help me?"

"I saw what you just did. I've been in many deadly battles and seen many deadly fights. What just happened was unreal. You are something special."

"Is that a yes?"

"Hell yes!" the guy replied.

"When Mike comes through that door and sees what happened, he'll start shooting. My girlfriend is in the room behind me, and I don't want her to be hit. I need to get close enough to stop him from shooting. I need you to distract his attention to allow me to get close. I have a plan. Before we get started, why don't you tell me your name?"

"Chad, sir. I mean, just Chad."

"OK, Chad, go pull that bulletproof vest off your friend. Put it on under your sweatshirt."

While Chad was doing that, Gus asked, "How well did you know Ike?"

"To me, Ike was like a brother. I loved him, man. He saved my life and Mike's, too. Ike wasn't the smartest guy around but loyal as hell to his friends. There was wasn't anything that I wouldn't have done for him. I have a question for you. Is Ike really dead?"

"Yes," Gus replied.

"Did Mike really kill him?

"He forced him to fall to his death to save himself."

Chad stared at Gus with his eyes wide open and said, "I believe you. I really do, man. What next?"

"Go stand over to the left of the door that Mike will come through."

Gus unloaded the semiautomatic pistol that he was holding and gave it to Chad. He took the gun and went and stood by the door.

Gus asked, "Did Ike carry a cell phone?"

"Yes, we all do. If any of us call each other during any kind of mission, the others have to pick up. It's one of our rules. Communication is always critical."

"Do you have your phone with you?"

"Yes, sir."

"Call Mike and tell him to get here immediately. Tell him that there's trouble. When he gets here, I want you pointing the gun at me. At some point, I need you to point the gun at him. Just follow my lead, and you'll know when it's time. Just think of it as being an actor in a play without a script. You'll have to make it up as it goes along."

Chad made the call, then said, "Mike is on his way."

Gus got in position in front of the door, with Chad to his left. Gus stayed far enough from the door to draw Mike into the room but close enough where he could try to disarm him before he could shoot. Gus knew it was risky and that the distraction he planned must work.

Mike came busting into the room with a large revolver in his hand. He immediately froze, pointing the handgun at Gus.

Chad yelled, "Mike, he got the jump on us! I got to my weapon and controlled the situation. What do you want me to do?"

Mike screamed, "Kill him! Shoot the fucker now!"

Gus then yelled, "Chad, before you kill me, remember, he killed Ike, and he'll kill you next!"

Mike yelled to Chad, "I order you to kill him now, soldier!"

Chad said to Mike in a slow but loud voice, "Where is Ike?" Then he turned his gun on Mike.

While keeping his gun on Gus, Mike slowly said to Chad, "What the hell are you doing? You're losing it, pal."

Chad reached into his pocket and pushed a button on his cell phone. A phone started ringing in Mike's pocket.

Chad then yelled, "That's Ike's phone!"

Mike looked at Chad and said, "You're an asshole."

He turned his gun on Chad and fired one round into his chest. The blow of the powerful revolver knocked Chad onto his back.

With amazing speed, Gus lunged forward, grabbing Mike's gun with his left hand. Then Gus let out a bone-chilling roar. With a surge of power and pinpoint accuracy, Gus solidly slammed a right-handed, one-finger strike into Mike's left eye. Toughened by years of fingertip pushups, his finger ripped through Mike's eye and sank deeply into his head. As Gus pulled his hand back, blood gushed from Mike's eye socket. His eyeball was hanging out, leaving an ugly hole.

Mike let out a loud cry of agony. He released his gun and fell to the ground. Helpless and disoriented, he squirmed on the ground in pain. Then he yelled at Gus, "You better finish the job, soldier! You better kill me now. If you don't, you'll pay! I'll kill you and everyone you care about. I'll kill them all, one by one, and then I'll kill you! This will not be the end. This will become the beginning! What's wrong, asshole? You think I'm lying? What's the matter? Can't do it? I bet you're one of those goody two-shoe motherfuckers that think that they only should kill in self-defense. Look around motherfucker at what you've done. It feels good, doesn't it? You are a killer! Do it, asshole. Do it. You are no better than me. We are of the same breed. Put a bullet in my head. Feel the pleasure of pulling the trigger. Do it now or suffer the consequences." Even in his pain, Mike managed to crack a slight smile.

Gus looked down at Mike, smiled, and said, "I remember you mentioning something about payback being an eye for an eye. Since your eye is no longer useful, I think it should be donated to someone for some evil thing that you have done to them. I want you to know that I am a peaceful, charitable-type guy. So for this reason, I have decided to donate your eye to charity. To someone who deserves it as payback. I'm sure you've developed a long list of people who would be very pleased to accept my donation. Since I don't know any of the other people you've hurt, I hereby dedicate your eye to somebody eye don't know!" Then Gus snickered.

Mike screamed, "Fuck you! You can't do it, can you, you fuckin' wimp?"

Gus looked at Mike with seriousness and said, "You are absolutely right. I cannot kill a defenseless man. And I do believe that if I don't kill you, you'll track me down and cause me great pain. But like many difficult problems, there is most likely a simple solution."

Just about then Chad sat up. The shot to the chest had knocked him down and broken some ribs, but the bulletproof vest had protected him.

Gus looked at Chad and said, "Here you go, buddy. Redemption time." Then he threw him the loaded clip to the unloaded forty-five that he had been pointing at Mike.

Chad grabbed the gun off the ground and slammed the clip in. Still sitting, he looked at Mike and said, "How could you? We took an oath. Ike saved our lives." Then he screamed, "Ike saved your life!"

Mike looked at Chad, sneered, and said, "I'II see you in hell."

Chad then fired five shots into Mike, threw down the gun, bent over, and started sobbing.

Gus knocked on the door that Lisa was behind. He said, "You can come out now. It's safe."

She opened the door and looked as pale as a ghost. Gus grabbed her hand and said, "Let's go."

Without saying a word, she tightly clutched his hand, and they left.

Gus found a service elevator to avoid people and got Lisa to his room. She looked tired and confused but did not look scared. He asked her to lay down on the bed and rest, which she did. He shut the bedroom door, went into an adjoining room, and called his father. Gus told his father everything that had happened then asked, "What do I do now?"

His father said, "Sit tight. Government people will be there shortly to clean this mess up. I am sending a private escort to pick up both you and Lisa. You will be flying out of Nellis Air Force Base on a private jet."

Within an hour Gus and Lisa were safely flying home. The plane was empty except for the pilots. It was quiet, and Lisa looked like she wanted to talk.

Gus asked Lisa, "Why did you come to Las Vegas?"

Lisa excitedly replied, "My father surprised me and said that my condition was improving, allowing us to go on a small vacation. He even said we were going to fly on a plane. I was very happy until he told me what we were going to do. My father told me that they had found a young man, my age, whose DNA was compatible with mine. He even joked and said that if we liked each other, maybe someday we could marry and have children. Gus, I don't want to marry anyone else except for you! Our trip got canceled and my father is away on business. I was alone and it was safe for me to travel, so I followed you to Las Vegas. I tracked you using your company-paid cell phone. Gus, I wanted to surprise you. Something is wrong with me! I can't stop from wanting to be near you. I am doing bad things, and it's causing bad things to happen to you. Can you forgive me?"

Gus compassionately replied, "There is nothing to forgive. Some of the things you have done turned out bad but were done for good reasons. Lisa, for now I need you to be confident that I will never leave you or let anything bad happen to you. I need some time to figure things out. You need to be rational and not do anything crazy without telling me first. Can you do that for me?"

Lisa smiled and said, "Yes."

After that, they cuddled and talked very little. They landed and Gus quickly and discreetly got her back to the company. Then he went home.

Chapter 10
GOOD HARD INFO.

The next day, Gus called his father with the contract phone his father had given him. He only used it for confidential conversations and felt comfortable talking freely.

Gus called and his father picked up. His father spoke. "I've been waiting for your call. After we talked yesterday, I did a little investigative work, and I wanted to let you know what I found."

With sarcasm in his voice Gus asked, "You did a little investigative work?"

With a snicker, his father replied, "OK, I oversaw the direction of a team that is now dedicated to this investigation. Would you expect anything less?"

"I know you, Dad." They both laughed.

Gus's father then switched to a more serious tone and said, "Let's talk about these guys known to you as Ike and Mike. Like I had worried about, they came to settle a score. The first time they met you on that mountain trip, they were there to collect information on you because you are high on the SIP list, Significantly Important People list. Any and all information on you is worth money, but that didn't turn out well for them. They were embarrassed and angry. This time, they were back for revenge. They could just as easily have performed an ambush-style attack and killed you but didn't do that for two reasons. First of all, that would have been too easy and would have made them look weak.

Very bad for their reputations. The second and more important reason is that anybody who kills a Significantly Important Person while collecting information on that person is immediately neutralized, aka... killed. It's part of the unwritten rules of the information-collection game."

Gus asked, "Who enforces the rules?"

"I wish I knew. It all goes on and is controlled through some dark part of the Internet. Thank you, new technology. They're years ahead of anybody watching them. With this in mind, and from what you've told me, I believe they were there to kill you but intended to make it look like an accident. Even when Mike could have killed you at the hotel, he didn't want to do it himself, so he tried to get Chad to do it. He knew the rules of the game. Gus, these guys were bad, very bad. You did what you had to do. How do you feel about it?"

"Strangely numb. I don't feel anything."

"If it starts to haunt you, remember to ask yourself, 'Did I do it in the name of good or evil?' I won't you tell what other things these guys have done, but I will tell you they were extremely evil. There's something else I wanted to tell you about: we found Ike."

"Is he dead? Did he drown?"

"He is dead. But I don't know if died from drowning or from the bullet Mike put in his head. Mike was evil, but now he and his evil crew are gone. I don't think you have to worry about retribution from anybody associated with these guys. Mike was their leader, and as a group, they acted alone. From what we know, they weren't well-liked even by the sleazy group of people they did business with. As far as I can tell, it's the end of the story when it comes to you and them."

Gus's father paused to take a drink of his coffee. After a couple of long slurps, he spoke. "What's more important is why you have moved up so high on the SIP list. I've been investigating some possible reasons. First, I investigated your acquaintances. You've picked up some interesting new friends, like the Mexican guy, Monolito."

Gus quickly replied, "Oh, you must mean Mono. Cool guy."

His father quickly answered back "Aka El Mono. Spanish for 'the Monkey.' Used to be a big-time gang leader. He seems to have gotten a little older, hasn't seen much jail time, and has not gotten killed. Now he's kind of retired. He still has his hand in a lot of barely legal stuff, and I'm sure he's making a lot of money. But he doesn't flaunt it and keeps a low profile. He seems to have been lucky enough and smart enough to have achieved gang leader retirement without getting killed or spending the rest of his life in jail. But I'm not here to judge him. I didn't find anything about him that would cause you to be high on the SIP list.

"Another interesting new acquaintance of yours is Mr. James P. Caldwell. Graduated from high school at sixteen years old. Had a PhD in physics by twenty-four. Started a company, Intellectual Design Systems, at twenty-six. Very respected in his field. A very high-achieving person but still a nerd."

"You're telling me. You haven't met the guy. I guess he's a super nerd."

"That's not all that your friend is about. He's into very kinky sex with Asians. Besides his local hookups, he travels to Thailand several times per year.

"Big deal, he likes Asian women."

"I did not say, 'Asian women.' I said, 'Asians.' He likes them all, and he likes them young."

"How young?"

"Let's just say if he were looking for a young bride right now, he couldn't find one. That's because she or he hasn't been born yet!"

"I get it." Gus coughed and said, "Pervert," at the same time.

"But I am not concerned with his sexual adventures. He does do a lot of work for the government and has a secret security clearance. He has access to a tremendous amount of video information in a lot of places. I believe that you have already discovered that. The problem is that he's civilian and not government. We think he's on our side, but we're not sure. We did find out that he's in some organization of limited members of very high intelligence. Occasionally, they publish a paper talking about good and evil and our duty to nature. Some of their stuff makes sense.

Other times, it borders on radical and crazy. My guess is that he's not on anybody's side but his own."

"There's some concern that his abilities would be in high demand for those who seek information. We thought possibly that might have something to do with you and the SIP list. But after careful analysis, my team decided that he was not the reason. As far as new acquaintances go, he and Mono fall into the interesting category. People to keep an eye on. Besides them, most other people you associate with on a nonwork basis seem harmless. Even that attorney guy, Harold." Then he laughed.

Gus asked, "Did you see the phone video?"

"Yes, I did, and it proves to me that even at my age, I can still kick your ass." They both laughed. Gus's father then said, "You may know karate, you may know jujitsu, but I have age and wisdom!"

"But I might just wrestle you down and put you in my crazy-boy headlock just like I used to do when I was about five years old."

"No, not the headlock. You're right...I don't stand a chance!"

They both laughed again. Then Gus's father changed back to a more serious tone and said, "Now, let's talk about your place of employment. First, let's talk about what you do. You've become a top scientist doing gene editing. You have the ability to alter a human's DNA. You're experimenting with the basic building blocks of nature. This is very controversial."

Gus quickly answered back, "I know what some people say, but we're working on many new and exciting things. We're introducing genes into mosquitos that eliminate them from carrying diseases such as malaria. Using a new technology called CRISPR, we are working on a cure for AIDS. We're developing genetically modified crops that are hardier, drought resistant, and more nutritious."

"I know about all the good stuff. It's the potential bad stuff I worry about. Gus, both you and I know that companies like yours have the ability to alter the genes of humans. Basically, they have the ability to produce predesigned human beings. Nobody has any idea of the consequences as humanity would reproduce and evolve after the changes they could make. You are very good at what you do, and my team believes that is why you have risen very high on the SIP list. You're definitely in a small group of people who could alter the evolution of human beings. Knowing about you would be important to a lot of people. My team has determined that for this reason, you're a Significantly Important Person. So now let's talk about your contacts at work. There is this guy Dave that you seem to have become friendly with—we looked into him. He's an interesting person. Dave is very well paid by your company. Almost two hundred and fifty thousand annually for a technician position. Your buddy has an odd history. He went to college to study electrical engineering. After three and a half years and a 4.0 GPA, he dropped out. He was only one semester away from graduation. After that, he spent a couple of years in South American countries traveling and doing charity work. When Dave was finished with that he returned to the United States and started working where you work. That was about four years ago. He has been there ever since."

Gus replied, "He's always seemed to be a worldly type of guy. From what you've told me, he just sounds like someone trying to find himself."

"What he did was not all that uncommon except for one other thing: Dave comes from an ultra-wealthy family. His family is worth billions."

"Well, maybe he's just one of those rich kids who had a falling out with his family and decided to take a different path."

"That's what I was thinking. But he visits them regularly. They seem to be on good terms. But then again, they don't seem to give him any money or expensive toys. Unless, of course, they give him cash and he spends it on something we're not tracking."

"Like what?"

"Drugs. Maybe expensive hookers. Who knows? Maybe he collects diamonds on the black market."

With a snicker, Gus replied, "Maybe he collects diamonds on the black market to give to expensive hookers."

"You sound like you might know something that I don't."

"Dave and I have shared some good times together. I kind of know how he thinks."

132

"To sum him up, I don't see anything bad about him. But then again, all the dots don't connect with this guy. I'll keep my eye on him."

Gus said with joking sarcasm, "Oh no! Dave the gadget geek is coming to get me!"

"Maybe he's a master of deception. Possibly he's not who he appears to be."

"What are you saying?"

"All I'm saying is that the geek might be a freak!"

Then they laughed. Gus's father paused, took a deep breath, and said, "Now that we've covered Dave, let's talk about the person I believe that you find the most interesting at work. This girl that you've been telling me about, Lisa. Gus, as far as I know, right now, she does not exist. No birth certificate, no medical or dental records, no educational history, no pictures, no anything. And this guy you say is her father, Hank Stewart, has never been legally married. Nothing shows him as being the father of any child anywhere.

"I also looked into that artificial environment and home you told me about that Lisa lived in. We tried to do a radar scan of the part of the building that you said it was in. In that area, they have installed some kind of electromagnetic shielding throughout the structure of the roof. We couldn't see past it with radar. After that, we tried infrared thermal imaging. They keep the upper crawl space of the roof very hot, essentially producing a thermal shield. In addition, they're heating the roof with some ingenious pulsed heating system. Even with the roof's outermost area being extremely hot, if it stayed constant, we could have gotten some information using highly sensitive equipment. But they have a ceiling of thousands of small, heat-producing electrical plates. They're all turning on and off hundreds of times per minute, each at a different rate. It produces a thermal image that saturates our equipment and renders it useless. We've never seen anything like it. They obviously don't want anyone to know what's going on in there.

"Gus, you need to be careful. My senses tell me that your journey is unfolding before you. As with me, the god dog powers were given to you for a reason. I'll always be there for you when I can, but your destiny is not up to me. It's up to you. My advice is to stay in touch with your inner self and, when in doubt, trust your instincts."

"Thanks, Dad. I will not forget what you've said."

"You need to find out what's going on at your company. I suggest you start with this girl, Lisa. Maybe she isn't who you think she is. Maybe she's there to keep an eye on you. Possibly faking that she's in love with you as a way of manipulation."

"I don't think so. I think she's real, genuine."

"Using love as a weapon in the art of deception has been practiced since the beginning of mankind. Are you sure that you're not wrong about her?"

"Dad, you told me to trust my instincts. They tell me that she's not evil and using me. If anything, I feel that she might be being used. I feel the need to protect her. Dad, she almost got killed because of me."

"Good point, son. I think she would have gotten killed if you hadn't stopped those guys. People aside, is there anything at work that you're involved with that seems odd or strange?"

Gus hesitated for a second, then said, "There's one project I work on called Project X. It's a special project run by the president of the company, J.P. Thorn. He works closely on it with the vice president, Hank Stewart, Lisa's father. None of us are given the whole big picture. We're given small problems, then are given the freedom to experiment and solve those problems. Getting assigned a Project X task is like a badge of honor at my company. If you solve the problem, you temporarily walk on water and are treated like a god."

His father asked, "Have you been given any Project X problems to solve?"

Gus replied, "I've been given the toughest Project X problems in the company and solved every one. My status and pay have risen significantly."

"We need to find out about Project X."

"I don't know how I could do that. Hank Stewart is shrewd and tough. I don't think I could get anything out of him. I don't want to involve Lisa, and I'm not close at all with J.P. Thorn."

His father was silent for a moment, then said, "OK. For now, just be normal at work to buy us some time. And Gus, don't solve any difficult problems on Project X until we figure out what's going on. I'll call you in a couple of days."

"Sure thing, Dad." They said their goodbyes and hung up the phone.

Two days had passed, and Gus had just gotten home from work when his contract phone rang. It was his father. They exchanged greetings; then his father got right down to business.

"My team can't get into your company's computers. They have a private server that's not connected to the Internet or phone lines. But we think we may have found a possible way to get in. We found out that they ran a two-mile fiber-optic cable from the company's private server to J.P. Thorn's personal residence. We can't get at the fiber-optic cable because it's on private land, so we need to get at the computer in his home. We came up with a plan, and it involves you. But before I outline the plan, I need to ask you a question. My friend, the short, fat, Eskimo man, told me that you were given the power of love. That you should be able to seduce any woman. Is that true?"

"Yes, Dad, it's true."

"Does it really work? Have you tried it?"

"I've tried it many times, and yes, it really works."

Then his father said slowly, "Really?"

Gus snickered and said, "Like shooting fish in a barrel."

"Damn, Gus! I didn't get that talent with my god dog experience. Now I know the true meaning of the line 'You lucky dog.' The powers of good gave you an additional talent to assist you on your journey. You lucky dog!"

Gus and his father both laughed deviously. His father continued with "OK, with that in mind, I'll outline the plan. J.P Thorn's wife is a wealthy, good-looking, sexually aggressive woman. She and several of her rich lady friends collect and share boy-toy sexual experience stories. We also know that twice she connected her husband's work computer to their home Internet connection and used it. It appears that her home computer wasn't working and she used his, most likely without his knowledge. If his computer is connected to the Internet for even five minutes, we can hack in and get what we want without anyone knowing.

"So here's the plan. We'll arrange a by-chance meeting between you and her. Your job is to get into her house and connect her husband's computer to the Internet. It must stay connected for at least five minutes. Then the connection must be moved back before he uses it again. You may have to use your power of persuasion. Do you think you're up for it?"

Gus sarcastically replied, "Don't worry, Dad. When the time comes, I'll be up for it."

With a chuckle, his father said, "I'm sure you'll rise to the occasion, you lucky dog." He got serious again and said, "We'll put the plan into effect tomorrow. She'll be driving home from a meeting with her friends around 7:00 p.m. As she approaches home on her dark, isolated country road, she'll get a blowout on one of her tires. You'll be the next car coming down the road behind her. You'll pull over to help her and offer her a ride home. From then on, it's up to you. Turn on your charm. Get into the house. Remove his computer's Ethernet cable from the wall and move it to the Ethernet connection for their home Internet service. I'm sure it's close, since she has done it twice before. Keep her occupied for at least five minutes while connected. After that, switch the cable back. Then you can leave. It is a simple plan."

"Your part is simple."

"I am sure that you will figure something out; just follow your instincts."

As planned, Gus waited in his car the next day, hidden from her view. He saw a brand-new Mercedes E-Class pass him. He pulled out and started to follow her. Just as planned, her tire blew out, and she pulled to the side of the road. Gus pulled up behind her in his Porsche 911 Turbo and got out of his car. He was wearing a nicely tailored business suit.

She got out of her car. She was a slightly older woman, approaching fifty years old. Despite her age, she was gorgeous. Her hair was cut short. She was thin and shapely. Her breasts were large, obviously implants, but her face looked natural with no plastic surgery. She was wearing a tight black skirt, stiletto high heels, and a sexy white blouse with a low-cut V exposing her breasts and dropping halfway down to her stomach.

Before they even spoke, their eyes locked on each other. The first thought in Gus's mind was, *Am I going to seduce her, or is she going to seduce me?*

They introduced themselves and began to talk. Gus inspected her blown-out tire to start a conversation. They immediately began talking and laughing. Gus offered her a ride home. She not only accepted, she insisted. During their conversation, he talked and listened, but Gus was retaining very little. He was turning on his power of seduction. As with other women he had seduced in bars, there was sexual attraction and tension. But this time, it was much more intense. She was obviously an expert at seducing men. She was using her art of persuasion. Gus was now in autopilot. He wasn't sure what he was saying or doing. He couldn't even remember her name!

Then things started to happen. She opened her door to get her purse so that Gus could give her a ride home. Bending over in her tight black skirt, she slowly turned and stood up. Gus was standing close. She had an intense, evil desire look in her eyes. Gus broke. They fell into each other's arms in a long, passionate kiss. She was breathing heavily.

Gus thought to himself, *This isn't the plan. I must get to her house first. I must control myself!*

He pushed her away and said, "Not here, not now. I prefer to take a woman as beautiful as you someplace nice. Why don't I give you a ride home and we can take it from there?"

She pulled him closer, and they fell into another long, passionate kiss. As it ended, Gus pushed her away again and said, "Not here, not yet."

She then smiled a wicked smile at him. She grabbed him by his tie with one hand and then slapped him hard across his face with the other hand.

Gus was stunned. He felt a strange feeling of both anger and sexual desire all at once. She kept a hold of his tie and put her other hand between his legs. She said, "You don't feel like you're ready to leave."

She squeezed hard, and Gus, now erect, felt the grab surge through his body. He started to push her away, but then while still holding his tie, she slapped him hard in the face again.

Gus snapped. His animal instincts were taking over. He shoved her against the car, grabbed her blouse, and ripped it open, exposing her breasts and sheer bra.

To his surprise, she just smiled at him and said, "Is that all you got?"

Gus was now in the animal world. He picked her up and threw her onto the hood of the Mercedes. He lifted her tight black skirt, ripped her nylons, lifted her legs, unzipped his pants, and slammed himself deep inside her. She screamed, and he started pounding like an enraged animal. He was sweating. She was holding him tightly, her hands underneath his shirt, digging her long fingernails into his back.

Then along the dark isolated road, a car's lights appeared in the distance. She told Gus, "Stop, someone's coming." She started to struggle and push him away.

There was no stopping him now. The more she struggled to get away, the harder Gus pounded. She screamed in ecstasy as the car passed. The exposure of the passing car had driven her wild. Gus finished, and they both fell onto the hood of the car, spent from their sexual adventure. Afterward, they talked, kissed, and laughed. Gus then gave her a ride home. He didn't attempt to get into her house. He knew it was the plan, but things hadn't gone as planned, so it just didn't seem the right thing to do.

As Gus was driving away, he got a call from his father.

"What the hell, Gus? You didn't even get in the front door. What were you thinking? I tried to break you up. I sent a car past you. You missed the opportunity to slow things down. Gus, really, on the hood of the car? You need to stay focused. Now what the hell are we supposed to do?"

Gus just laughed and said, "You told me to follow my instincts, so I did. Dad, don't worry. Disrupt her cell phone and computer, and then just wait for her to hook up her husband's computer. I would advise that you do that now. Believe me, Dad if she's the kind of woman who shares stories with friends, I'm sure she's dying to tell someone now. I would guess that this is her most exciting story ever!"

"That's a lame plan, but I've stopped her cell phone and personal computer from working. I can't do this for too long, or we'll be exposed. Gus, sometimes I wish you would just do as I say…hold on. Son of a bitch! She just hooked up his computer to their home Internet connection. I'll get back to you."

About two hours later, Gus's father called him. Gus picked up. He immediately answered with, "So how was Plan B?"

"If Plan B stands for 'better' or 'big time,' then Plan B was the best pick. We've found some very interesting and sensitive information. I want to take a little time and analyze the data. I'll call you tomorrow on your regular phone and offer to take you to lunch. I'll come over and pick you up. I know a place where we can have lunch and talk. We will have this conversation again tomorrow on your regular phone. When I call tomorrow, talk to me just like it's one of our typical Saturday talks. Remember, the world has ears. That conversation will be for whoever might be listening."

Gus replied, "OK Dad, sounds good." They said good night and hung up their phones.

Chapter 11
THE HIVE

As planned, Gus's father called the next day. He came over and picked him up. They went to one of his father's favorite restaurants. It was the little French sandwich shop. Gus had been here several times before with his father but now found himself wondering if his father went there often because he liked the food or because he knew it was secure.

They sat down. Gus could tell his father was trying hard to hide his seriousness and must have something important to tell him. They ordered their meals, and then Gus's father said, "Gus, this is big-time serious. We found out that Project X is a large-scale gene-editing program to produce designed people. But it's not what we had expected. We knew somebody would try it someday, but we always expected that they would try to create super humans with superior intelligence, tremendous strength, and even super-good looks. Project X is working to design something different. They want to design a human that is docile, easily controlled, extremely loyal, hardworking, and of medium intelligence. The easiest way to describe the people that they're trying to design is the term they use themselves: the Worker Bee. Their plan is to develop all these people and put them into one place. This place they called the Hive.

"Project X is a massive, heavily funded plan to develop a super company. It would consist of employees who are dedicated, easily satisfied and controlled, and willing to work night and day for the company, or the Hive, as they call it. Right now, we know what they plan on doing, but we need to know more about how they plan on doing it. We know that the Hive is being built somewhere down in a remote South American jungle. Someone who knows and understands the kind of work you do needs to go down there and look around. Gus, reluctantly as your father, I need to let you know that you are the best person to go. It could put you in harm's way."

"I know I'm the best person to go. That is why I am going."

"I'll set it up soon and let you know when it's time to go. Gus, there is one other thing that I need to talk to you about. I am sure that there are people watching you. I'm also sure that the people who are watching you know that I'm your father and are watching me with anything that concerns you. I know somebody has you under surveillance, and I want to find out who it is. I can't use any of my own people because the stakes are too high. We need somebody to occasionally watch you who's on our side. Maybe they watch you when you leave home or work, just to see if anyone leaves at the same time you do. Or maybe they see a car or a person that shows up right before you get home or go to work. All I need is a small piece of information, and my team can take it from there.

"We need somebody who is below their radar. Somebody that they wouldn't suspect. Somebody that you can trust.

"You've made three new acquaintances lately and probably want to ask one of them to help you: You have Dave the Gadget Geek, rich boy freak, or the notorious ex-gang leader El Mono, aka The Monkey, or Mr. James P. Caldwell, the sexually twisted genius. I've noticed that all three of them have done something special for you, which would gain your trust. I can't tell you which one you can trust. Maybe you can trust all of them. Then again, maybe you can't trust any of them."

Gus replied, "Interesting. Every interaction I've had with these people you have just mentioned seems to have been very natural and unplanned."

"Was it very natural and unplanned or a very well-planned hoax? I can't tell you who you should ask for help. You need to follow your own intuition. I could make a recommendation for you, but by the look on your face, I believe you've already made a decision."

Gus sighed and said, "Dad, you know me too well. But before I tell you my pick, you tell me yours."

His father quickly answered "I would pick Dave. OK, now you tell me your pick."

Gus smiled a devious grin, showed his teeth, and blurted out, "Ouu, ouu, ouu, ahh, ahh, ahh!"

His father looked at Gus, shook his head, and said, "I knew it. The Monkey! My last choice." Then they laughed together. They finished their lunches and left.

A couple of days later, Gus's father called him on the contract phone. He said, "Gus, I have a plan. I'll call you later on today on your regular phone and invite you to go fishing. We'll go for three days. You'll come to my house on Friday morning, and we'll leave from there. We're going to take that opportunity to fly you down to some very isolated part of South America. I am sending you down to the Hive. We found its location. Now would be a good time for you to set up your own surveillance. Let's see if you can catch somebody watching you leave. I can't use my people, so you will have to figure out something on your own. Oh, and one last thing: don't shave before you come over. I'll explain later."

Gus simply replied, "OK, Dad, sounds like a plan. I'll start preparing." Then he hung up.

Gus decided that now would be a good time to call Mono. He called him and invited him to meet downtown to have a burrito. The location was near the place where Gus had saved Mono's son's life. Mono knew that Gus had never invited him to lunch before. He caught on fast and knew something was up.

He agreed to meet. They met downtown. Upon meeting, they shook hands, ordered, and sat down. Mono smiled a devious smile, his gold tooth shining in the sun. Gus acted normal around Mono but knew he should be cautious. Mono appeared to be a good friend, but he was also an ex-big-time gang leader. Gus now knew that Mono truly was bad-ass and was not to be messed with.

142

Mono started with, "Gus, my man, I am honored that you have invited me to lunch. What's up, amigo?"

Gus replied, "I may be crazy, but I think somebody's watching me. Maybe our friend Harold has hired somebody to watch me and is planning something. I don't know. Maybe it's just my imagination."

"No big deal, man. I'll get the word on the street to some people I know. I got you covered."

After that, Gus and Mono had a couple of beers and just talked and laughed. They said their goodbyes and went their separate ways. On the way home, Gus thought to himself, *That was easy. Sure is nice to have an ex-gang leader as a friend.*

Gus knew before he left he had to tell Lisa that he would be gone for a couple of days. He would also hide the truth from her and tell her he was going fishing with his father. In his heart, he felt that she wasn't part of this evil plot, but he always heeded his father's advice. Maybe he was blinded by love, and she wasn't who he thought she was. For now, Gus felt that she was at a safe distance. He wasn't putting her in any danger, and she was in no position to hurt him.

Friday morning, Gus got up early, packed his things, and drove to his father's house. When Gus arrived, he went inside. He met his father, they hugged, and then his father said, "We have to get you ready to go. You have a plane to catch."

"I'm ready."

"No, you're not."

About then, another military-looking man walked into the room. Gus's father said, "This is one of our facial recognition technology experts. He's going to disguise you so that your photographed face will not be able to be identified using facial recognition technology. I'm sure that you'll be photographed sometime during your arrival. If they want information on your identity, I'm sure they'll turn to the Internet. Using your photograph and facial recognition technology, they'll make the digital equivalent of a fingerprint of your face. If your face exists anywhere on social media, driver's licenses, or even high school yearbooks, they'll find you. My friend will make you a disguise that will change your facial recognition technology fingerprint."

The man looked at Gus and said, "Have a seat, and we'll get started. I'll explain what I'm doing and why."

Gus sat down. The man opened a large briefcase, exposing his tools of the trade. He began to speak. "First, I'm going to shave the bottom part of your face and attach a chin extender with a low-cut beard. I'll shave the top part of your face to make it blend in. That's why your father asked you not to shave. When the FRT…facial recognition technology analyzes your face, it will calculate the length of your facial hairs and digitally remove them to calculate the contour and shape of your chin. Your analyzed chin won't match your real one. On your forehead and nose, I'm going to apply a waterproof makeup that reflects light back at a different wavelength. In a photograph, your nose and forehead will appear to have a slightly different shape."

"Am I going to look like some kind of freak?"

The man laughed and said, "No, the shape changes aren't noticeable to the naked eye, only when analyzed by FRT. I'll also give you these glasses to wear. They're coated with a substance that produces a glare in a photograph, therefore hiding your eyes. And last but not least, a thin-knit ski cap. You'll need to keep this pulled down, covering at least half of your ears. In essence, I'll have kept the FRT from correctly analyzing your eyes, ears, nose, forehead, and chin.

"Some last things here. I'll attach the chin with a fast-drying acrylic adhesive most commonly known as Krazy Glue. I'll give you a solution to remove it. It's acetone. You can't remove it without it. If you lose it, you can typically find acetone in a hardware store in the paint-removal section. Or when you're at the airport, you might want to pick up a bottle of fingernail polish remover with acetone in it. The makeup I'll put on your nose and forehead is invisible and waterproof. It's OK to rub your forehead or nose; it only comes off with warm soap and water. Don't wash it off until you reach your hotel room."

The man applied the disguise. Then Gus's father spoke. "Gus, you now have two faces. We have given you one to match an ID that identifies you as a technician working for a company that's installing a large medical x-ray machine. I would wear the glasses, beard, and ski cap during the day. If you need to sneak out at night, remove the disguise. That way, if you're spotted, you can run back to your room and change back into your new identity."

Gus replied, "Sounds good, but you want me to wear the ski cap all day? Isn't that kind of odd?"

His father answered, "It's a thin-knit ski cap, and it's not unusual if you're a hat guy. Hat guys always wear their hats wherever they go. I am sure you know of hat guys."

Gus smiled and said, "I always wanted to be a hat guy, but why not a baseball or military cap?"

His father said, "Because they don't cover enough of your ears. Would you prefer a wig?"

"I love my new ski cap."

His father laughed, then continued. "We're not sure why, but for some reason, they're installing a medical x-ray machine into the building they call the Hive. This new identity will get you into the building. You will be posing as a technician showing up to do a final calibration and turn-on of the equipment. I'll give you some manuals to read on the plane. In reality, you'll install one small interlock, and everything will turn on and work. Once you're in the building, you must figure out a way to look around.

"Now it's time to go. Your flight leaves in an hour. Have you noticed how much my friend here looks like you? He's going to change into your clothes and vice versa. When we leave my garage, he'll sit in the front seat and appear to be you going fishing with me. You'll lay down in the back seat. On the way there, you'll switch to another car, which will take you to the airport."

Gus did as his father said. He changed clothes, they drove out, switched cars at a secure location, and he was dropped off at the airport. He was flying to some South American city that he had never heard of on a private jet. Gus boarded the plane. He was the only passenger. There were two pilots and a female flight attendant. They all smiled and said hello but had a seriousness about them. The female flight attendant approached Gus about every two hours but offered only direct questions and responses. She seemed to avoid any nonessential conversation.

After flying for nearly ten hours, the plane landed. It was dusk. Gus got out and walked to the bottom of the ladder. The airstrip was interesting. It was a very new and modern asphalt runway with a well-lit and modern two-story building. Other than that, it was surrounded by jungle.

A short, dark-skinned man approached Gus. He put out his arm to offer a hand shake and said, "Welcome, Mr. Brown. My name is Pedro. I am your official escort to the area and facility in which you will be performing your services."

Gus thought to himself, *Almost forgot that my fake identity is Mr. James Brown.* One of his father's favorite singers. James Brown, the father of soul. Gus shook his hand and said, "Nice to meet you, Pedro. You can call me James."

"Very good, Mr. James. I will drive you to your room, which is in the same compound as the facility. Everything that you will need for your stay is available at the compound. I have already retrieved your bag. Please follow me to my vehicle."

Gus followed and got into a brand-new Jeep Grand Cherokee. Pedro drove. On the way, he asked Gus, "Is there anything I can help you with or questions that I can answer for you?"

"Actually, yes. I'm just a technical guy, but my company sends me all over the world. I'm always interested in the people and cultures of the places I visit. What can you tell me about the people and cultures of this area?"

Pedro turned to Gus with a large smile, his bright white teeth glowing against his dark skin. It was like Gus had just pushed Pedro's On button. He looked like a salesman about to tell you why you should buy this car.

Pedro laughed loudly and said, "I am glad you asked! But first, let me tell you about the facility that you are here to visit. It is simply called 'the facility' for now until it is given a proper name. It is to become one of the most premium orphanages in the world! It is a whole new concept on how to truly take care of the world's orphans.

"Once it is completed, orphans from all over the world will be selected to live here. As soon as they arrive, they will be assigned a mother who will care for them for life. Unlike other orphanages, they will be individually nurtured and loved. They will get a superb education and will be taught working skills at a very young age. And unlike other orphanages, they will not be kicked out onto the street at the age of eighteen. They will not be expected to leave until they feel mature enough and want to leave. If they decide to stay beyond eighteen, they will be offered internships. When they do decide to leave, they will venture into the world a stable, intelligent, and skilled individual. It is a very beautiful concept!"

Gus said, "It does sound very beautiful, but it must be expensive."

Pedro replied, "Yes, it is expensive, but many large donations have come from very wealthy people. A lot of these people have become frustrated with giving money to charities and orphanages that seemed to take their money and do very little. They would rather spend a lot more money on a lot less children and achieve positive results. And as a benefit to the individual donors, they get to watch the children they have sponsored grow and develop into successful human beings. It is part of the concept of people with more, donating more per child, to achieve more with children who have less. Everybody wins!"

"Interesting. But why build it out here in the middle of nowhere?"

Pedro Immediately replied back, "For many reasons. The cost is very low. The local people are very friendly. But maybe most importantly, the children get to grow up without the crime and temptations that are common in populated areas."

"What about things that civilization provides, like police, firemen, and hospitals?"

Pedro laughed a phony laugh and said, "Everything will be provided here, even a hospital. That's why you're here! We are installing a new full-body x-ray machine in our medical facility. We need you to turn it on and ensure it is working properly."

"Impressive," replied Gus.

About then, they pulled up to the compound. It looked like a massive prison. It had a guard tower and large concrete walls. A huge gate opened, and they entered. Inside was a small city. It was like nothing Gus had ever seen. There were many small buildings and one very large building. The buildings had no names, just numbers. All the small buildings seemed to have a purpose. There was laundry cleaning, an auto mechanic, a grocery store, and even a gasoline station. Several people were working. They were all wearing blue uniforms. Besides that, there were many armed soldier types.

Gus looked around and said, "As far as civilization goes, I think you have the police part covered. Why are there so many armed soldiers?"

Pedro replied, "We have many hungry wolves outside the gates and in the jungle. There was a serious drought in the plains that forced all the antelope to leave. They were the wolves' food supply. All that is left for the wolves to eat is us. But don't worry. We are very well protected."

Gus sarcastically answered back, "I feel very safe. Who are the people in the blue uniforms?"

"They are from the local tribe. We have supplied them with many good-paying jobs. They are very happy and supportive."

"If they're so happy, why aren't any of them smiling?"

"They never smile when they are working. It is their custom. They are a very serious and hard-working people. To smile while working is an insult to their god of work."

With a grin, Gus said, "They must save all their smiling for after work. In fact, I would bet that they're laughing all the way to the bank."

With a serious look on his face, Pedro asked, "What does that mean?"

"It's a joke."

Pedro immediately laughed his fake laugh, then said, "Oh, Mr. James, you are a funny man! I will now take you to your room. I will escort you to your equipment in the morning. Anything that you need before then, you can call me on your room phone."

Gus went to his room, ordered some food, ate, and went to bed.

Gus got up early the next morning and decided to go have a look around. He walked toward the laundry cleaning building. On the way, he passed a young girl. He said hello to her. She said nothing back. She just stared at him with her eyes wide open.

Gus sensed fear. She turned away from him. He then tapped her on the shoulder and said, "Excuse me."

She turned to Gus and in a loud voice said, "No!"

Immediately, two armed men started walking briskly toward Gus. The girl put down her head and scurried away. The guards approached Gus with their hands on their guns. They yelled, "Do not move!"

Surprised, Gus said nothing and froze. Then he saw Pedro come running from around the corner. He blurted out as he approached, "Mr. James, is there something you need?"

Gus said, "A bulletproof vest might be nice."

Pedro replied, "Oh, Mr. James, the guards are very protective of their people. It is also the custom of the people to not talk while working, or they will offend their gods. The guards' strong reaction is only in defense of their people. Come, Mr. James, I will take you back to your room and then to the facility."

Pedro walked with Gus back to his room. Pedro spoke. "Mr. James, please retrieve your tools and manuals, and I will escort you to the facility. I will wait outside your room until you are ready."

Gus replied with a sarcastic tone, "Please do wait for me. I wouldn't want to get lost. Just in case we separate on the way, let me guess, it is the large building labeled Number One? It looks like that building right there?" Gus pointed to the largest building directly in front of them.

Pedro smiled a big smile and said, "Oh, Mr. James, you are a funny man. A very funny man."

Gus grabbed his manuals and some hand tools and went with Pedro to the facility. They entered the building. Gus was amazed. From the outside, it just looked like a very dull, large, box-shaped building. The inside was another story. It looked like the mixture of a hotel and a boarding school. As they entered, there was a lobby, and off to the left was a nicely decorated conference area. It also appeared that there were some guest rooms, most likely for VIP visitors. As they passed through this area and down a hallway, it led to a large open area, well-lit with skylights. There was a plush garden that bordered what looked like four open floors of a hotel. Each floor appeared to cater to a certain age group. They appeared that they were designed to take care of people from infancy to adulthood. Gus guessed that this was where the orphans would live.

Gus looked at Pedro and said, "Why would anyone ever want to leave? This is a fantastic place. The whole world should know about the great things that you're doing here!"

Pedro did not smile. He slowly said, "Noooo…Mr. James. We want to keep it quiet until we are ready. I am sure that your company has talked to you about the secrecy of our project."

Gus smiled and said, "Pedro, I'm just joking."

Pedro laughed and said, "Mr. James, you are a very funny man."

Pedro escorted Gus to the equipment. As they walked, Gus noticed that, just as outside, there were only two types of people throughout the building: soldiers and people dressed in blue uniforms. All the soldiers were staring rudely at Gus, while all the people in blue uniforms did not make eye contact.

Gus and Pedro reached an area labeled Medical Assistance. It was staffed by people in blue uniforms and had a lot of very new, expensive-looking medical equipment. Pedro took Gus to the x-ray machine that he was there to work on. Surprisingly, Pedro told Gus to call him on one of the building phones when he was done, and he left.

Gus looked over the equipment. He inserted the interlock and ran through the turn-on procedure. The equipment was up and running. He had been there about an hour. He decided that now would be a good time to look around. If anyone asked what he was doing, he would say that he was looking for the power room. He needed to check the circuit breakers to make sure that they were sufficiently rated to protect the equipment.

Gus left the room and started walking around. He carried his tools and papers to look like a contractor. As he walked down the hallway, he found all the doors to be locked. He had passed two soldiers who stared at him but did nothing. He passed several workers in blue uniforms who never made eye contact. Then, as he was walking down the hallway, he passed a worker leaving a room. The worker looked at him out of the corner of his eye and then quickly looked away.

Gus thought to himself, *Is this man evil and disobeying his god of work, or is he trying to tell me something? I choose number two.*

Gus walked about halfway down the hallway, turned around, and started walking back. As he passed the door of the room that the man had come out of, he turned the doorknob. It was unlocked. The worker must have left it unlocked for him.

Gus went inside. It was a storage room. There were several boxes of files. Gus quickly started looking through them. All of a sudden, he found a large red box that was labeled Company Confidential in bold letters on all sides and the top. In the box were several folders labeled Presentation to Investors. Each was labeled by a year. Gus grabbed the oldest one.

It was basically a marketing presentation to investors about the concept of the Hive. It described the plan and methods of how orphaned children would be transformed into Worker Bees of the Hive. In the presentation were younger pictures of J.P. Thorn and Hank Stewart.

Every folder was labeled with the next consecutive year and had a presentation showing the progress.

Gus grabbed the most recent folder and quickly flipped through it. He was stunned by what he saw. In one section called Scientific Advancements was a picture of him! In another section that he did not quite understand, he saw a picture of Lisa.

There were several copies of each year. Gus took one copy of each year and left the room. He locked the door on the way out. He had what he needed. He went back to the x-ray equipment and called Pedro on one of the facility's phones. Pedro showed up and escorted Gus back to his room.

After returning to his room, Gus arranged to call his boss back at the factory. Pedro called the number and sent the call to Gus's room. Gus picked up the phone.

"Hello, James, this is Frank. How's it going?" It was his father.

Gus answered, "Everything went really smoothly. I got everything I needed done. You know, we've had some finicky units before, but this setup was easier than I expected. Even with the humidity down here, everything went fine."

His father replied, "Are you sure? That humidity can be a killer. You never know. When things go too easy, maybe it's because you're overlooking something. I always worry about these high-humidity environments. What kind of room is the machine in? Do these people know what they're doing? Are they on top of it?"

"It's in a state-of-the-art air-conditioned facility. These guys really know what they're doing. They are on top of it. In fact, I would say that this place is run with military precision."

"Maybe you just got lucky. Sounds like these guys know what they're doing and made your job easy for you. Well, you know me. I always worry when things go too easy. You're done a day early. The next scheduled flight out is day after tomorrow. We're busy here and could use you back at the factory. I could send a chartered jet to come pick you up."

"I think I'll take a day off. There's a trail I want to hike on, check out the local vegetation."

Even though Gus had the information he needed, he wanted to get outside the compound and talk to the locals without the soldiers being around. His intuition was telling him that there was more he needed to know.

His father said, "If you go, remember to take your GPS in case you get lost. I'll look into a chartered jet and see what your options are. If you do want to leave early, give me as much advance notice as you can. Other than that, call me if you need anything, and I'll see you in a couple of days."

"OK, see you in a couple of days."

Gus thought about what his father had said. It was too easy. He decided to do a little surveillance on his own. He grabbed a chair and pulled it outside in the sun in front of his room. He knew this would irritate the soldiers. Especially the two that were obviously guarding his room.

Gus laid his head back and quieted his brain. He appeared to be sun bathing. When relaxed, he found that his superior hearing improved tremendously. The guards were over two hundred feet away. Gus could easily hear what they were saying. They spoke Spanish, but he understood enough to know what they meant. There were two guards. A younger, more muscular one and an older, overweight one.

The younger one said to the older one, "Look at that whore. I wish I could put a bullet in his head right now. He can't be trusted. They gave him too much freedom. He's up to something. I know what we should do with him. Tomorrow we can invite him for breakfast. He can have scrambled ranch eggs. But he can only have two. We have no bulls available, so he'll have to supply the eggs!"

They both looked at Gus and laughed. With his eyes closed and listening, Gus just smiled.

Then the older guard said, "Do not worry, my friend. He will have an accident before he leaves, just like many of the others."

"What will they do with this one?"

"Tonight, when he goes to sleep, they will let the special spider go in his room. The spider will bite him, and then it will die. The gringo will get very tired and will keep falling asleep, and then he will die. Within twenty-four hours of being bitten, his heart will just stop."

"What if someone gives him an antidote?"

"The spider leaves a very little scar. The stupid Americans do not even know about this spider. They have no antidote! They will just think he had a heart attack."

The young guard looked at Gus and said, "Good night, Mr. Gringo." They both looked at Gus and laughed again.

Gus now knew what he needed to know. He smiled at the guards and went back into his room.

It was too easy. Gus now knew getting out of there would not be that simple. He could act very tired, like he had been bitten by the spider. He might be able to get on a chartered flight out if they thought he was going to die before he got home. From there, he could possibly hijack the plane. His other option was to have his father pick him up, military-extraction style. That would have to be someplace outside of the compound.

In his room on the wall was a basic map of the compound. It also showed a little bit of the area outside of it. The map showed a clearing about two miles away. It looked like a place that might work for a military style pick up. Possibly where some sort of aircraft could land.

Gus decided to sneak out at dusk to go check out the clearing. He would make it look like he was in bed sleeping. He would put some pillows in the bed and add the ski cap and the beard to make it look like it was him. Since they expected him to get bitten by the spider and be very sleepy, nobody would check upon him until the morning. By that time, he could have arranged an emergency extraction from his father and gotten out. If that wasn't feasible, he still would have enough time to sneak back to his room. He could then kill the spider and act like he had been bitten. He could plan his escape from there.

Chapter 12
WOLVES

It was dusk, and Gus decided to go check out the clearing that he had seen on the map. He packed his most important things with him just in case he was not coming back.

He snuck out, hidden in the shadows. He was fast, nimble and had excellent hearing. He could also see in the dark. Gus easily snuck by the guards and roaming soldiers. He climbed two roofs and reached the top of the compound wall. With the agility of a cat, Gus quickly ran along the top of the compound wall to a heavy drainpipe. He slid down the drainpipe to the ground on the outside of the wall.

Gus pulled out a map that he had drawn in his room. He followed a path on his map that took him to the clearing. When he arrived there, he was surprised by what he saw. In the distance, he could see approximately fifty dark-skinned South American men in military uniforms. They were wearing the same type of uniforms as the men back at the compound. A large campfire was burning. They were drinking some sort of liquid in glass bottles. By the way they were passing the bottles and yelling, Gus assumed it was some kind of hard liquor like whiskey or rum. There was lots of laughter. It looked like they were having a party.

Gus thought to himself, *This could be where they recruit the locals into their military. Maybe they're paid to join. Possibly they're tricked into joining. Or maybe they're just good people who've been forced to become puppets of the evil people developing this place.*

About then, Gus heard the men start cheering. He decided to hide in the bushes and just watch.

All of a sudden, he heard a girl screaming, "No!…No!"

It was the girl that he had tried to talk to in the compound! Two men were holding her arms. They pulled her to the front of all the other men. As they held her, another man walked up to her with a knife.

Gus thought to himself, *He's going to kill her.*

Using the knife, he brutally cut and ripped off the girl's clothes. The men cheered. She was nude except for her shoes. Gus thought, *They're going to rape her.*

Then another man approached the girl with a bucket of liquid. He threw it on her. It looked thick and oily. It slowly dripped down her bare body. The men all cheered again. Gus thought, *That must be some sort of flammable sticky liquid. They're going to burn her.*

The men started chanting, "*Lobo, lobo, lobo,*" which Gus understood meant *wolf* in Spanish.

They threw the girl into the clearing; then one of the men fired a rifle at her feet. She started running. The men cheered again. Gus was confused. He thought to himself, *What the hell are they doing?*

As the girl ran, they shined a big spotlight on her. The men were yelling and holding up money as if they were betting on her. She was about halfway across the clearing when Gus heard growling. First, he saw one wolf. Then two more. Then six or seven more. The wolves were all heading for the girl. They looked very lean and hungry. Gus now knew what the men were doing. They were feeding her to the wolves!

Gus thought to himself, *Forget the good people thing. These guys are evil.* He felt the hair standing up on the back of his neck. He could feel himself growling. Like a bolt of lightning, Gus raced about one hundred feet ahead of the girl. He turned to face her, put up his hand, and yelled, "Stop!"

She ran up to him and stopped. They were now surrounded by as many as fifteen hungry, angry wolves. The soldier's spotlight was now focused on him, the girl, and the wolves.

He told the girl to lay down, which she did. Then he threw his backpack beside her.

Gus walked a couple of feet away from her, toward the wolves, then stopped. The wolves all started to snarl, saliva dripping from their mouths. Gus looked them in the eye and loudly snarled back. They were telling him to leave or die. Gus understood this and sent his own message back, essentially saying the same thing. Then the snarling stopped.

Gus knew they were preparing to attack. It was the calm before the storm. Gus pulled out his knife. He closed his eyes to calm his mind in preparation for battle. He knew that he was fighting an enemy that was not human. An enemy that he had never trained for.

Gus half opened his eyes. He had put his mind into a meditative state. He now could feel a sense of 360-degree vision. He could not only see all the wolves around him in his mind, he could feel their presence in his body.

Then the wolves attacked. Gus stood in one place, drawing their attack into him. With tremendous speed and agility, he blocked their angry jaws while spinning, cutting, slicing, and stabbing. No block or strike was planned. Every move was completely reactionary. Within seconds, Gus looked around, and five dead or dying wolves lay near him.

The others had backed off and were now hesitating but circling.

Then one of the wolves howled very loudly. Gus knew it was a call for help. In the distance, he heard a wolf respond. It was a loud, grisly-sounding howl. It almost sounded like mixture of a wolf and a bear. All the wolves turned and retreated into the jungle.

Suddenly Gus heard shots ring out. The soldiers were firing at them. The girl screamed, "We must run! They are coming to kill us!" Gus was surprised at how well she spoke English.

Gus looked toward the men and saw two jeeps approaching rapidly. They each had machine guns mounted on the back. Each had a driver and a soldier manning the machine gun.

The girl stood up. Gus told her to go run and hide behind some rocks. She ducked her head and quickly ran for cover. Gus ran toward the jeeps to draw their attention away from her. He ran to the bottom of a small valley, crouched down, and waited for them to get closer.

The first jeep came flying over the hill, charging for Gus. As it barreled him toward him, he leaped into the air, landed on the hood of the oncoming jeep, and immediately flipped, landing perfectly on the back of the jeep. He grabbed the soldier manning the machine gun by the neck in a chokehold. In one fatal move, he flipped off the back of the jeep, spun in the air, and slammed the guy to the ground like a cowboy taking down a steer. He broke his neck upon impact.

The driver spun around and came charging toward Gus with the intention of running him over. Gus looked over his shoulder. The second jeep had just come over the hill and was approaching fast from behind. Gus stood directly in front of the first oncoming jeep and waited. Within a tenth of a second of getting hit, he stepped right to the driver's side of the jeep. As the vehicle passed him, Gus spun and grabbed the steering wheel with his right hand. In one quick move, he yanked the steering wheel down. It caused the jeep to make a sharp left turn. The quick turn of the wheel and its high rate of speed made the jeep flip, becoming airborne. Gus had timed it perfectly. The first jeep landed, slamming into the second jeep that had been approaching fast from behind. They slammed together with an explosive crunch. The jeeps were destroyed. None of the men were moving.

Gus ran back to the girl. He said to her, "I think we're safe for now, but we should leave."

She looked at him strangely and said, "You look different without your beard and glasses. Your face is bare."

Gus replied, "You look different without your clothes. Your body is bare."

She shyly turned her head down and smiled. Gus opened his backpack and threw her some lightweight rain gear. While he turned his back to allow her to dress, Gus asked, "What is that awful smell?"

"It is rancid hog fat. They threw it on me to attract the wolves." The girl quickly dressed and said, "Let's run."

Gus said, "I agree, but where are we running to?"

"We must run through the valley of the wolves to reach my people."

"Let's go. You lead the way."

They started running. Gus could hear the soldiers approaching in the distance. The girl was running fast, but Gus knew that the soldiers were catching up. They were on ATVs and were on some other road heading their direction. Gus told her to stop.

She looked at him in panic and said, "Are you tired? We must keep going."

He took off his backpack and told her, "Put this on."

She looked puzzled but did what he said. He then told her, "Get on my back."

"What are you doing? I am not injured." She hesitated but did what he said and got on his back, piggyback style.

Gus said, "I'll drive you direct. Are you ready?"

"Yes," she replied.

"Hold on tight. Which way?"

"Just keep going straight."

They were now on some crudely cut road. Gus started running. Then he picked up the pace and started running faster. He let out a yell and pushed his body hard. To the girl's amazement, they were approaching sixty miles per hour. Eventually, the sound of the motor vehicles of the men in chase could hardly be heard.

After a while, Gus had put a considerable distance between himself and them. Gus was tiring. He said, "Let's stop for a quick break."

The girl now seemed less panicked. Gus asked her, "What is going on down here?"

She said, "This used to be a beautiful place. I am part of what used to be a thriving village of happy people. My people have existed here in harmony for thousands of years. Then men showed up one day telling us they wanted to build a beautiful orphanage here. My people would be instrumental in running it. We would have good-paying jobs, medical facilities, and education. Our way of life would be enhanced, not destroyed.

We would become an example to the rest of the world. It would be a beautiful place where compassionate people took care of the world's homeless children.

"It all started out that way. Then, overnight, it changed. They brought in their own people who resembled us. After that, they started killing my people. They stole our jobs, took our land, and even stole our identities! They assumed our names and traditions. To the outside world, it appears that they are working in harmony with my people. In reality, they have killed most of us. We once numbered over two thousand. Now, there are barely two hundred of us left, most of which are hiding in the jungle. Many of us have been forced to work in the compound. We are the ones wearing the blue uniforms. They mix us with their own people in blue uniforms. As they learn our ways and customs, they kill us off and replace us with their own people. We are not allowed to speak or communicate in front of strangers. That day when I said 'No', I spoke to you, so I was selected for this week's kill."

Gus said, "This week's kill?"

"Yes. Each week, they kill several of us. They know that my people worship the wolf. To be cruel, each week they feed several of us to them. We have lived in harmony with the wolves for centuries. But these evil men killed off the antelope and anything else the wolves have to eat. The wolves are starving. The men douse us in hog fat and force us to run. They watch and laugh as the hungry wolves attack and kill us. If any of my people run out to help us, they shoot them. My people have no choice. They either do nothing and watch us die, or they die trying to save us. They must kill all of us. Every single one of us must die for their plan to work. Feeding us to the wolves is their cruel way of pulling us out of the jungle. If they don't kill us, the wolves will!"

"That explains a lot to me. These people are evil. They must be stopped. But right now, I think we're out of immediate danger. Let's get to your people."

With an excited look on her face, she said, "We are not out of danger. We are in the valley of the wolves! I will pray to the Black Wolf, the leader of all wolves, to let us pass."

"I'm more worried about soldiers than wolves."

"In the valley of the wolves, you should worry more about the wolves. I think that you are a good person. Maybe if you pray to him, the Black Wolf will listen to you."

Gus smiled and said, "Maybe so. We're both of the same family. Let's get moving."

They briskly walked for over an hour. It was now dark, but there was a full moon. Everything was visible, especially to Gus, who had the ability to see in the dark. The girl stayed very close to him as they walked. She looked scared. She wasn't talking, but her lips were moving. Gus looked at her and said, "What are you doing?"

"I am praying to the Black Wolf."

Gus did not say anything to her in response. The look in her eyes and the way her lips were moving left him with a strange, uneasy feeling. Something wasn't right. He felt like they were being watched. His mind and body were alert.

All of a sudden, out of the bushes walked a huge black-and-gray wolf. It was the size of a cow but had the muscular body of a wolf. It was a very large animal. Gus estimated that it was approaching a thousand pounds!

Gus stopped in his tracks. He put his hand on his knife but knew it would not stop an animal of this size.

The girl quietly said, "Black Wolf."

Gus instinctively started to growl. The wolf locked eyes with him and growled in return. It looked fierce. They were both growling loudly at each other. Suddenly, Gus could hear the wolf communicating with him. It was talking to him. This creature was of a much higher intelligence than the wolves he had fought earlier.

He felt the wolf say to him, *You have killed five of my kind in defense of one of your kind. I must now kill five of your kind. The five of my kind that you killed were renegades. They do not obey our laws. But they are still my kind.*

I understand why my renegades do what they do. I also understand your reaction. Beyond that, I also understand what the right thing to do for all species is. I will try my best to choose the renegades of your kind. Do you understand?

Gus felt himself replying, *Yes, I understand.*

The Black Wolf replied, *I am not sure that you do, but you soon will.*

Gus found himself thinking, *The girl and I are going to die.*

Then he heard someone from behind him yell, "Stop! Put your hands up, now!"

He slowly turned to see several soldiers pointing guns at him. The men chasing him had parked their ATVs several miles back and quietly ran down the trail. Gus turned his head back to look at the Black Wolf. It was gone.

He and the girl put up their hands. One of the men, who appeared to be the leader, yelled out, "Get on your knees!"

Gus and the girl did as he said. He feared that they were about to be executed. Gus looked over at her. She appeared to be in some sort of a trance. Her head was shaking, and her eyes were starting to roll back in her head. She was mumbling, *"Lobo negro, lobo negro, lobo negro,"* over and over. He understood this to mean *black wolf* in Spanish.

Gus could tell that some of the soldiers were scared. In English, the leader of the men laughed and said, "Fuck your Black Wolf. The Black Wolf does not live. And soon, neither will you!"

What the men did not realize was that while they had their guns trained on Gus and the girl, wolves had been gathering behind them. Gus could see ten or more wolves. They were being very quiet. He decided to buy some time as more wolves were entering the pack. Gus yelled out, "The Black Wolf told me to tell you something."

The leader of the men asked, "What would that be?"

Gus replied, "He says, 'Eat shit.'"

Some of the men laughed. In a somewhat confused tone, the leader asked, "The Black Wolf says, 'Eat shit'?"

Gus replied, "Yes, he says, 'Eat shit.'" More of the men laughed.

The leader of the men yelled in anger. "Tell the Black Wolf he can eat your dead body!"

About then, one of the wolves started to growl. The men froze. Behind them were now over thirty wolves. Even though the soldiers had guns, there were only five of them. The wolves were very close and ready to pounce. The men did not stand a chance. In addition to the first growling wolf, another one joined in. Then several more started growling.

One of the men looked back, then quietly said, "We are surrounded by wolves. Prepare for attack."

The leader of the men turned and fired his handgun. Instantly, the wolves lunged, biting, ripping, and tearing the men apart. Within seconds, the men were on the ground being destroyed by the angry, hungry wolves.

Gus looked at the girl and said, "We should leave."

She said nothing and just nodded her head, implying yes.

Gus turned as he stood up. Once again, in front of him was the Black Wolf. It was just silently staring at him. It communicated to Gus, *I have just killed five of your kind. I believe I have chosen your renegades. The score is settled. Our laws are that if you kill one of our kind, in return we kill one of your kind. If you kill five of our kind, in return we kill five of your kind. The only other time we kill your kind is in defense of our lives. If one of us disobeys our laws and kills one of your kind for no reason, then we expect your kind to kill him or at least one of us. We do not retaliate. This balance has worked between my kind and your kind for thousands of years. Now renegades of your kind kill as many of us as they can. In retaliation, renegades of my kind do the same. I believe I have the ability to understand who the renegades of your kind are. I believe you are not a renegade of your kind. I have tried my best to follow our laws and restore balance between us. Five of my renegades for five of your renegades. I hope I have chosen wisely. Forgive me if I am wrong.*

Gus replied, *You are a wise and noble creature. You seem to understand the difference between good and evil. The rebels of my kind are evil. They plan to destroy the good of my kind. They also plan to destroy all of your kind. I believe I was sent here to stop the evil rebels of my kind.*

The Black Wolf replied, *Your belief is correct.*

Gus blinked his eyes, and the Black Wolf was gone.

Gus realized that he had just intelligently communicated with this animal. While he had felt some level of communication with other animals, mainly dogs, this communication was of a much higher level. It amazed

Gus that an animal of this intelligence existed that was not human. It would always be treated as less intelligent than a human simply because it cannot communicate with man. Gus realized that we as humans have been taught that if some person or creature does not understand us, then they are not as intelligent as us. Maybe it is we who are not intelligent because we do not understand them. He also wondered how many other intelligent creatures existed that simply do not have the ability to communicate with man. Gus also understood something else about this creature: It had just saved his life!

Gus and the girl ran back to where her people were hidden. As they approached, armed men jumped out of the bushes and turned guns on them. "Halt!" they yelled.

The girl walked in front of Gus. She put her hand up and, in a strong tone, said loudly, "Put your weapons down." She was definitely more aggressive now amongst her own people. She continued with, "He is with me. Take me to the Wise One." She then screamed, "Immediately!"

They kept their guns on Gus as he followed the girl down a path to a hidden cave. Inside were two younger men in military fatigues and one very old man in some sort of traditional native-type clothing.

The girl ran up to the old man and hugged him.

She said, "Grandfather, this man saved my life. He is special. He easily killed many wolves in my defense. He throws soldiers in jeeps like they are toys. And he runs faster than the fastest antelope, even with me on his back. And, Wise One, he speaks silently with the Black Wolf."

One of the younger men said, "You have been tricked."

The other one said, "It is another one of their tricks. I don't trust him. Wise Father, we should kill him now!"

The girl then said, "Wise Father, I saw the Black Wolf myself. The Black Wolf protected this man."

The old man slowly approached Gus and grabbed his hand. He stared silently into Gus's eyes for several seconds. Then he smiled and said, "I have awaited your arrival for several months. I have seen you in my dreams. We are in desperate need of your guidance. My people are trapped. The invaders have burned the prairie that feed the antelope. The antelope have all left. If we try to cross the prairie to follow the antelope, we are killed. If the wolves try to cross the prairie, they are killed. While we can survive with food that we find in the jungle, the wolves cannot. The wolves are trapped in here with very little to eat but us. They have turned our scared friends against us and are using them to help slowly kill us off. I am sure after they use the wolves to help kill us, they will also kill all of them. We have many strong men who are ready to fight. But when the invaders took over, they took most of our weapons." The old man's eyes teared up. He squeezed Gus's hand and said, "Please help us."

Gus grabbed the old man's hand with both of his hands and said, "I don't understand exactly why I have ended up here, but I know what I must do before I leave. I must stop these evil people." He looked over at the two younger men, who were fiercely staring at him. Gus then sternly said, "Let's send these bastards to hell where they belong!" The two men smiled.

Gus knew he needed some help. It was time to call his father. His father had given him a satellite phone that worked even in the jungle. He had told Gus that he shouldn't call on this phone unless it was absolutely necessary. When he did, it would break radio silence. Gus knew he had to call his father first. His father would not call him. Gus called. His father picked up the phone.

"Gus, I've been waiting for your call. What the hell is going on down there?"

"Well, like you said, Dad, it was too easy. I had to start evaluating my exit options. I went out of the compound to check things out. To make a long story short, I can't go back to the compound and need to leave. But I have some things to take care of before I go."

"You need to wrap things up as soon as possible. I put a tracking circuit in your GPS hiking equipment. I know exactly where you are. There's an army coming your way. It appears to be about three hundred men. They are heavily armed. They have six tanks, ten Humvees, ten jeeps mounted with .50-caliber machine guns, and a wide assortment of mortars and automatic rifles. And they're headed straight for you! You need to wrap things up fast. What's it going to take to get you out of there?"

"What's it going to take? Dad, it takes a village."

"Now is not the time for joking."

"Part joke, big-time serious. That army isn't coming for me. It's coming to wipe out a village of local people. The last of their tribe. There's some evil shit going on down here, and that army is part of it."

"Gus, this isn't your war. You need to not lose sight of the big picture. You have the information you need; now it's time to get out of there. The future of mankind might be at stake. Now's not the time to get killed trying to save a village."

"Dad, I to have to try."

"Damn it, Gus, you're just like me…OK, let's see what we have to work with and come up with a plan. First of all, I've been tracking you since you left the compound. They have planted their own tracking device on you. I picked up an additional tracking signal about thirty minutes after you left. One tracking device is mine. The new one is theirs."

"That's impossible. They couldn't have planted a tracking device on me after I left the compound." Then he looked over at the girl. He saw a small scar and lump on her neck. He said, "It's not on me, but it has been very close to me."

His father proceeded to ask, "How many men do the locals have and what kind of equipment?"

"They have about eighty in-shape, strong men. They have an assortment of rifles and pistols. No tanks, no jeeps, maybe an ATV or two."

"They're outnumbered by more than three to one and have no weapons to speak of. Right now, they don't stand much of a chance. Gus, I wish I could tell you that I can send in fighter jets and take care of the incoming threat, but I can't. I would be starting a war with a foreign country. It would be an international incident.

"We would look like the bad guys. We need to figure out a way to help your guys win. They need weapons. Here's what I propose. I have a Predator UAV flying at about twenty-five thousand feet. It's above the cloud cover where no one can see it. It is equipped with a Hellfire missile that has a special ordinance on it. We developed it to attack terrorist zones that are populated with civilians. It's essentially a very large stun grenade like the police use. It will detonate approximately one thousand feet above the ground. Once it goes off, it will put out a blinding light and ear-deafening sound, accompanied by a large shock wave. Anybody within a mile diameter will be severely stunned. They won't be able to see, hear, or function for approximately twenty minutes after it detonates. After twenty minutes, they will start to recover. Within twenty-five minutes, some will have recovered enough to start functioning and fighting back. The goal of this plan is to detonate, then have the men of the village attack before the enemy recovers. If they're successful, they can take all of the enemy's weapons and equipment. The beauty of this bomb is that it doesn't damage equipment.

"There's one problem. Outside of the bomb's one-mile stunning capability is an additional five-mile diameter that's unpredictable and can be lethal. This means that the men of the village must stay six miles away when we detonate. The problem is, if they're on foot running at twenty miles per hour, which is about the top speed of a man who's in shape, they'll cover a little over six miles in twenty minutes. They will reach the enemy just about when the effects are starting to wear off. If they're five minutes early, they can capture or kill the enemy and confiscate the weapons and equipment. If they're five minutes late, they may all be massacred. If I were to calculate their odds of success, I would put it at fifty percent."

"Let's do it."

"What's your plan?"

"If I told you, you wouldn't believe me."

His father quickly shot back, "Gus, I need to know your plan in case things don't work out."

"My plan is that you let the incoming army get within six miles of where I am now. Then you fire the missile. The army is coming across the flat lands, and we are up on the mountain. When the villagers attack, they'll have the advantage of running downhill. In addition to that I will take a small group that will travel faster than twenty miles per hour. We'll attack before the second, larger group arrives. I'll be with the fast group, and you can track me using your tracking device signal. The other signal that you're tracking is a transmitter that they planted in a young girl's neck. She'll stay with the slower group so that you can track them."

"Sounds workable. Let's put this plan into action. We're running out of time. Check your watch. I will fire the missile in exactly fifteen minutes from now. And one last thing: promise me that whatever happens, you will get the hell out of there if things go to shit. I'll have a chopper in hot standby. They'll pick you up within five minutes of your call."

"I promise," said Gus. Then they hung up the phones.

Gus got together with the villagers and explained the plan. He asked the girl and wise man to travel with the group. He needed the girl because of the tracking signal implanted in her neck, but he also needed her and the wise man to help him control this army. Especially in the heat of battle. Gus didn't discuss his plan of using a fast team and a slow team. There was no reason to. He knew he was the only man on the fast team. Gus got the men of the village prepared. They would run as planned. The girl and wise man would follow on ATVs.

Gus could feel their desire for battle. They had no fear. Their only wish was to kill or be killed. By looking at them, Gus understood what his father had told him about taking another man's life. There is a time when it is required for defending you or someone else from harm. But it may also be required in a time of war. To these people, it was war.

Gus looked at his watch. Just as his father had said, the missile was fired right on time. It came out of nowhere. It was glowing as it approached but was eerily quiet. Gus told everybody to look toward the ground and not directly at the missile. Then it exploded. The light was an intense, huge flash. It was followed by a large sonic boom. The concussion could be felt even though they were six miles away.

Gus looked at the anxious men of the village and yelled, "Attack!"

They started running toward the enemy. Gus started running. He passed them up like a bolt of lightning. He didn't know exactly how fast he could run, but he knew it was around sixty miles per hour. At that speed, Gus calculated that he was running a mile a minute. That meant he would be there in approximately six minutes. As he ran, for the first time, he could understand the feeling of war. He had a plan but didn't know how things would truly turn out. He might die fighting, but he felt no fear. He was just doing it.

As Gus reached the battlefield, he was surprised by what he saw. Some men were lying on the ground, not moving at all. They appeared to be dead. Many were stumbling with blood dripping out of their ears. They were bumping into things like they were very drunk. It was obvious that many of them couldn't see. A lot of men were just lying and moaning. Some were crawling on all fours. Gus knew he couldn't just start massacring all these helpless men. But he also knew that if he did nothing, it could result in the end of the villagers. It was time for Plan B.

When Gus had fought off the wolves while saving the girl, one of the wolves howled when they were losing. Gus knew it was a call for help. He had memorized that howl. He put his head back and howled his loudest. It was immensely loud and ended with an echo.

He heard nothing in reply. He did it again, and no reply.

He did it again and got the response he had hoped for. The loud, grisly-sounding howl of the Black Wolf. Gus knew the Black Wolf was coming. He knew that a wolf could run around forty miles per hour and maintain that speed for some time. He felt that even though the wolves were about the same distance away as the men of the village, they would be twice as fast. They should easily get here before them.

Much to Gus's surprise, the Black Wolf came charging in within minutes. As he approached the battlefield, he was leading an army of wolves. In a triangular formation the Black Wolf was leading the pack. The biggest, strongest, and fastest wolves were close behind. Behind them were hundreds more. There were wolves as far as Gus could see.

The Black Wolf charged toward Gus and stopped within ten feet of him. They locked eyes. The Black wolf was snarling and growling, but Gus could feel him communicating with him. All the other wolves stopped behind the Black Wolf. Gus could feel their desire to attack.

Interesting, Gus thought to himself. *They seem to have the same rage as the attacking villagers. It was the rage of war. I wonder if they somehow understand that these are the bad guys?*

The Black Wolf communicated to Gus, *My kind are hungry and smell blood. I have the power to tell them to attack. I do not have the power to stop them after that. Why have you called me?*

Gus replied, *These are the renegades of my kind. They plan to kill all the good of my kind and all of your kind if they are not stopped. I have made them weak and vulnerable. I need your help stopping them. I am asking you to help me restore the balance of this land. Do you understand?*

The Black Wolf responded, *I understand. You must leave now, or my kind will attack you, too. You must stop the people of our homeland. If they arrive, my kind will also attack them. Leave now!*

Gus turned toward the mountains and started to run. As he did, all the other wolves snarled and growled but moved aside to let him pass. Gus started running fast. He had to reach the villagers as quickly as possible. He passed many wolves running toward the battlefield. They now ignored him. In the distance, he heard a loud howl by the Black Wolf. He knew that meant "Attack!"

Within minutes, Gus reached the quickly advancing group of villagers. He went straight to the wise man and told him to tell them to stop. They stopped.

The two younger men, whom Gus had met in the cave with the wise man, started yelling, "Wise One, we must not stop. This is our only chance. We have been tricked before!"

All of the other men stared at their young, aggressive leaders. Gus could see that they didn't want to stop. The war switch was turned on. The wise man looked at Gus and said nothing. Gus grabbed a pair of binoculars from one of the men and handed it to one of the young leaders. Then he simply said, "Look."

The young leader grabbed the binoculars from Gus, put them to his eyes, and froze. The other men anxiously awaited his reply. His facial expression completely changed from one of anger to disbelief. He dropped the binoculars from his eyes, turned to the others, and said, "Our enemy has gone to hell."

All the others started looking with binoculars and rifle-mounted scopes. There were gasps from the men as they observed the carnage. The wise man put down his binoculars and said, "What do we do now?"

Gus answered, "Go in after the wolves leave. Take their weapons and reclaim your land!"

The men all cheered. One of the men who was looking through his rifle scope yelled, "Wise One, two of the soldiers are escaping on a motorcycle! I can kill them. Should I take the shot?"

The wise man smiled and said, "No, let them go. They are messengers and have a purpose. Let them tell the others what they have seen today. Let them spread the legend of the Black Wolf."

While the villagers were all staring in amazement and horror, Gus snuck away. Someone realized he was gone and said to the wise man, "The good white man has left."

The wise man replied, "That was not a man. That was the answer to our prayers."

Chapter 13
THE TRUTH COMES OUT

Gus slipped away from the villagers and found a private spot to call his father. They arranged a pickup. Within ten minutes, Gus was being flown out in a helicopter safely guarded by a team of marines. They flew for about thirty minutes before landing at a small runway. His father was waiting for him in a private jet. Gus quickly boarded. Upon seeing his father, they embraced in a long, hard hug.

His father said to him, "I have a lot of questions, and we have a very long flight. Before we talk, why don't you get some food and water, then take a rest. I'm sure that you're still running on adrenaline. We can talk after you've had some time to recharge."

"Sounds like a plan."

Gus ate a meal of microwaved spaghetti and meatballs, and drank a large bottle of water. After that, he reclined in his seat, leaned his head back, and closed his eyes. Gus didn't realize how much energy he had spent. He thought he would take a quick nap. Instead, he fell into a deep sleep.

After several hours, he awoke. He got up, used the bathroom, and poured himself a cup of coffee. Then he went and sat back down. The plane was dark, and everyone was sleeping. He wasn't tired, so he opened his backpack and pulled out the information that he had taken from the Hive. Gus studied the annual presentations to investors. For each year since its inception, there was a candid report on the annual plans and progress of the Hive. He studied the documents. Gus now had a very good understanding of their devious plan.

His father came and sat down beside him. He said, "Are you ready to talk?"

"I'm dying to talk!"

"An interesting choice of words. You did almost die in order to talk. So what's going on down there? Give me the big picture first."

Gus spoke. "The Hive is being disguised as an orphanage. The Worker Bees will, as they call them, will all start out as orphan children. They will be raised in a controlled environment where everything is supplied for them. Under the disguise of education, they will be taught working skills at a very young age. At the age of twelve, they'll start working for the Hive. They won't receive pay. They will not need pay. Everything will be taken care of for them; food, clothing, and shelter will be provided. When they're young, they'll be provided with love. As they get older, they'll even have their sexual needs taken care of. Kind of like living in a commune and being raised by a cult. It will become their family. It will be all that they know.

"To the outside world, it's being sold as a beautiful place where or- phan children get the best in nurturing, education, medical facilities, and work-related training. They'll come in as a disadvantaged orphan child and leave as a strong, educated adult. They even brag that they can stay well past eighteen years of age. As adults, they'll be offered working in- ternships until they're ready to leave. That's where it starts to get sinister. The internships don't pay, but everything is taken care of for free, and they can stay for life. What that really means is that they'll work for free and they don't ever intend for them to leave. So now you have your Hive of Worker Bees. Smart, hardworking, educated, dedicated employees who work for free. Your only costs are those needed for their basic survival.

"Then it gets even more sinister. They pushed that concept even fur- ther. It was decided that if they chose just any orphan children, it could become chaotic. Too many different personalities. It could grow out of control. So what was their solution? To design the children to have the perfect controllable personality before they were born. That's where my company comes into the picture. We're developing genetically altered sperm to mass-produce Worker-Bee-mentality children. As it turns out, I'm helping design the perfect Worker Bee. That is Project X. That is the big picture.

"Now a little more detail. I was right about Lisa. She's not part of this evil plot. She's a major part of their experiment. As it turned out, they needed to design the genetically altered sperm to work with a certain group of females they had determined would be suitable mothers. The females had to be genetically compatible with the sperm and available amongst the general public. While developing the sperm, they decided they needed to study one of these genetically compatible females. They decided they needed a test specimen. A very young specimen. They found an infant girl who met their specifications and kidnapped her. That infant was Lisa. They have studied her entire life. She will be the first female who will become pregnant with the genetically designed Worker-Bee sperm.

"If her pregnancy and child are a success, they'll move into mass production. They'll start kidnapping women from around the world who have been determined to be genetically suitable mothers. They will become birthing slaves. They're even considering putting these women into induced comas. They believe the women would still be able to give birth while in a coma. They would be easier to control that way. Those children from these women would become orphans and end up in the Hive. If their plan works, those orphans will grow into adults that will never want to leave. They're genetically designed to become people who are introverted and very nonaggressive. They want smart people with weak, submissive personalities. They believe that if they create an environment that provides all the basics of life, these weak-willed people won't have the mental capacity to leave, especially after being raised with a cult mentality their whole lives. Why leave your family? Everything you need is here.

"Of course, in their literature, they do realize that they may, on occasion, produce imperfections. They don't say what they would do about them, but they do say they are committed to continually tying up loose ends. I believe that's their nice way of saying that anyone who doesn't conform or wants to leave will be killed."

His father said, "Wow, these are a bunch of really sick bastards. What I find the most disgusting is that they're using modern science to develop weaker, less capable humans. As these newly developed humans evolve, civilization will be downgraded. It's more than a crime against humanity—it's a crime against the future of civilization. Well, we know what they plan on doing and how they plan on achieving their goal. Now we need to stop them."

Gus asked, "Is it over if the locals destroy the orphanage?"

"Unfortunately, no. It would be a major setback, but it won't stop them. We have to cut off the head of the snake. We just have to make sure it's the right snake."

"What happened after I left? Do you know how things turned out?"

"I monitored the situation right before I came and sat down. I have some guys on the ground and some good satellite surveillance. It couldn't have worked out better. The men of the village took all the weapons and equipment and headed back to the orphanage to take over. They expected a fight, but when they got there, all the opposition was gone. Any remaining soldiers and about half of the workers had left. Eyes and ears on the ground reported that many had left in a panic. They were screaming, '*Lobo negro.*' You know Spanish. What does that mean?"

"Black wolf."

"Interesting," his father replied; then continued. "The villagers took over the orphanage without a fight. And here's the best part: The bad guys worked so hard at stealing the identities of the good guys that the good guys had no problem stealing them back. The villagers came back and found that they had desk phones, business cards, and offices with their names on them. Now the people running the orphanage truly are who they claim to be."

"What do you think will happen to the locals and the orphanage?"

"My guess is that there are a lot of wealthy investors that know the risks of getting caught at what they are doing. They'll probably stick with the concept of the beautiful orphanage. They'll claim that it was always their plan and to have no knowledge of anything illegal, dishonest, or immoral. They'll act very sorry for any injustices that happened. The people with the money will be very eager to right the wrongs. The locals now run the orphanage, and the investors won't change that. In a way, the people with the money are now being held captive by the villagers. And in order to cover their asses, the investors will most likely continue to fund the orphanage for some time. They could end up investing so much money to cover themselves that the beautiful orphanage idea becomes a reality. Imagine that!"

Gus's father paused for a moment, then said, "After reviewing the satellite images, I do have a question for you."

"What's that?"

"Where did the villagers get all those trained attack dogs?"

"They were wolves."

"OK, wolves. Where did they get all those attack wolves?"

"You wouldn't believe me if I told you."

"Just tell me."

Gus smiled and said, "I talked to the Black Wolf and asked for help. He sent them in."

His father laughed and said, "You're right. I don't believe you! Sounds like another story on a different day."

Then they both laughed together.

Gus's father said, "Tell me more about Lisa and her situation."

"Lisa has no idea of what's really going on. She thinks that Hank Stewart is her real father and that her mother died in an auto accident. They've told her that she has an incurable disease that prevents her from going out in public. She believes that she lives in isolation to stay alive. They have told her that she was chosen to be studied as they work to find a cure for her disease and that she was very lucky to be chosen. She feels very lucky."

"Give me some history. Why did they pick Lisa, and where did they find her?"

"According to what I read, they did a lot of research to determine what kind of women would be genetically suitable to become birthing mothers. The women all had to have what they called less dominant genes. The Worker-Bee sperm was developed to have dominant genes. When the dominant genes combine with the less dominant genes, the outcome is determined by the dominant genes.

"They collected massive amounts of data on women around the world to make sure that the women would be available when needed. They then predicted that they needed at least fifteen years to develop and perfect the Worker-Bee sperm. It was determined that during this development period, it would be good to study a genetically suitable birthing mother. They wanted a female that they could study for at least fifteen years without interruptions. Their final conclusion was that they needed to start with an infant. They would study the female in parallel with developing the sperm. That female would be the first one to become pregnant with the Worker-Bee sperm.

"After combing through data, they found a lonely prostitute who had just had a baby girl that met their needs. The baby wasn't born in a hospital, so there were no records of her birth. The mother was estranged from her family, and they didn't know that she had a child. She didn't know who the father was, and no men had claimed the child as theirs. Hank Stewart befriended this woman and her infant. The woman then conveniently died in a car crash. Hank Stewart took the infant and claimed her as his. The infant was Lisa."

"So that's where Hank Stewart fits in. He controls Lisa for them."

"He's using the trust that's between a parent and a child for his own personal gain. What's interesting is that lately, Hank has been telling Lisa that they're making progress on a cure for her disease and that she can occasionally go out in public. He's even telling her that she may be able to marry someday and have children. They must be making significant progress toward completion of the worker-bee sperm."

His father smiled and said, "You must be doing a good job."

Gus just shook his head and said, "Ya, thanks Dad." He continued with, "I think they're preparing to get her pregnant with the genetically developed sperm. They will most likely continue her fantasy and set her up to believe she's happily married and having a child. Little does she know the child would become the first Worker Bee."

"In the information you found, did they say what happens to Lisa after she has the baby?"

"No, after that, she's not part of the discussion. My guess is after that, she becomes a loose end. And they already said that they take care of all loose ends."

His father leaned back in his chair. With his elbow on the armrest, he put his hand to his chin, then said, "We have to carefully think about where we go from here. Hank Stewart is an integral part of their plan, but there's definitely somebody bigger. We need to figure out who they are."

"Dad, I'm not sure what we should do, but I know something I must do. I have got to get Lisa out of there."

"Well, I have an idea. When you go back to work, I don't think you'll be under suspicion. The Hive was lost while you were gone, but you were fishing with me. I'm very confident that your picture will not be identified in an FRT sweep. Here's my idea: Lisa believes that she may be able to soon marry. Use your power of seduction to get her to elope with you. It's a way to get her to leave without trying to explain to her what's really happening. Of course it would only be temporary. It would flush out the real serious people in this evil plot if both you and her temporarily disappeared. After that, you can tell her the truth. You may be breaking her heart, but it's a sacrifice you may have to make to save her life—not to mention, saving the future of mankind."

"Dad, I really like your plan. And I think it would work. But there's one other thing that I haven't told you about Lisa. I have not told you that I love her. She's the most unique and beautiful woman I've ever met. Lisa has grown up in near-total isolation from people but not from the Internet. She knows more than most, as she has had access to a computer since she was a child. As a person, she knows a lot about a great many subjects but has had very few real-life experiences. Dad, if I let her go alone into the world after this, I fear she would be crushed. I feel this overwhelming need to protect her. I don't know if you understand."

His father smiled and said, "I understand. When I left with your mother for South Korea, I was twenty, and she was ten. I was a man and she was a little girl. Although I was not attracted to her as a woman, I felt the overwhelming need to protect her. Even after I had gotten her to safety, that need to protect did not go away. As she became of age and developed into a woman, that need to protect turned into love. But to tell you the truth, as I looked back, I always wondered if it was truly love from the beginning. There are many components of love. Are you sure that your feelings go beyond the need to protect her?"

In an excited tone, Gus answered, "Dad, the first time I met Lisa, I was amazed. By the time I met her, I had already truly tested my power of seduction. No woman was able to resist. The first time I met Lisa, I got it going. I wanted her, and I could tell she wanted me. But she knew in her heart that it wasn't right. She snuck away before it could happen. She was the only woman who was able to resist me. I was amazed by her strength and integrity. I've sometimes wondered why I was given the power of seduction. Maybe it was given to me as a tool to help me along this journey. Or maybe that was not the reason at all. It could have been given to me to help find the only woman who could resist me. Possibly my power of seduction drove me to find Lisa.

"And there's one other thing I'm sure that would you be interested to know. Lisa saw the dog. She's the only other person who has seen it besides me. Lisa was watching me even before I knew who she was. I was walking the dog in the park when she saw me."

Gus's father leaned back in his chair then said, "Your mother told me about it. I wasn't sure if Lisa was the same girl. The only people who saw the dog with my experience was your mother and her father. Lisa is an important part of your journey. Let's stick with the plan. Gus, get her out of there. How you decide to do it is up to you. We'll move the cheese and wait for the rats to come looking for it. For now, why don't you get some more rest. You go to work two hours after we land. Just enough time to go home and clean up before you go in. Take these with you when you go to work." His father handed him an envelope.

"What's this?"

"Fishing pictures of you and me. I have some really good Photoshop guys on my team. Oh, and one last thing: stay in touch and let me know what your plan is and what you're doing."

"Sure thing, Dad."

After a couple of hours, they landed. They went to Gus's father's house, and Gus drove home from there. He ate and showered. He had about an hour before he had to leave for work. To kill time, he checked the messages on his phone recorder. He saw several calls from Mono with no message. Gus called him.

Mono picked up on the second ring. The first thing he said was, "Gus, my friend, we need to talk."

"Sure, what's up?"

Mono just said, "Meet me outside of your house in ten minutes." Then he hung up. Gus thought to himself, *That was strange.*

Within nine minutes, Gus saw Mono's Escalade pull into his driveway. The driver got out and stood near the back of the vehicle. Mono got out of the passenger side and got into the backseat.

Gus started thinking to himself, *What's this, some kind of gangster hit? Maybe people know that I wasn't really on a fishing trip. Maybe I'm wrong about Mono. What if he's one of the bad guys and he's here to take care of business? Just like in a movie, I'm getting into the backseat with a gang leader. Is this where he shoots me?*

Gus opened the door and got into the backseat. He looked at Mono and said, "What's up?"

Without his normal smile, Mono said, "Gus, my friend, we had a problem while you were gone. I had one of my people watching your house. He told me he had something to tell me. I was to meet him an hour after talking to him. He never made it to our appointment. He was shot in a part of town I know that he never goes to. The cops are calling it drug- or gang-related, but I know that's not true. Also, someone is making it very hard for me to find out any information. I want you to know, man, that the guy who was killed was my cousin. This is personal to me. Gus, my friend, I think that you are in some deep shit. More than you have let me know."

Gus answered, "I'm sorry, and you're right. At the time I did not know how deep the shit was. It got very deep very fast."

Mono was silent for moment. Then, looking straightforward, he asked, "What can you tell me without lying to me?"

"All I can tell you is that, somehow, destiny has cast me into a place that I never intended to be. Because of the work I do, I've become a very important piece of an extremely evil puzzle. The players are well funded and very diabolical. That's all I can say for now."

Mono looked at him and said, "So, wealthy and diabolical people would expect me to be scared and lay low. I know how to play that game. Gus, you may be in more trouble than I can help you with. I've always lived for my family. When you saved my son's life, I told you that you were family. But even family has its limitations. Because of you, my son lives. Because of you, my cousin has died. While you will always be my family, the debt for my son's life has been repaid. I do not blame you for my cousin's death. And even if you know who did it and cannot tell me, do not worry. I need to find out for myself. The punishment I will release to honor my cousin must be justified in my soul. Your word alone would not justify it."

Mono then turned to Gus, smiled, and, while offering a handshake, said, "My friend, it is time to part ways. Take my advice. Lay low and stay safe. It will keep you alive longer than a healthy diet and exercise!" Then he laughed a crazy laugh, his gold tooth somehow shining in the dimly lit Escalade. Gus sensed a level of craziness that he had not seen in Mono before. It was a scary kind of crazy.

Gus got out of the vehicle and went back into the house. Mono's driver got in, and they left. Gus had hoped he could count on Mono for more help, but it now seemed that wasn't possible. Mono had made it clear that their relationship had changed.

Gus prepared to go to work. Things in life were becoming very tense, but now was not the time to lose his cool. He needed to appear like he had just come back from a relaxing fishing trip. Gus went into work. He could feel the tension among the higher-up management. The news of the Hive must have spread. Shortly after he entered the building, he saw Hank Stewart approaching him. Being more aggressive than usual, he walked up to Gus, flashed his evil grin, and said, "How was your time off, Mr. Shepard?"

Gus smiled and answered, "Had a good time. Did some fishing."

Hank immediately asked, "What kind of fish were you fishing for?"

Gus pulled out one of the pictures his father had given him. It was a picture of Gus holding a fish by the tail. He had no idea of what kind of fish it was. He replied to Hank, "This kind of fish."

Hank looked at the picture. He obviously didn't know what kind of fish it was, either. He replied, "I don't catch them. I just eat them. Have a nice day, Mr. Shepard." Then he abruptly turned and walked away.

Gus knew that Hank's question was a test to determine his where abouts while gone. Hank seemed satisfied.

Gus started working on his projects like nothing had happened. He didn't want to draw attention to himself. After a couple of hours, he called Lisa. Gus always called her at this time of day on the special phone she had given him. She picked up, and they talked for several minutes with flirtatious back-and-forth comments. Then Gus said, "Lisa, I want to talk to you seriously. Can we meet somewhere?"

She immediately said, "Gus, what's happening? Something has changed. People are acting strangely. My father will be in an important meeting at two o'clock. I can get away for an hour. Meet me in the Environmental Test Lab in Section Two. It's closed for upgrades. Nobody will be there."

Gus said, "See you then," and hung up.

Gus met her there, and she looked radiant. He knew in his heart what he was doing was the right thing. He said to Lisa, "I can't explain everything to you, but there has been a big change at this company, and it will affect you. I can't explain the change and how it will affect you, but the change will happen fast. The most important part of this change that you must understand is that if we don't act fast, we will never be together. If I don't take you away from here very quickly, I'll lose you for life. I need you to trust me."

Lisa replied, "Gus, life is very confusing for me. I can watch TV and have access to the Internet, but until recently, I was never exposed to the outside world. I have a lot of knowledge, but I know nothing. I don't know what to believe about anything because I never had anybody who I could ask questions to. I never had anybody I could trust. But then, I found you. My life is now simple. I can ask you a question, and I trust your answer. No more second-guessing. Gus, with you, I'm alive. My whole life, I've grown up with the fear of dying. That fear is gone. Now, I only fear losing you. I will do whatever you want. I will trust you to make the right decisions."

Gus smiled at Lisa and said, "You are amazing. We're going to elope. I'm stealing you away, and we'll get married. This will make your father and many people at this company very angry. They'll come looking for us. They'll be especially angry with me. Some of them may want to hurt me."

"Will they try to hurt you like they did in Las Vegas?"

"Yes, that's possible."

"Will they want to hurt me?"

"That's also possible."

Lisa looked at Gus and said, "I would rather die with you than live without you. When do we leave?"

"Pack lightly. I'll pick you up at seven tonight."

Chapter 14
LET'S GO TO MY HOUSE

Gus showed up back at work promptly at 7:00 p.m. He called Lisa, and she came out with a duffel bag. She got into Gus's car, and they left. Everything seemed happy and joyous. He knew it wouldn't stay that way for long.

They drove back to Gus's house. Lisa had not seen his house and everything in it was interesting to her. Time was going fast. Gus planned on calling his father and letting him know that Lisa was now with him. His father could decide what to do next. About an hour passed, and Gus decided to call his father. He used the contract phone his father had given him. It appeared to have a weak signal and wasn't making a connection. He decided he would try again in a couple of minutes. Then Gus heard the doorbell.

He answered the door, and in front of him was a woman from the local gas and electric company. She told him that there was a gas line emergency and that they would be digging in the street in front of the house. The gas and electricity would be temporarily shut off for a short period of time.

Gus looked out at the street and saw a large utility truck from the company pulling up. She said that there would be some noise from generators and a jackhammer. It would take approximately one hour to complete the noisy stuff. Gus asked when all of the work would start. She told him in about ten minutes.

Gus shut the door and went into the kitchen. He tried calling his father again, and there was still no connection. He decided to try the landline. Gus went to the phone and saw that his answering machine was flashing.

There was a message from his father. It said, "Hello, Gus, this is Dad. I let myself in and dropped off your fishing gear. It's in the garage. The key is by the coffee machine. Great time. See ya."

Lisa was standing next to Gus, listening. She spoke, "That was very considerate of him. Your father sounds like a nice man. I would love to meet him. That was nice of him to bring back your fishing gear."

Gus replied, "That would be very nice of him except that I don't have any fishing gear."

He looked over at the coffeemaker and saw a key. He grabbed it and headed to the garage. Lisa followed. In the garage was a large locked box that Gus hadn't seen before. He unlocked and opened it. Inside was a large canvas bag. Inside the bag was a note and several weapons.

The note read: Gus, a couple of things I thought might come in handy over the next couple of days.

Then there was a list of equipment with some comments:

1. Two *bulletproof vests. Adjustable, one size fits all.*
2. *Beretta 9* millimeter. A great semiautomatic handgun. Sarge's favorite.
3. Smith & Wesson 627. Eight rounds, .357-caliber. A powerful and reliable revolver. Automatics sometimes jam. A great handgun if things get dirty.
4. Winchester 20-gauge Defender-style shotgun with pistol grip. Not as loud as a 12 gauge but still powerful enough for cleaning house.
5. 38-caliber snub-nose five-shot revolver with hollow-point shells. One body holster. Lightweight and easy to carry, but still packs a sufficient punch.
6. AR-15 assault rifle. For when the shit hits the fan.

The end of the note said, "Gus, I hope that you don't need to use anything that I've given you. Just remember that it's better to have something and not need it than to need it and not have it. Be careful. Love, Dad."

Lisa was looking over Gus's shoulder. She said, "I like what your father told you at the end of the note. It makes a lot of sense. He must be a very smart man. I noticed that he left you a Winchester 20-gauge Defender-style shotgun with a pistol grip. Did you know when that shotgun first came out, it was called the Lady Defender? It was like the 12 gauge was for the man, and the 20 gauge was for the woman."

Gus looked at Lisa, somewhat puzzled, and said, "No, I did not know that."

"He also gave you a 38 snub nose with hollow points. I noticed that it has been modified to include a large rubber easy-grip handle. Did you know that handgun is highly recommended for self-defense for a woman? It's powerful enough to stop an angry man, but the kick isn't too bad. They recommend hollow points for home defense."

Gus looked at Lisa in amazement and said, "How do you know all this?"

"After what happened in Las Vegas, I realized that I knew nothing about weapons and self-defense. I've been studying them on the Internet."

"Have you ever shot a gun?"

Lisa enthusiastically answered, "Well, kind of. I purchased target-practice software. It came with a battery-powered handgun that produces a simulated kick. I coincidently had the kick when fired to simulate a .38 caliber. I'm a very good shot!"

Gus looked at Lisa, smiled, and said, "When we're married and living together, I wouldn't want to anger you. I promise to always lift the toilet seat before I pee!"

She had no idea what he was talking about. She just smiled back and said, "Thank you."

Gus then said, "I'm going to call my father and thank him."

He used the contract phone his father had given him, but it still wouldn't connect. All of a sudden, Gus could feel the hair standing up on the back of his neck. Something did not feel right. His intuition was telling him that something was wrong. He grabbed the canvas bag and told Lisa, "Let's go back to the kitchen. I'm going to call my dad from the landline. My cell doesn't seem to be working."

They both went back to the kitchen. Gus picked up the landline. It was dead. Then he tried the cell phone that Lisa had given him to call each other. It also wasn't working.

Gus looked at Lisa and said, "The landline isn't working, and I think the cell phones are being jammed. Something is not right."

Lisa replied, "Maybe it has something to do with the work that's going on outside."

Gus replied, "Maybe", as he cracked open the shade to look out in front of his house. Then the power went out taking the lights with them.

Looking out the window, Gus realized that his was the only house without lights. He looked over at the utility workers. They were carrying weapons and looked like they were preparing for an assault! The woman who had come to the door and two men looked like they were preparing for a stealthy, quiet attack. They were carrying handguns, knives, and were putting on night-vision goggles. He saw them split up and come running toward the house.

Gus looked at Lisa and said, "We're in trouble. I knew it might get dangerous, but I didn't expect it to happen this fast."

"Is it as dangerous as it was in Las Vegas?"

"Yes, maybe worse. Open the bag. Let's put on the vests."

To Gus's surprise, Lisa didn't look scared. She grabbed the bag and opened it. She handed Gus a vest, then put on hers. She smiled and said, "What next?" It was obvious to Gus that she had been sheltered from reality for so long that she didn't understand how serious the situation was. She had no fear.

Gus told her, "I think they're planning a silent attack. My guess is that they're coming to kidnap you and take you back. I'm not sure what they plan to do with me. I don't think that they want to attract attention. They have cut off all the phones and power so that we can't call for help. I think we should play their game. I have the ability to see in the dark. While they're quietly sneaking in, we'll be quietly sneaking out."

Gus started preparing. He chose some of his quiet weapons first. He grabbed his favorite knife: a small, lightweight, ten-inch, razor-sharp Japanese sword. In addition, he added six custom throwing stars to his arsenal. He looked at Lisa and said, "You carry the bag and follow me."

Gus could feel his animalistic defense mechanisms kicking in. With his superior hearing, he heard someone breaking in from the living room window. He turned to Lisa and said, "They're coming in through the front first. I don't want to sneak out the front. But now I'm forced to deal with that threat first. I don't want to use a gun because I don't want them to know that we know what's happening. Stay close to me, but stop when I tell you."

Gus and Lisa quietly walked down the hallway toward the living room. He could see a man entering through the window. Gus pushed Lisa to the wall and whispered, "Stay here."

He heard the guy quietly say, "I'm in." Then he heard the reply in his earpiece: "Do not harm the girl. Neutralize him quietly if possible."

It was just as Gus thought. They wanted to take Lisa back. They must have felt that he was disposable. Gus knew that this was going to be a quiet fight. Neither of them wanted to attract attention. Gus thought of an old saying that he had heard before: "Don't bring a knife to a gun fight." But in this case it was the opposite. This was a quiet fight. This time it should be, "Don't bring a gun to a knife fight."

There was some light coming in from the window in the center of the room. Gus walked into the center of the room and made his presence obvious. He pulled out his knife, and the attacker froze upon seeing him. Then the guy smiled and pulled out his knife. He had a large Bowie-type hunting knife. He took off his night vision goggles and mumbled, "Won't be needing these."

They both knew this was going to be a knife fight. Gus had received martial arts weapons training at a young age. His father had trained him in *Eskrima*, a Philippine form of stick and knife fighting. Gus dropped into a crouched position with his knife in his right hand. Instantly, two things popped into his mind about knife fighting. The first thing was to never take your eyes off your opponent's knife. This was opposite his weaponless martial arts training, which taught him always to focus on the eyes and head, not on the striking hands and feet. The second thing was something his father always said about knife fighting: "One guy goes to the hospital. The other guy goes to the morgue."

Gus saw his opponent put his knife in his right hand with the blade dropping below his wrist, parallel with his forearm. Gus recognized this as a style of knife fighting that was different than his style. It was more of a kill or be killed style than a competition between two men fighting with knives.

Suddenly, the attacker lunged at Gus, holding the knife close to his forearm for protection. Then he swung at Gus's head with a backhand-style stabbing move. Gus jumped backward, avoiding the potentially lethal strike. The guy quickly tried the same backhand stab again but followed up swinging in the return direction, the blade up barely missing Gus's throat. This guy was good. Gus had quickly moved backward, avoiding the strikes while continuing to circle him. Then the guy whipped the knife away from his forearm and dropped his arm low. He now had the blade facing forward. Crouching down, he dropped into a position similar to Gus's, then he quickly lunged at Gus with a forward stab.

Gus jumped back, but the strike nicked his stomach. The guy smiled. Gus had been hit but had gained an important piece of information about his opponent. He had seen his attacker glance at his eyes before his stabbing motion. That meant for a moment, he had taken his eyes off of Gus's weapon. He was going for do-or-die body shots. It was now time to counterstrike.

Gus waited for his attacker's next strike. He didn't take his eyes off his opponent's weapon. Then the guy lunged forward with an aggressive stab toward Gus's midsection. With the quickness of a snake, Gus whipped his stomach inward, avoiding the strike. At the same time he delivered a slashing blow to his attacker's knife-yielding hand. It resulted in a deep cut.

The guy knew he was hit. In anger, he swung at Gus's throat, then charged forward with a stab toward his body. Whipping around his body to avoid the strikes, Gus counterattacked with the speed of a cobra. He cut the guy's knife-yielding arm two more times. His opponent was now bleeding badly. The guy hesitated for a second and looked at his injuries. He now knew what Gus knew. If this fight didn't end soon, he would bleed to death. In a knife fight in the street, a fighter could just run and hope he made it to the hospital in time. Here, there was no place to run.

Gus kept the action going but stayed out of the way of his attacks. He knew the more active his opponent, the more quickly he would bleed. Gus could see that the guy was starting to fade. His attacks were becoming sloppy. Then, in an act of desperation, the guy grabbed a statue off the mantel with his left hand and threw it at Gus's head. He then came charging in for the kill. With the knife in his right hand, he attempted a low stab. Gus easily grabbed his knife-yielding arm with his left hand and held it tight. Then he slammed his Japanese mini-sword deep into the guy's stomach! Gus held his opponent in this position until he slowly crumpled to the floor.

Gus pulled his knife out, leaned straight back, and listened. He could hear someone coming slowly down the hallway. He went to Lisa, who was still standing in the hallway near the living room, and whispered, "Stay here."

Gus looked down the hallway. At the opposite end of the hallway he saw a soldier-looking-type guy in military type pants and a tank top. His arms and face were covered with black camouflage paint.

Gus moved past Lisa, toward his opponent, and pulled out his knife. The guy saw him. His attacker then slowly moved one hand to his side and appeared to be pulling out a knife. His other hand then went behind his back. From behind his back the guy very quickly pulled out a handgun. In one hand he had a gun. In the other hand he did not have a knife. He had a silencer. This was not a knife fight! The attacker was rapidly attaching the silencer to the gun. The assembly was almost complete.

Moving quickly, Gus threw down his knife, stabbing it into the floor in front of him. From a pouch behind his shoulders, Gus grabbed his throwing stars. With a right-left-right combination, he hurled three throwing stars at the attacker. The first two stars slammed into the guy's forehead, sinking deep into the bone. The force of the strikes whipped his head back, exposing his neck. A perfect landing pad for Gus's third strike. The third star hit hard, ripping directly into the guy's throat! He hit the wall with a thud. The camouflaged soldier dropped his weapon and fell to the ground. He rolled to his side, choking up blood. He was still alive but effectively neutralized.

Gus went back down the hallway toward the living room and got Lisa. He quietly said, "Follow me. I think we can sneak out the side garage door."

Gus and Lisa quietly went down the hallway to the garage. He whispered to Lisa, "Wait here. I'll go check it out."

As Gus entered the garage, he heard a woman's voice say, "Freeze or die."

He recognized the voice. It was the utility company woman who had come to the door earlier. She then said, "Hands on your head and move."

The woman turned on a flashlight and directed Gus to the center of the garage. She asked, "Where's the girl?"

"What girl?"

The woman sternly replied, "Get the girl, or I'll just kill you and go find her myself."

Lisa moved into the doorway and said, "This girl?" She had the .20-gauge pistol-grip shotgun in her hands.

The woman laughed loudly and said, "Look what the guinea pig has. Now, listen, sweetie, why don't you just put that down, and I'll get you something that you know how to use? Like a broom and a dustpan." She laughed again.

Lisa, looking slightly confused, replied, "I know how to use it. The instructions were clearly defined on the Internet. I see no reason why it shouldn't work."

The woman raised her voice and sternly said, "You don't see any reason why it shouldn't work? It won't work because of the idiot who's trying to use it. Now, just put down the gun before I kill your friend. Last chance. What do you say, sweetie?"

Gus saw Lisa's forehead tighten. She looked angry. He had never seen her look that way before. Then, in a sarcastic tone, Lisa replied to the woman, "You should have brought me a broom and dustpan."

The woman gave her a puzzled look and said, "Why's that?"

Lisa smiled and said, "Because it's time to clean house...bitch!"

As the last word left her mouth, Lisa fired the shotgun. She immediately cocked the gun and fired two more times in rapid succession. The hail of fire hit the woman three times. With each shot, she stumbled backward, landing flat on her back.

Lisa looked at Gus and said, "Your father was right. This gun isn't too loud but powerful enough to clean house!"

Gus looked at Lisa and said, "Damn, all that because she called you an idiot?"

"She also called me a pig. Gus, what's a guinea pig?"

Gus just smiled and said, "I'll tell you some other time."

Lisa got a serious look on her face and said, "She was going to kill you to find me? Just because we want to get married?"

"All I can tell you right now is to trust me."

With his excellent hearing Gus then heard a voice in the downed utility woman's earpiece. It said, "Team One, Team One, we heard gunshots. Silent Night program is terminated. Switching to full-frontal assault. Infrared indicates possible targets in garage. Switch from extraction to elimination. Full-frontal assault will begin in ninety seconds, starting now!"

Then Gus heard a very loud generator turn on outside. After that, someone started using a jackhammer. They were creating noise loud enough to disguise gunfire.

Gus looked at Lisa and said, "We're in trouble. I can't call for help because they've disabled our phones; they've turned off all the power, and are tracking us with infrared sensors. They've created loud noise to cover their gunfire as they charge in to kill us."

Lisa replied, "If we were in the forest and had no phones to call for help, we would light a fire."

Gus said, "That's a very good idea."

He grabbed a five-gallon gas can, then opened the big garage door using the mechanical latch. With the door cracked slightly open Gus quickly started pouring gas back and forth, out of the bottom of the door. The gas was running out down the driveway. He grabbed a long wooden match from the shelf and lit the gas. Instantaneously, flames shot up in front of the house.

Gus turned to Lisa and said, "That will attract attention. Plus, the heat of the flames will keep their infrared sensors from seeing us. The sensors won't be able to detect our body heat as long as we stand behind the flames. You need to stay here. I have to stop the attack. I need to strike before they do."

Lisa grabbed the AR-15 assault rifle from the bag and said, "Your father's note said this gun is good for when the shit hits the fan. Gus, has the shit hit the fan?"

He grabbed the gun and replied, "Yes, it has." Then he smiled at her and said, "I think my father is going to like you."

Gus slammed the clip into the rifle and put another through his belt. He ran toward the living room. Gus knew that once away from the flames, they would track his body heat. He must keep moving, or he would be shot. He entered the living room, and the gunfire started. They were shooting at him. Gus could see four young soldier types moving in formation across the front lawn. He could tell that their infrared tracking was locking on. They were blindly shooting at him through wall. He was stationary, but their shots were coming dangerously close. Gus knew from his Las Vegas gun training that it is much harder to hit a moving target than a stationary one. So he ran across the room, did a forward flip, popped up, and fired through the large front window. With amazing accuracy, he hit one soldier in the foot with a single shot. The guy fell to the ground.

He ran back in the opposite direction, flipped, and popped up again, shooting a second soldier in the foot with a single round. The second soldier fell to the ground. He easily could have killed both men, but that wasn't the goal. The goal was to get them to stop the attack. Killing any one of them might have caused anger and rage. That could drive them to attack even harder.

It appeared to be working! Out of the four attackers, two were down. One of the standing soldiers started pulling one of the downed men to safety. The other standing soldier dropped to one knee with his rifle up in a defensive position. He was providing cover, not attacking.

Gus ran across the room again and used his foot to propel himself off the wall. Becoming airborne nearly horizontal to the window, he shot a burst of gunfire at their generator. It was a perfect hit. The generator shut down. It caused the jackhammer to turn off. All the loud noise quit. There was now no noise to mask the sound of gunfire. Gus could see the flames from the large fire in the driveway. In the distance, he could hear sirens. One of his neighbors must have called the fire department. Gus saw the attackers retreating. They were quickly packing up and leaving.

Chapter 15
WEDDING PRESENT

Gus knew it was time to leave. As he ran back to the garage, he heard the large utility truck driving away. He opened the big garage door all the way. Gus grabbed the bag of weapons, and he and Lisa got into his car. They ripped out of the garage and through the driveway of flames. As Gus drove away, he realized that he had left all the cell phones in the kitchen. There was no way to call his father. With very few options he knew that he had to get somewhere safe so that he could call. Someplace no one would suspect he went. He decided to race to Caldwell's company, IDS.

In his Porsche 911 Turbo, Gus was flying. He got to IDS. It was a very secure-looking building. The gate was locked. He pushed a large button that was below a video monitor. He heard a voice reply, "Gus, is that you?"

He was lucky that Caldwell was there. "Yes!" Gus replied. "I'm in trouble. I need your help."

"Come in. The doors will unlock for you."

The gate opened. Gus raced inside. He and Lisa got out of the car and ran into the building. They went through several locked doors. Each door buzzed and unlocked, leading them to where Caldwell was waiting. They entered a very large room that looked like something out of a science fiction movie.

Gus said, "I'm in trouble. Let me explain."

Caldwell replied, "Gus, you don't need to explain. I know who you work for and what you do. I probably know more about your situation than you do. We can talk later. Right now, I need you to know that you've been followed. A team of armed men are heading this way. Don't worry. You're safe here."

About then, Caldwell turned on several video monitors. On the monitors were as many as ten armed soldier-looking types. They were coming in from all sides of the building. Leading the charge was Hank Stewart. Hank the VP now looked much more intimidating dressed as Hank the soldier.

Lisa yelled out, "It's my father! He has come to save us!"

Gus and Caldwell looked at each other. They knew that wasn't his purpose. Gus could see that the soldiers were blowing the doors open with explosives. Caldwell just smiled and said, "No need for so much damage. I'll just let them in and see what they want."

Caldwell waved his arms, and all the doors unlocked. The attacking team quickly entered the room with guns drawn. Caldwell was still smiling.

Hank entered the room and yelled, "Hands up; you're all surrounded!"

Lisa yelled, "Father, you've come here to save me!"

Hank looked at her seriously and said, I've come to take you home." He had his gun aimed at Gus.

Lisa said, "You must have gotten my letter and found me."

Hank replied, "I can always find you." It was obvious that Lisa had some sort of tracking device on her.

Lisa then smiled and said, "I've decided to elope and marry Gus, as I told you in my letter."

Hank replied, "You can't marry him. His DNA is wrong. If you marry him, you'll die due to your condition."

Lisa looked at Gus, who replied, "Lisa, that's not true."

Hank sternly looked at Gus and said, "I would like to take Lisa home and leave you alive, if that's possible. I think you should shut up."

Gus looked at Hank and said nothing. Then Caldwell spoke. "I've been watching your organization for some time. You're Hank Stewart, the senior vice president. I know what your company says they do and what they really do. I'm also involved in research of the same subject. I believe we have common interests."

Hank turned his gun toward Caldwell and said, "I did not come here to talk to you. I told you to put your hands up."

There were eight soldiers who had come in with Hank. Immediately, six of them turned their weapons onto Caldwell. The other two kept their guns pointed toward Gus and Lisa.

Caldwell just stood there, calmly smiling, and then said, "I think you and all your men should put *their*...hands up."

As soon as he said "hands up," laser pointers put a red dot in the center of all the attackers' foreheads, including Hank's.

Caldwell then pointed his finger at Hank and said, "Not you, so that we can talk." The red laser dot disappeared from Hank's forehead.

Hank looked at Caldwell and said, "Neat trick. I know who you are, Mr. James P. Caldwell. You may be some kind of rich genius, but you're out of your league. I think you've been watching too many movies. You're bluffing with your little light show. Even if they were backed by firearms, I'm sure one of my men is going to get at least one bullet in you before you can take them all out."

Caldwell replied, "Mr. Stewart, do you know what is faster than a speeding bullet? The speed of light. I have developed my own small-scale missile defense system. My system doesn't use firearms. It uses high-power laser light. It will not only kill all your men, it will destroy any bullet fired at me in midair. Would you like me to demonstrate?"

Hank replied, "Enough of your hocus-pocus bullshit. I am giving you to the count of three to put your hands up."

Caldwell shook his head like a mother scolding a child and said, "I don't want to do this, but I am doing it for your own good. Hank, please do not fire your weapon unless you want to die. You're not targeted, but the system will eliminate anybody who fires at me."

Caldwell then looked up at the ceiling and rapidly blinked his eyes three times. All of a sudden, a loud buzzing sound and gunshots went off at the same time. All eight soldiers dropped to the ground with perfectly round holes in the middle of their foreheads. Smoke exited the holes made by a precision, high-power laser. A handgun and an assault rifle lay on the ground smoking. Their barrels were exploded with a single strike from the high-power laser, the result of two of the men firing their weapons during the laser strike.

Hank didn't fire his weapon. He just stood there, training his gun on Caldwell. Then he smiled his sinister grin and said, "OK, Caldwell, you proved your point. So tell me; what the fuck do you want?"

Suddenly Caldwell got a serious look on his face and answered, "I know that your company is creating a genetically engineered master race of people. It was inevitable that someday somebody would do it. I also know that you have to base it upon a living human's genetic makeup and work from there. I believe that you would greatly benefit if you based it upon humans with superior genes. I would like to work with you. I am considered to be a genius. I am involved in an organization consisting of geniuses from all over the world. We comprise an extremely small group of the smartest, most intelligent people on this earth! We would be willing to donate our superiorly intelligent genetics for integration into your master race."

Hank laughed loudly, then said, "Sure, buddy. I can arrange that. We do need superior intelligence integrated into the future of mankind. I'm sure that we can work something out."

Caldwell's eyes lit up, and he gave a huge smile.

Gus looked at Caldwell and said, "James, don't believe him. They are not developing a master race needing superior intelligence. They're creating a race of working slaves! Their goal is to develop a group of easily controlled, hard-working humans. They call them Worker Bees. After that, they'll get them all in one place and use them to do their bidding. These people aren't enhancing the evolution of mankind. They're destroying it to enrich themselves!"

Gus watched Caldwell's smile disappear as his facial expression turned to anger. His face got red, and his eyes bulged. He stared directly at Hank and said, "I know Gus. He would not lie about a thing like this." Then he yelled, "Your plan is evil! You are evil! You and your plan must be destroyed for the future of mankind!"

Hank laughed loudly again then said, "You're right. He is too damn honest to lie. I guess that only leaves me as the liar." He looked at his watch and said, "The only real reason I've listened to all your shit was because I needed to buy a little time. But I think you've given me all the time I need."

Suddenly, the power went out, and emergency backup lighting turned on. A door kicked open, and in walked a large man dressed in military fatigues. It was Hans from where Gus worked, whom Gus hadn't seen since he had broken his nose.

Hank yelled out, "Is everything secure?"

Hans bellowed back in a deep, raspy voice, "Everything's secure. Including any backup system. It doesn't take a genius to know that they won't work without wires." He put his head back and laughed loudly.

Hank pointed his handgun at the ceiling and fired, destroying a sensor in the center of the room that Caldwell had been communicating with. Hank smiled and said, "Houston, we have a problem."

Instantly Caldwell pulled out a chrome revolver and pointed it at Hank. Hank whipped back around and pointed his gun at Caldwell. Gus and Hans immediately pulled out semiautomatic handguns and pointed them at each other.

Hank then yelled, "Looks like the genius has gone low tech on us. It's now two against two. The odds are even. Looks like we have us one of those Mexican standoffs."

Hans then yelled to Hank, "The boss said to take her alive and everyone else is expendable."

Hank said, "I would like to make the boss happy, but we have a logistics problem. Too many guns on the side of the opposing team. But I do have an idea that could change the balance. Hans, you always said that the next time saw Gus you were going to kick his ass."

Hans blurted out, "The boss says he's mine."

Hank said, "Listen up everybody. I have a proposal. Hans and Gus, why don't you both put down your weapons and fight it out hand to hand?

Once one guy beats the other, he can go retrieve his weapon. That will change the balance. His team will have two guns and the other team will have one. The standoff will be ended. It will be a winner-takes-all battle. Of course, our other option is that we all start shooting one another now, in which case there would likely be no winners, as we will all probably die. What do you think, Gus? Would you at least like to try? I think you owe it to Lisa to at least try."

Gus knew he had very few options. Hank was right. If the shooting started now, they would all most likely die. Gus said, "I like your proposal, Hank. Or maybe I should just call you Dad. I want you to know when this is over, I really am going to marry Lisa."

Then Gus looked directly at Hans. He knew a fight was imminent. He wanted to anger him to mentally throw him off. Gus smiled and said, "Look at this idiot. He may be big, but he's stupid. Did they design this pig at work? Talk about poor genetic engineering. Somebody fucked up bad, real bad. You know what they say: if you can't do it right, you can always do it over. I think it's time to eliminate this mistake. Hank, just for you, I'll take this pig to the slaughter house." Gus then snickered.

Hank laughed and said, "What do you think, Hans? Sounds like a challenge to me."

Hans yelled in his raspy voice, "Fuck your bullshit. Let's do it! We'll both put down our guns at the same time and kick them to the side. Then I'll crush you like a bug!"

They both started lowering their guns.

Lisa screamed, "Gus…nooo!"

Hank loudly and sternly said to her, "Stay back!"

Gus said to Lisa in a slow and even voice, "Do as your father says."

They slowly put down their weapons and stood up straight. Simultaneously, both Gus and Hans kicked their guns to the side of the room. Hans looked at Gus and smiled. They started circling each other.

Hank yelled out, "Come on, Hans! Don't take too long. Show us that you're everything that you say you are."

Hans then blurted back, "Fuck you. This problem should have been solved a long time ago. Now I have to take care of it for you. You should have fired him and kept me. Maybe the problem is you. Maybe after I kill him, I should just let this Caldwell guy eliminate you."

Hank laughed and said, "What, eliminate me so that you can run the show? I hate to tell you, pal, we didn't bring you on because of your brains. Just do your job, and let's clean up this mess up before the boss gets here."

The talking stopped. Hans now turned his full attention to Gus. At six foot five and 380 pounds, his size was intimidating. Hans wasted no time and came charging in, throwing punches like a trained boxer. Gus blocked, dodged, and sidestepped his powerful strikes. This continued for several minutes.

Hans was starting to tire from the flurry of punches he had thrown. Then he started to slow down. He realized Gus was not fighting back. Hans yelled to Gus, "Looks like somebody has some training." He now knew Gus was too quick and nimble for him to just simply mow over. Also he could tell Gus was just trying to wear him down.

Hans decided to change his strategy. He abruptly stopped and positioned himself to one side of the room. Hans hesitated for a moment, then started walking toward his gun. He had set himself up so that he was closer to his gun than Gus was to his. He knew what Gus's reaction would be, had to be.

Gus charged and faked a front kick, getting Hans to drop his hands low. Then he threw three hard punches, each landing solidly in Hans's face. As Hans pulled his hands up in a defensive position, Gus slammed a roundhouse kick into his ribs. Then Gus backed off.

Hans was smiling. He appeared to be unaffected by the strikes. Then he laughed loudly. He gestured with his hand, egging Gus on while yelling, "About time. Bring it on!"

Gus charged in, throwing several more roundhouse kicks, hitting Hans solidly in the ribs. He followed up with more good punches to his head. Gus also hit Hans with many solid kicks to his stomach. He even threw a very powerful spinning back fist, hitting Hans squarely in the jaw. Hans stumbled back, shook his head, and smiled.

Gus was giving it everything he had, but nothing seemed to hurt this guy.

Gus was starting to tire. He realized that Hans was throwing few counterattacks and was saving his energy. The shoe was now on the other foot. Hans was trying to wear him down. Gus knew this would be no easy battle. Hans was big, trained, and tough. Gus decided to slow down. He knew he had to outthink and outmaneuver this big man.

Both men were tiring. They started circling one another, each looking for the killer strike. Gus noticed that Hans had switched to a slightly wider stance, keeping his legs father apart, possibly to give himself a longer reach for his deadly punches. Gus saw an opportunity. He lined himself up for a Krav Maga-style front kick, developed to hit hard and upward between an opponent's legs. Having the same effect as a good old fashioned kick in the balls. He saw an opening and delivered a full-power kick between Hans's legs.

Immediately, Gus felt pain on the top of his kicking leg. Instantly, he knew Hans was wearing a protective cup. Hans had set him up to draw him in close. Before Gus could back off, Hans lunged forward and grabbed his shoulders. He then delivered a full-power knee strike to Gus's stomach, lifting Gus's body off the ground. Before Gus could counter, Hans delivered another vicious knee strike. As Gus pushed away, Hans threw him across the room.

Gus hit the floor with a thud. Hans charged in with a stomp to Gus's head. His stomp narrowly missed as Gus rolled and jumped back to his feet. Hans obviously had more skills than just boxing. Gus could feel the pain in his stomach from the strikes. He decided to take advantage of the situation. Bending slightly over and crinkling his face, he wanted Hans to think that he was hurt more than he actually was.

It worked. Hans came charging in, leaving his face wide open while trying to throw a knockout punch. Gus quickly stepped to one side and delivered one quick counterpunch, breaking Hans's nose. The blood squirted out as he whipped his head back. Hans paused, stepped back, and put his hand on his nose. His eyes bulged in anger when he realized Gus had broken his nose, again!

Gus had achieved what he wanted. Hans was now furious and mentally off balance. Hans rushed in, wildly throwing punches. Gus danced around, easily blocking his attacks. Then Gus delivered a precision front snap kick, hitting Hans in the groin. A soft area on the front of his body that was below his stomach and above his testicles. A sensitive area not protected by strong stomach muscles or a protective cup. He could tell by the look on Hans's face that it hurt. Gus had found a weakness, and Hans knew it. A soft spot Hans could not easily protect. Gus's leg speed was just too fast for Hans to counter. While Hans threw wild punches in desperation, Gus delivered several precision, hard-hitting kicks to Hans's groin. In pain and exhaustion, Hans paused his attack. He backed off and crouched over with his hands dropped low. Breathing heavily, he was catching his breath and studying Gus, obviously trying to develop a new strategy.

Gus immediately saw an opening. He quickly shuffled forward, then fired a spinning back heel kick and hit Hans perfectly on the tip of his jaw. Hans fell to the ground!

Gus stopped and just stared at him for a moment. He could feel the pain in his heel from the impact with Hans's jaw. Hans wasn't moving. He must be unconscious. Gus walked up to him and kicked him hard in the side. He didn't move. Gus turned and started walking toward his gun.

In an instant, Hans jumped up and grabbed Gus from behind. The big man picked Gus up over his head and slammed him to the ground! He hit the ground hard. Hans had faked being out, and Gus fell right into his trap. Then Hans quickly jumped on to Gus, over powered him, and moved into position sitting on Gus's chest.

It was now a ground war. Due to Hans's size and strength, Gus was at a big disadvantage. The huge man on top of him started raining down punches. Pinned and in a defensive position, he blocked Hans's massive fists from smashing in his head. Gus knew he was in trouble. One strike from Hans would put him away. The weight of the 380-pound man on his chest was restricting his breathing. He had to do something fast.

With lightning speed, Gus whipped his body into a half-sitting-up position. While blocking Hans's deadly punches, he hit Hans in the eyes with a quick two-finger strike. Hans roared in pain. Gus dropped back down and whipped up again, this time hitting Hans in the throat with a knife-hand finger strike. Hans started gagging. With his eyes closed and choking for air, Hans opened his massive left hand and slammed it into Gus's face, pinning his head to the ground. He raised his right hand and prepared to crush Gus's head with his huge fist. Before Hans could deliver, Gus bit hard into his left thumb, crushing it to the bone. Hans bellowed in reaction. Gus then grabbed the two smallest fingers of the same hand and snapped them back, breaking them like pretzels. Hans yelled loudly then rolled off to the right of Gus to break the hold.

Hans started standing up, but Gus got to his feet faster. With ten feet between them, Gus got a running start, jumped into the air, and hit Hans in the head with a flying sidekick! Hans's head jerked backward, and his eyes rolled back as his limp body dropped to the ground.

Gus just stood there staring at Hans. There was absolutely no movement. He decided not to check him his time and started walking toward his gun.

Just as Gus reached his gun and was bending over to pick it up, he heard the deep raspy voice of Hans yell, "Freeze!"

Gus turned around and Hans was sitting up with a gun in his hand. He apparently had a gun hidden on him the whole time.

In a loud voice Hans bellowed, "Congratulations! You're much tougher than I thought. You have earned my respect. But now, you must die!"

Then Hank yelled out, "You were starting worry me, Hans. I'm glad to see that you were smart enough to carry an extra weapon. Especially after he kicked your ass!" He laughed very loudly and said, "*He* broke your nose!" When he stopped laughing, Hank said, "Now that we know who's tougher, could you just point your gun at Caldwell so that we can take control before the boss gets here? Gus isn't leaving, and he's unarmed. Caldwell first. Then we can take care of Gus."

Hans kept his gun on Gus and yelled to Hank, "You think I'm stupid, don't you? Do you really think that I'm going to pass up this opportunity? First, I'll shoot Gus while you and Caldwell shoot each other. After that, I'll shoot whichever one of you is left standing. When the boss gets here, the only ones alive will be me and the girl. I will be a hero! They'll probably give me anything that I want. And with you gone, asshole, do you know what I want? I want the girl when they're finished with her. And do you know why? Just so that I can hear her scream for her Daddy!"

Then Caldwell yelled out to Hans, "You have neglected one thing, sir. My firing accuracy is very, very good. I have six bullets, and all I need is three. By the time you've finished shooting Gus, I'll have killed Mr. Stewart and will be putting a bullet in your head. You are both evil, and you both must die!"

Hank asked Caldwell in a loud voice, "You said that all you need is three shots? Which one of us gets two?"

Caldwell looked toward Gus and said, "The third bullet is for the girl. I'm sorry, Gus, but the girl must die. She is key to their plans, and the only way to stop them is to kill her."

Gus looked at Caldwell and said, "James, I can't let you do that. You know how fast I am. By the time you've killed both of them, I'll have grabbed my gun and will be shooting you."

Hank laughed his sinister laugh and said, "What a predicament we are in! If Caldwell wins, I die, and Lisa dies. If Hans wins, I die, and Lisa lives in hell. If Gus wins, I'm most likely dead, but he marries Lisa, and they live happily ever after." Then he yelled, "Lisa, I've been an evil man and done some very bad things, all for money. I've deceived you your whole life, and for that, I'm truly sorry. But somewhere along the way, I realized that I do love you, like a father loves a daughter." He looked toward Gus, smiled his sinister grin, and said, "I wanted to get you a wedding present, but I didn't make it to the store. So here's what I got you instead."

Hank winked at Gus, whipped around, and fired, hitting Hans in the head, killing him instantly.

In doing so Hank knew what would happen next. Caldwell fired two quick rounds into his chest. At the same time, Gus dove for his gun, rolled, turned, and fired. Caldwell had turned to fire at Lisa, but Gus was quicker to the punch. An instant before Gus fired, Caldwell yelled, "Shields!"

Bulletproof glass came shooting up from the ground, protecting Caldwell, stopping Gus's shot. Caldwell did not get a chance to fire at Lisa. Gus and Caldwell locked eyes through the glass. They knew their relationship was forever changed. Then trapdoors below Caldwell opened, and he dropped from sight.

Lisa ran over to Hank. She grabbed his hand and sobbed, "Father, you're dying!"

He squeezed her hand like a reassuring father and said, "We all start dying the day we're born. Maybe we all start living the day we die. Don't worry. Gus will take care of you."

Then he grabbed Gus's hand. Hank smiled his sinister grin, looked at Gus, and said, "They forgot to factor love into their calculations. Never underestimate love." With very little life left in him, he pulled Lisa's hand and Gus's hand together, squeezed them between his, and said, "Gus, you win. Take care of my little girl." With a look of satisfaction on his face, he closed his eyes and died.

Chapter 16
THE SNAKE

Lisa sat crying over Hank. Gus grabbed her hand and said, "We have to leave now. They said several times that the boss will be here soon."

Suddenly, he heard someone from behind him say, "You're not going anywhere. Put your hands on your head and turn around."

Gus did as he was told. He turned to see J.P. Thorn. The owner and president of the company he worked for. He was pointing a gun at his head.

Gus said, "Looks like the boss is here. Hello, Mr. Thorn."

J.P. replied, "Hello, Mr. Shepard. No need to leave so soon. I've actually been here for some time. I thought that it was best for me to sit it out until everybody killed each other. It couldn't have worked out better. Losing both Hank and Hans this close to completion will save the company a lot of money. All that's left is you. Once I take care of you, all will be well again."

Just when Gus thought Thorn was going to pull the trigger, he heard someone yell, "What the fuck are you doing?"

It was a voice that Gus recognized. It was Dave, the Gadget Geek. He looked different with a gun in his hand. He was pointing it at Thorn.

Looking scared, Thorn said, "I'm taking care of business. He kidnapped the girl. I tracked him down. We had some casualties, but the situation is now under control."

Dave looking around said, "Some casualties?" Then looking tough, in a loud voice, he said, "Whose decision was it to kill Gus now, and who decided to eliminate him back at the house? You don't need to answer that—it was you! Did you ever stop to think that we might need him? Did it even cross your mind to ask me first?"

Thorn said, "Sorry, boss."

Dave shook his head and replied, "I also told you to never call me that again. You're fuckin' useless."

Then, to Gus's surprise, Dave fired three quick shots into Thorn! He stumbled back and fell to the ground, dead.

Gus quickly pulled the forty-five he had tucked into his waistband and pointed it at Dave. Gus looked at Dave and said, "Thorn was not the boss. He called you the boss."

Dave put his gun back into his shoulder holster and smiled. He didn't look scared. Then he said "You're a smart man, Gus. Looks like you figured it out. You're right. I'm the boss. Thorn was my puppet. I let everyone think he was the boss. Day to day, I preferred to just be Dave the Gadget Geek. It was easier to keep an eye on things that way."

Gus said, "You sure had me fooled. I thought you were an exceptionally smart rich kid who was on his own path. I understand that you were a straight-A engineering student that dropped out just before graduation. From all the technical abilities you had I thought that you were probably one of those genius type people was that actually too smart to stay in college. I also found out that you then left college to travel South America while working for charities. It explained to me your worldliness. I did wonder if maybe you had a falling out with your parents, like many children of wealth do. If that was driving you to seek your own path. But most of all, I respected you because you appeared to be one of those men who follow their hearts. Actually, I hate to say it, but I admired you. I never thought of you as the kingpin of this whole evil plot."

Dave laughed and said, "Wow, you've done your homework on me. Your father must have helped you. Thank you for the compliments. It almost makes me want to cry—just kidding, now the truth. The college thing was a big scam to buy time and make me look legitimate. I just hung around the school and partied. My transcripts and grades were all fixed. When I left, school I wasn't traveling and working for charities. I left school searching South American countries to find a suitable place to build our factory. Also known as the Hive. And last but not least I have had no falling-out with my family. We get along great. In fact, they're the ones financing this whole thing.

Gus, the world as you know it isn't what you think it is. My family is very rich and powerful. Rich and powerful people throughout history have determined the future of mankind. I am only following my destiny. We're developing a race of people who are bred to work and will be very happy doing it."

Gus looked sternly at Dave and said, "You're not creating a race of happy workers. You're developing a race of controllable slaves!"

"I know that you don't share my vision, but I'd officially like to ask you to join me. You're a brilliant scientist, and we need you. On top of that, I like you. If you and Lisa agree to cooperate, with me you can marry and obtain wealth beyond your wildest dreams. If you decide not to help me, then I'll forcefully take what I need from both of you and eliminate you both when I'm done. I'm sorry that I can't give you more time to think about it. I need an answer now. So, Gus, what do you say?"

"What do I say? I say you're crazy. I have a gun on you, and I think that I should just kill you. That would be the end of all this evilness."

Dave looked at Gus seriously and said, "I put my gun away because I needed you in control so that I could get a truthful answer out of you. I guess your answer is no. Well, Gus, I was prepared for that."

As Dave finished speaking, Gus heard the familiar sound of the hammer being cocked on a revolver. He felt the cold steel of a large-caliber handgun being pressed against his head. Then he heard someone say, "I think you should put your gun down, my friend."

It was another voice that he recognized. Gus dropped his arm and slowly let his pistol fall to the floor. He turned around, and it was Mono. He was pointing a shiny chrome .44 Magnum at him. He smiled, and the shine of his front tooth strangely matched the shine of the large revolver.

Gus looked at Mono and said, "I can't believe that you're also a part of this whole thing."

Mono replied, "Hey, man, I don't know what this whole thing is, but everybody is part of something. I really don't know or even care what your friend Dave's plans are. For me, this is just business."

Dave said, "Sorry, Gus. Your friend works for me. His cousin got killed by somebody who was watching your house. The guy who killed him was employed by me. I found out that your buddy Mono was searching real hard for who was responsible. I knew I was responsible as it was one of my guys who did it, but I did not authorize it. The situation just got out of control. It was a mistake. So I contacted Mono and, like a gentleman, explained the situation. We worked things out."

Gus said to Mono, "You worked things out? He killed your cousin. I thought you were all about family."

Mono replied, "Yes, I am all about family. Normally, I would have handled this differently, but your friend Dave offered me two million dollars. My cousin has a wife and kids. The money will help them survive without their husband and father. I am about family, but I am also about business. I just consider this taking care of family business."

Gus angrily said, "What else has he paid you to do?"

Mono meanly answered, "I think that it's time that you quit asking questions and be satisfied that you're still breathing air."

Dave then yelled, "Enough idle chitchat! I have a plane to catch. Let's get this show on the road. As we discussed earlier there will be four teams in four vehicles. The first two teams will be Mono's men. They'll be in the leading car with Lisa and in the car behind them with Gus. The third team will be my explosives guys in car three. The last and fourth vehicle will be my SUV and my security team. OK, let's move. Team One, take the girl. Team Two, take Gus. Team Three, wire this place to explode. Team Four, follow me. I want all teams in front of the building, in their vehicles, and ready to leave in fifteen minutes!"

Gus could do nothing but observe and obey. He saw Mono's guys surround Lisa. She looked back, and Gus just nodded to her. He knew that they would not harm her until they got what they needed from her. She seemed to understand Gus's reaction and did as they told her. They directed her out a side door.

Gus looked at Mono's men who were taking Lisa out the door and the others that were surrounding him. They were all armed and looked tough, but they weren't as well armed as Dave's guys. Mono's guys looked like thugs with handguns. Dave's looked like soldiers prepared for war. Mono's people numbered about the same as Dave's, but in a firefight, Gus didn't think Mono's guys stood much of a chance. He found it interesting that Dave kept his men separated from Mono's. Gus sensed that Dave might be planning some sort of double-cross against Mono. In a battle of wits against Dave, Mono was probably in over his head.

Gus then felt a hard push against his shoulder. He turned and recognized him. It was the big Aztec-looking guy that he fought in the park, one of Mono's inner circle. He loudly said to Gus, "Let's move."

He marched Gus out to the front of the building. There were three cars parked in a line with a large SUV parked in back. The moon was bright and there were no clouds in the sky. Gus saw Mono's men putting Lisa into the first car in the front of the line. Gus was put in the backseat of the second car, surrounded by Mono's guys. Four of Dave's military-looking guys who had been setting explosives got into the car behind Gus. Then Dave came out, escorted by four very tough-looking military guys. They got into the SUV. Two in the front and two in the very back. Dave and Mono sat in the middle seat. Gus heard somebody yell, "Let's move!" The car in the front with Lisa got the caravan moving.

They drove for about ten minutes when Gus turned to the Aztec guy and said, "I think you're being set up. At some point, I think these guys are going to overpower you and kill you all."

To Gus's surprise, the big guy replied, "I'm glad that's what you think. I hope that's what they think. That means everything is going as planned."

"What is the plan?"

"Your friend Dave's plan is that your girl and his SUV are going to a deserted runway where a small jet is waiting for him. You and I and the car behind us will split off and take you to a very secluded hiding spot. We're being paid to keep you captive there."

"You know when you get there that the guys in the car behind you will probably try to kill you."

"I believe you are correct, my friend. That's why I'm talking to you. Mono has his own plan. I can't tell you everything, but he told me to tell you that you need to trust him. He said forget what he told you back at your house. He had to tell you what told you in case they were listening. You are and will always be family. With family, there are no debts and payments. If you do your part and the plan works you, and your girl will be safe."

"I have very few options, so I choose to trust him. What do you need me to do?"

"Soon, we'll split off from the rest of the group and drive to the secluded spot. The car behind us will follow. We believe they'll wait until we get there. That's when they'll make their move. But we know that they don't want to kill you. So we'll stop before we get there and let you out to pee. That's when you'll hit my guy who's watching you and run.

"You'll run up the valley toward the mountain. My guys will panic, jump out of the car, and start chasing you. We think they won't try to kill us until we capture you and bring you back. We need about ten minutes. Don't let us capture you before then. By that time, a group of very mean people will show up to help us out. Mono rented the secluded hideout from a very notorious drug lord, who will be supplying the backup. They're on their way and are about ten minutes behind us."

Gus said, "Sounds like a plan. But how do I know that I can trust you?"

The Aztec looked intensely at Gus and said, "Take this gun."

Gus smiled, took the gun, and checked to make sure it was loaded. He then said, "I trust you."

Soon, the car Gus was in split from the caravan and drove down a dusty gravel road, with a carload of Dave's explosives team close behind. The first car with Lisa in it and Dave's SUV continued in a different direction. After about fifteen minutes, the Aztec smiled and said to Gus, "Do you have to pee?"

Gus replied, "Yes, I do."

The car stopped, and the guy on the other side of him and Gus got out of the car. The guy kept a gun pointed toward Gus. The car behind them started honking their horn. Gus unzipped and started peeing. The honking stopped.

Gus stopped, zipped up, then quickly spun around and hit the guy watching him with a back fist. Then he took off running. All of Mono's guys in the car got out and started chasing Gus.

The only one staying was the one Gus hit. He was lying on the ground. Gus didn't run too fast. He didn't want to lose them. Gus turned to see three of Mono's men chasing him.

All of Dave's guys were back near their car. He could hear a lot of yelling but no gunfire. The plan was working.

Gus ran up the valley, making it look like Mono's guys almost had him. He did this for about ten minutes until he saw a large armored vehicle full of heavily armed men come driving down the road. The plan worked. The backup was here. Gus was surprised when the vehicle pulled up behind the car of Dave's men. A man with dark sunglasses got out and shook the hands of one of Dave's guys.

Gus, hidden in the bushes, saw the Aztec and asked, "What's going on?"

"I don't know. Stay hidden. Let's keep playing our game of cat and mouse. Maybe the situation has changed."

Then he whistled to his guys. They moved around the area, each bending down and coming up with UZIs with large-capacity clips. They had hidden guns in the rocks where they had stopped.

Then the Aztec said, "We have an alternate plan if we can't trust the drug lord. The plan is to keep you alive at all costs. If we start shooting, you run as fast as you can and get over that ridge. We'll provide cover as long as we can."

"All of you will be killed."

"That is true, but I'll take a lot of those *putas* out before I go. I may have to strike first, or I'll lose the element of surprise."

"What if the drug lord hasn't changed the plan and is really here to back you up?"

"If that's the case and I start shooting, I've fucked up. You still should run, and I will still die."

Gus said, "I have superior hearing. Before you attack, let me just listen to what the men down there are saying."

The Aztec hesitated and then said, "Maybe I shouldn't move too quickly. I still have one guy left at my car, the guy that you hit. He's the drug lord's cousin. He's my insurance policy. The guy who just showed up with the sunglasses is one of the drug lord's generals. I was hoping for the drug lord himself because he and my guy are family. But before I make a decision, I need to know, can you really hear from here?"

To make him feel comfortable, Gus simply said, "I can read lips."

"Cool, man. The general is talking to my guy. What are they saying?"

"They're talking in Spanish, so I will translate. The general just said to your guy, 'How's it going, you stupid whore?'...Your guy just said back, 'I'm only a stupid whore because I let you lick my precious balls but I never collect any money!'...The general just pushed him and said, 'Fuck you.' ... Your guy pushed him back and said, 'You can't fuck me because your tiny cock doesn't work!'" Gus then said, "This does not look good."

The Aztec smiled and said, "No, man, this is good."

"The general just said to your guy, 'If I can't fuck you, I should just shoot you, you pig!'...Your guy just said, 'If you shoot me, you won't get to drink good tequila with me.'...The general replied, 'Then I guess I cannot shoot you!' They're laughing and hugging."

"Dave's man is talking to him. What's he saying?"

"Dave's guy just said to the general, 'What about the plan?'...The general just replied, 'I plan to drink tequila with my friends.'...Dave's guy just asked, 'What about our plan?'...The general just said, 'The plan between us has changed. Now I plan to just kill you!'...One of Dave's guys just said to the general, 'I drink tequila.'...The general replied, 'Then you can leave your weapons and come drink with us.' Another of Dave's men just said, 'I love tequila!'...The general just said, 'You may also leave your weapons and join us.'" Gus then said, "Looks like all of Dave's men are putting down their weapons. They're all saying how much they love tequila."

The Aztec said, "The drug lord is a smart man, just like Mono. He only kills when needed. These guys will probably end up working for him! I think it's time that I went down and talked to the general. I'll tell him that he and my guy, the drug lord's cousin, should move down to the hideout and drink tequila. We'll pretend that we're still trying to catch you. I'll tell him that I'll catch you soon and meet him at the hideout later."

Gus replied, "Sounds like a smart move. I think this is a much healthier environment."

The Aztec smiled and said, "The air out here is much fresher. Also, we have much better weapons and big rocks to hide behind. Mono's plan will be reaching completion in about ten minutes. I plan to stay out here for about fifteen minutes. Until then, I believe that you're the safest with us."

Gus asked, "Where's the jet and airstrip that Dave plans to take off from at?"

"It's about ten miles over those two ridges. There's no possible way for you to get there before Dave plans on leaving. I think you should just be calm and let Mono do his thing. This is his gig. This is what he does, man. I've seen him in action. Mono is like a champion chess player when it comes to this shit. He never loses. Your girl will be safe, and all will be well soon."

Gus said, "I wish I could do that, but I have to run."

The Aztec looked at him seriously and said, "I figured that. Good luck. Don't get yourself killed. Stay alive, because I want a rematch for that fight in the park!"

Gus grinned and said, "I do owe you that. Nobody wants to leave this earth owing people. I'll stay alive just for a rematch. You're on, amigo!" Then they both laughed. The Aztec turned and started walking toward the men below.

With every ounce of his will and might, Gus charged up the valley to the top of the first ridge. He was going for Lisa! With an intense rage burning in his body, he reached the top of the ridge in seconds. When he reached the top, he put his head back and howled. Then he closed his eyes and sniffed the air. He had memorized the smell of the car Lisa was in when she was in front of him. Gus faintly smelled it in the distance. He ran his fastest in that direction.

He reached the top of the second ridge and looked out across the valley. He could see the jet on a small runway. Then he saw Lisa's car being followed by the SUV. They were about two miles away from the jet on a road approaching it. Gus judged the distance. If he ran fast enough, he could cut them off before they got to the plane. He had a plan. The plan was to run down to the driver's side of the car that Lisa was in. He would run up with his gun drawn and point it at the driver. He would then quickly pull him out of the car, jump in, and drive away before Dave could stop him. It was a gamble that Mono's guys would not try to stop him. Gus was also counting on that Dave's guys would not shoot out of the fear of hitting Lisa.

Like a rocket, he charged down the valley toward the cars. Gus reached the junction point. He was an instant too late, and they passed him before he got there. Gus bolted toward the passing cars, running up from behind. He passed Dave's SUV running at over sixty miles per hour.

Dave looked out the window and said, "What the fuck was that?"

Mono looked out the window and said, "That's your boy, Gus. What the hell have you been feeding him?"

"This is unbelievable. He must have genetically altered himself."

Gus passed them and ran up to the car with Lisa in it. Running at nearly seventy miles per hour, he pointed the gun at the driver's head. As expected, the guy stopped the car. Gus grabbed the guy by the shoulder and was about to yank him out when he looked in the backseat. Lisa wasn't there! It was a girl disguised to look like Lisa.

Gus froze. He wasn't sure what to do. The driver slowly got out of his car with his hands up. He said, "We switched her back at the building before we left. Pretend like it's her, or we're all going to die. Go with the plan."

Gus just stood there with his gun pointed at the driver. The SUV stopped about forty feet behind them. Two armed men quickly jumped out and pointed assault rifles at him. Then Dave got out and yelled, "You are truly amazing! Gus, I am very, very impressed. I've changed my mind. I'll take Lisa and you with me. Why don't you put down your gun and get in with me? Our plane is waiting."

Gus threw his gun off to the side and walked over to the SUV. Without saying a word, he got inside and sat between Dave and Mono.

They drove for about ten minutes when Dave said to Mono, "We're almost there. I hope for your sake you're not trying to pull something on me. No matter what you may think, your people are my people. I know the hideout that you had planned for Gus was supplied by a well-known drug dealer. You paid him fifty thousand. That's why I paid him an extra five hundred thousand. Also, all the guys in your cars, I paid twenty thousand cash each. And if for some reason things get ugly, I told your guys they each will get one hundred thousand for every one of their own kind that they may have to kill. So you see, everyone 'works for me!" Then he laughed loudly.

Mono leaned back in his seat, turned his head, and said to Dave, "You are a very smart and resourceful man. I know you paid my drug-dealing friend five hundred thousand. He told me. But that was after I promised him two million. And the guys in my cars all gave me the money that you gave them. They trust that I will compensate them with more in return. And do you know why all these people do these things for me? Because we are family. So, my friend, you need to consider that if many of my people are your people, then many of your people are my family."

Dave, looking slightly irritated, said to Mono, "Give me a break. You're bluffing. Where are you going to get that kind of money?"

Mono smiled, showing his shiny front tooth, and said, "From you." They were just pulling in the runway entrance. Then Mono said, "I want fifty million for the girl."

Dave said, "I already have the girl."

"No, you don't." Mono held up a cell phone showing a live video of some of his guys and Lisa at another location.

In a rage, Dave yelled, "Stop the car! Go get the girl!"

The two guys in front jumped out. They ran to the car ahead of them, grabbed the girl, and brought her back.

Dave screamed, "You idiots! That's not her!"

Mono said to Dave, "I can have her here in less than ten minutes. Make up your mind. Don't you have a plane to catch?"

Dave, appearing angry but calm, said, "I don't have time for this shit. I will live to fight another day. Let me out." He told Mono, "Wait here."

He got out, opened up the back of the SUV, and hooked up a laptop with video chat. He was contacting his father. There was a lot of yelling between Dave and his father. Then Dave brought the laptop into the back seat of the SUV and said, "He wants to talk to you."

He handed the laptop to Mono. On the screen was Dave's father, an older, meaner-looking version of Dave. In a loud voice he yelled at Mono, "I want you to know that you have made a serious mistake fucking with me! I am a man of my word, so I will give you one chance to change your mind and I will forget everything that has happened up until now. Just give us the girl and go. We will still pay you what we owe you."

Mono calmly replied, "Now you owe me fifty million. I will give you an account to wire the money to. Then I will do as you wish."

With a scowl on his face, Dave's father said, "I will pay you your money. Give me the account. But remember, I will not forget that you fucked us. And the rest of the day better work out well. If there are any new surprises or things go wrong, I will kill you and everyone in your family. I will kill everyone you know! Do you understand me?"

Mono replied, "Yes, sir." He typed in the account number.

Several minutes passed. Then Dave's father said, "OK, the money is transferred. Check your account."

Mono glanced at his phone and said, "Looks good. The money is in."

Immediately after that, Mono's phone rang. He answered and said, "Are we good?" There was a voice talking in reply, then Mono said, "Thank you, Mr. Shepard."

An instant later, on the laptop, they heard Dave's father yelling and then saw his door being broken down. A SWAT team was charging in, yelling, "You're under arrest!" Then they saw Gus's father walking in right before the screen went blank.

Dave yelled to his guys in the car, "Kill them! Kill them both!"

His guys did nothing. Mono grinned and said, "These guys are not my family, but you were only paying them ten thousand each. I promised them two hundred and fifty thousand each. Of course, that was only if my plan worked. I think they know it did."

Dave screamed, "My family is wealthy! You will all pay! My father will not go to jail!"

Mono laughed and said, "I have been told that your father will not go to jail."

Dave said to Mono, "You're no better than me! You did all this for money."

Mono then replied, "No, man, I did not do all this for money. I did all this for family. You killed my cousin, and you would have killed Gus. My cousin and Gus are my family. I did this for them. Speaking of family, look out the window, my friend. My uncle and some cousins are here. They would like to speak to you. And guess what my friend, I did not have to pay them any money. They do not want money. They just want you!" Then Mono laughed a wild, crazy laugh.

Dave got out of the SUV and started running toward the jet. A single shot rang out, hitting Dave in the leg. He fell to the ground but kept crawling. A group of farm worker looking Mexican men came over and threw Dave, struggling and screaming, into the back of an old pickup truck. Then they drove away.

Gus asked Mono, "Will they kill him?"

Smiling, his gold tooth shining, Mono said, "When they are done satisfying their anger, they will kill him. Maybe not today, but soon. It really does not matter when they kill him, but he must die. Like a poisonous snake, if you don't kill it, the snake may come back and kill you or someone close to you."

Mono's phone rang, and he handed it to Gus. "He said it's for you. It's your father."

Gus grabbed the phone and said, "Daaaaad!"

His father replied, "Are you OK?"

Gus replied, "Doing great."

His father then said, "I guess you can see that I teamed up with your friend Mono. It was you who told me that he was the one that you trusted the most. I worked with him to get the data I needed. All I needed was Dave and his father on video and the money transfer. With that, I was able to cut off the head of the snake. I'm sorry I lost track of you back at the house. Things happened faster than I anticipated. We followed Dave because we knew he would lead us to you."

"Will Dave's father go to jail?"

"No, he's going to hell! Right after my guys came in to arrest him, he ran and jumped over his high-rise balcony, falling to his death. Can you imagine that?"

"Convenient," Replied Gus.

Then they both laughed. Gus then said, "What happened to Caldwell? You were right about him. He talked about the fight between good and evil, but I think he was just all into himself. He got away."

"Yes, he escaped and is on a plane to Thailand. But as he went through security, we downloaded child pornography onto his laptop. All of under-age Thai children. Some of which he has actually seen. Do you know what they hate most over there? Rich white men who come over to rape their young children. Do you know what they hate more than that? The ones that our government won't let them touch. Do you know what they love more than anything in the world? When our government gives them one. He'll soon be crying for his mommy and daddy as he squeals like a pig!"

Then Gus and his father laughed again. His father continued. "We may need Caldwell someday. We'll leave him over there for a while. I'm sure he'll be begging us to let him come back and do whatever we need."

His father then said, "Gus, you have successfully completed the journey of the god dog. Powers that were given to you helped you accomplish things that may not have been humanly possible. But in addition, they helped you unlock your own hidden potential. One power that was unlocked but may not be visible to you was your own wisdom. Not all things can be overcome with strength and violence. In many cases, the outcome of events is determined by correct decisions. The ability to make the right decisions at the right time is directed by one's own wisdom. You made many wise decisions. The powers of good chose you to help them stop this evil plot. They also made a wise decision.

"So, to sum it up, good has triumphed over evil! You have successfully completed the journey thrust upon you by the god dog. Lisa is safe. Let's get you both home. We have a lot to talk about."

The End

Made in the USA
San Bernardino, CA
14 January 2019